THE PIRATE'S PURCHASE

CHARLESTON BRIDES ~ BOOK 1

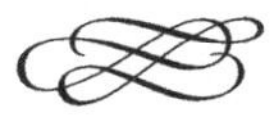

ELVA COBB MARTIN

Originally titled Marisol ~ Spanish Rose

ISBN-13: 978-1-942265-49-8

PRAISE FOR THE PIRATE'S PURCHASE

What do you get when you cross a Spanish lady on the run for murder with a handsome pirate who used to be a priest? A great adventurous romance with tons of twists and turns, romance, danger, suspense, and well, everything you'd want in a good book. I immediately connected with the characters, felt sympathy for them, and rooted for them as they faced one harrowing situation after another. Rarely does a book keep me on the edge of my seat through the entire story! Ms. Cobb has a real knack for keeping the action and romance going without cluttering things up with unnecessary details. You'd be a fool to pass on this one.

— MARYLU TYNDALL, AWARD-WINNING AUTHOR OF THE LEGACY OF THE KING'S PIRATES SERIES

[23] They that go down to the sea in ships, that do business in great waters;
[24] These see the works of the LORD, and his wonders in the deep.
[25] For he commandeth, and raiseth the stormy wind, which lifteth up the waves thereof.
[26] They mount up to the heaven, they go down again to the depths: their soul is melted because of trouble.
[27] They reel to and fro, and stagger like a drunken man, and are at their wit's end.
[28] Then they cry unto the LORD in their trouble, and he bringeth them out of their distresses.
[29] He maketh the storm a calm, so that the waves thereof are still.
[30] Then are they glad because they be quiet; so he bringeth them unto their desired haven.

Psalm 107:23-30 (KJV)

ACKNOWLEDGMENTS

I give a hearty thanks to my encouraging writer friends and critique partners like Yvonne Lehman, Cindy Sproles, and all the great partners and friends of our South Carolina Chapter of American Christian Writers; Fran and David Anderson, Angela Major, Edie Melson, Diana Carnes, Kelsey Messner, Arlene Dove, Ruth Camp, Carlene Brown, Mike Whitworth, Jay Wright, Tammy Karesek, Sigrid Fowler, and Karen Turner. Thanks for your timely critiques.

I am also eternally grateful to my diligent prayer team who have prayed for me and my writing journey including Pastor Phil & Teresa Sears, Lana Barbusca, Nancy Walker, Nancy Deal, Cindy Burriss, Angela Major, Fran Anderson, Deb Barrow, Cathy Frankel, Catherine Mazza, Towanda Phillips, Rae Hall, Sandra Fowler, and Phyllis Burroughs and Sonya Garris (my sisters).

I am so thankful for my forever hero husband, Dwayne, who not only prays for me daily, but also puts up with my hours at the computer, faster meals, and pitches in with household tasks.

Most of all, I thank my heavenly Father and Lord and Savior Jesus Christ and the Holy Spirit who have been with me, inspiring me, helping me, and keeping me on task.

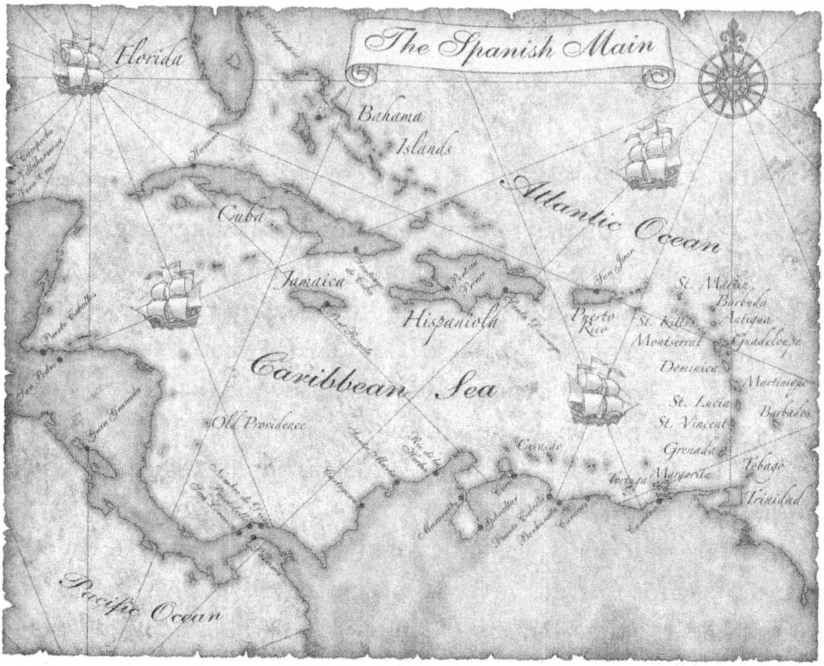

The Spanish Main

Florida
Bahama Islands
Atlantic Ocean
Cuba
Jamaica
Hispaniola
Puerto Rico
St. Martin
Barbuda
Antigua
St. Kitts
Montserrat
Guadeloupe
Dominica
Martinique
St. Lucia
St. Vincent
Barbados
Grenada
Tobago
Margarita
Trinidad
Caribbean Sea
Old Providence
Pacific Ocean

CHAPTER 1

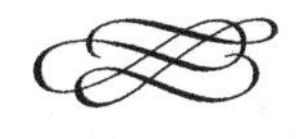

Cadiz, Spain
1740

Marisol Valentin pressed her tearful face against the warm neck of her beloved mare, blocking out for a moment the sickening smell of human blood in the barn corridor. "Goodbye, my dear Jada."

The horse nickered and nuzzled her, as if understanding. Dragging her feet out of the pregnant Andalusian's stall, Marisol could no longer squelch the sob that escaped her lips.

She averted her eyes from the form lying in the moonlight near the tack room entrance. The still body of Diego Vargas, nobleman of Spain, sprawled across the dirt passage.

She'd killed him, but she'd not had a choice.

Her breath strangled in her throat as she inched by. Somehow she made it across the shadowed stable courtyard and up the rear stairs of the hacienda. Bursting into her bedchamber, she shoved the door closed, and leaned against it. The pressure in her chest, the awful bile churning her middle, they both rose up to strangle her.

She drew in ragged breaths as tears flooded down her cheeks and onto her ripped gown.

Her maid Carmela dropped the camisole she was setting out on the bed. "Oh, my lady, what has happened?"

"Diego Vargas came into the foaling barn after I entered to check on Jada and he..." Her voice broke down. She wrapped her hands around herself and clenched her eyes to block out memories of his savage attack. "He's ruined me, and I stabbed him." Her lips trembled. "I only meant to stop him. Not kill him."

Carmela gasped and her hand flew across her mouth. "*Madre de Dios*!"

Marisol's shoulders slumped, and she swayed toward the wash stand. Every movement of her body ached. She would have bruises everywhere by morning.

Yes, Mother of God, if you're there, I need your help. Would God aid a murderess? She plunged her hands into the tepid water in the basin and scrubbed them raw. "I must flee tonight. His family will never believe my story or be content until I sit in the garroting chair. My blade is in his side."

The woman hastened to Marisol's side, her face pale and tense. "You will not go alone, dear one. I'm going with you." She darted to the chifforobe and stood on tip toes to reach for the travel bags on top.

Marisol turned from the washing bowl, wishing she had more time to sponge away the man's dreadful smell of unclean linen and wine that clung to her. But there was not a moment to spare. She frowned at her maid flinging clothes into both their valises. "No, my friend. I'll be a castaway, a criminal fleeing justice. You must not come with me."

Seeing her words had no effect, she continued, "You can go back to your brother's house tonight. Say you weren't even here."

Carmela shook her head. "You cannot travel alone. I'm coming. I have a little savings of my own, my lady. We need to find a ship to the New World and you will be safe." The woman squatted, loosened a floor board, lifted out a small leather pouch, and stuffed it into her bodice.

Watching her, Marisol sighed and ceased trying to discourage her. She didn't have time to protest and, in truth, having a friend along on this midnight flight would be a relief.

She rushed to the wardrobe and snatched a garment. Escaping to the colonies of Spain in the West Indies would likely be their best option. Carmela helped her peel off her ruined clothing and change into the simple, dark blue silk dress. She'd forego a hoop or layers of petticoats. They would have to travel fast and on foot.

She agreed with her maid about the type of shoes—her thick, black leather boots. Who knew how long they would have to walk and over what kind of terrain to the harbor? Heretofore, she'd only gone there in a carriage and by the main road.

Marisol opened her jewel case and scooped up her valuable necklaces, pearl comb, and the Valentin rose-cut ruby brooch, her precious last gift from her mother. *Dear Madre.* How she missed her.

She pressed an emerald choker into Carmela's hand. "For our passage when we get to the harbor." She stashed the rest of her jewels in a concealed pocket under her skirt. But she tied the thin leather strap bearing the ruby pin around her neck and thrust the gem deep into the top of her gown. Then she dropped her mother's miniature into her bag.

Her heart faltered as she thought of her departed father and how his proud Valentin name would now become a byword linked with murder. Another tear ran down her cheek. She swiped at it and cast her mind again on the New World. Maybe they could make it to her father's sister in Cartagena on the Spanish Main. Aunt Lucia would help her, and that destination should be far enough away.

She reached to the rear of the chifforobe and withdrew a short Sevillian steel blade, similar to, but longer than, the navaja left in Diego's chest. She cast aside the memory of his glazed, shocked eyes and slid the weapon into the top of her boot. Her father's brother, who now managed the estate, didn't know about the rapiers her dear Papa had given her. Nor had she told him about the sword fighting lessons Papa had insisted she take.

Her maid touched her arm. "I will go as your *dueña* and you'll be safer on the road and on the ship."

Carmela dressed her own dark hair as an older woman's, then donned a plain black dress, headpiece, and wrap. She handed Marisol a blue cloak and thick lace mantilla to cover her tresses and shadow her pale face. Then she moved to the cold supper tray and stuffed every sandwich and biscuit she could into her pockets.

A glimmer of a smile touched the corners of Marisol's mouth. Dear Carmela, only ten years older than her own eighteen summers, but so sensible. They would require food on their long journey. Her maid resembled a stern governess, clad as she was. Marisol loved and trusted the woman like the sister she'd never had.

Before leaving the room in which she grew up, Marisol marked her reflection in the walnut framed mirror over her marble-topped dresser. Her mantilla covered most of her thick, ebony hair. But the lace edge pulled close did not mask the paleness of her face or the bruise on her left cheek where Diego had knocked her to the barn floor.

Careful not to awaken the servants on the top floor, they glided like silent ghosts down the hall, the staircase, and through the shadowed kitchen toward the back door. Carmela lifted a leather waterskin from the servant's pantry and draped it across her sturdy shoulder.

Carrying her own valise, Marisol followed the woman outside and to the farm road. The moon drifted in and out of clouds like a stealthy galleon tracking its prey.

Carmela unlatched the wide gate, and they passed under the arched sign above the entrance. Marisol stole a look backward. *Valentin Andalusian Stud Estate.* Her heart broke anew. She loved the famous Spanish horses they bred, the spacious home her mother had once graced, and the large estate her papa had run like a gentle lord. Would she ever see it again? Nothing had been the same since her uncle took over at her father's death. A tear slipped down her cheek. The man had several faults, but one most costly —gambling.

The taunting words of Diego tripped back across her hot mind. *Don't think your dear uncle will come to your rescue, my girl. I've won all he owns tonight, including you. And he's passed out drunk in the Vargas game room.*

"Walk faster, my lady." Carmela urged her on the narrow path winding through the forest below the main road. "We must reach the harbor before dawn."

Marisol cast her sorrowful thoughts aside and forced her feet to move faster. The breeze rustled through leaves, and the screech from a pursued animal sent a shiver down her spine. She took a deep breath. The woodsy smell of wild mint, sweet cedar, and verdant growth encouraged her, and she continued on as fast as she could.

They passed the last majestic oak on the Valentin estate. No lights or shouts followed them from the house or stables. The tightness in Marisol's shoulders eased, but not the heaviness in her heart. *Murderess.* The word stung her mind like a scorpion.

The unpredictable moon covered their flight one moment and revealed their hasty passage the next.

"How long should it take us to get to the harbor, Carmela? Surely we can count on the night for travel before they will miss us in the morning." *Before the stable hands find Diego's body.* Marisol shuddered and ignored her tiring legs. The humid evening air promised rain. Something else to worry about.

"We must walk fast, my lady. I'll not have any peace until we're on a ship setting sail. And we can't go the easy road. We have to stay in the forest shadows *cuatro millas más.* But never fear, I know the way."

Four more miles? How many had they traveled already? Her maid wasn't even breathing hard. Her own legs ached from the continued rapid walk, and she switched her valise to her other hand for relief. Carmella must have sensed her tiredness, for she soon left the path and stopped at a log lying deep in the trees. Marisol dropped her baggage and sat. Her partner did the same.

"We can rest now, my lady. But merely for a moment." She swung the waterskin from her shoulder and passed it to Marisol. The welcome water soothed her dry throat like a cool breeze across her face on a hot day.

Too soon, Carmela stood up. Marisol forced her own weary self to rise and follow her back onto the path.

When she felt she couldn't take another step, the scent of the sea and cry of seagulls lifted her heart and renewed her energy. They had to be close to their destination. When the moon moved out from the clouds, she could see in the distance a row of waterfront buildings lit by feeble lights. And beyond them, the tops of ship masts bobbing in the water. The harbor of Cadiz.

Thunder rumbled, and the sound of horses on the high road made Marisol tremble. Carmela pulled her from the path into the forest and stopped at a large oak stump.

"We're entering the most dangerous part of our journey, my lady," she whispered. "And it may rain. We must wait for time to buy passage on one of the ships at dawn, but we won't have our cover of darkness. I'm going to look for a merchant ship heading to Hispaniola."

"But I want to go to Cartagena. I have an aunt living there who will help us."

"You have someone who might offer you shelter? That's good news, my lady. And don't fret, from that island we can gain passage to your aunt's city and to any other Spanish colony. It's the right port to find our way in the West Indies."

"Oh. I'm so glad you know all this, Carmela."

The woman smiled. "Well, that comes from having a father and brother who were sailors. Now would you like to rest here until I check things out?"

Marisol nodded and sank onto the tree stump. She dropped her valise next to her aching feet.

Her tired mind kept replaying the face of Diego Vargas. Her

ears still heard his contemptuous voice as he clamped her hands behind her back. *Since I saw you dance the flamenco at the harvest gathering, I knew I would have you. And I guessed right you would check on your prize mare tonight to see if she had foaled. I have plans for this stud farm. Europe is begging for our Spanish horses.*

Marisol shook her head and forced away the memory. She propped her elbows on her lap and leaned her chin onto her hands. For just a moment, she closed her eyes.

Cool raindrops on her face made her jerk awake. It took a moment to realize she lay on the damp forest floor next to the stump. She sat up and looked around, biting back a groan from her aching body. Pink and purple streaks spread across the horizon. Where was Carmela?

Marisol stood and grabbed her valise. She followed the path from the woods her maid had taken and came to the outskirts of the harbor town. Continuing through the narrow, sleepy streets of Cadiz, she passed store fronts whose owners had yet to open their shutters. Somewhere, a baker cooked bread, the smell of the fresh loaves making Marisol's mouth water. The shrill cries of two cats fighting in a nearby alley startled her, and she dropped her bag.

Heavy footsteps sounded behind her. Before she could turn about, thick arms, strong as iron bands, wrapped around her. The odors of sweat, rum, and unwashed clothing clawed in her throat, blocking her chest from inhaling. In another quick movement, her captor grabbed her hands and clapped a cuff on her wrists. She tried to scream, but a foul-smelling hand clamped down on her mouth. She bit into the fingers and the metallic taste of blood flowed onto her lips.

The man's slap reverberated through her head, sending flashes of light through the darkness that closed in like a haze around her vision.

But then a guttural whisper next to her ear sent the darkness fleeing. "If you try that again, you'll be sorry, Señorita. And don't scream or you'll die, and I mean a painful death. We thought there might be more of you heading to the harbor."

Others? Poor Carmela. Had they caught her, too? If only she'd had time to reach for her knife in her boot before he'd twisted her hands behind her.

The grimy paw pressed harder over her mouth as the man, twice her size, pulled her into an alley. No matter how hard she fought, his steel hands held her tight. Carmela lay bound on the ground before a tall ruffian with a full red beard and wild hair. Her maid twisted her head around and groaned through her gag when she saw her mistress.

The larger captor holding Marisol jerked her to a halt. "Now we have two fine señoritas to help colonize the King's colonies. These ought to bring plenty of gold, Jacque."

The man kicked Carmela, and her moan made tears spring to Marisol's eyes. "Yeah, well this one put up quite a fight. But she ain't going nowhere, except to that ship awaiting a few more warm bodies for the Indies."

The ruffian called Jacque ripped the mantilla from Marisol and gagged her with it. Then his rough hands wound her cloak around her body like a mummy, preventing all movement.

Carmela's captor pulled a sack over her head. He lifted her and slung her across his shoulder as if she were a sack of potatoes. Everything in Marisol wanted to spring forward and claw the man who would treat a woman like that. She had to save her friend. But the way she'd been bound, she could do nothing but watch as her middle churned with anger.

Before she realized what was happening, the monster standing over her stuffed a covering over her own head, cloaking her in a darkness that sent fear clawing through her chest. His hands gripped her arms, lifting her into the air and over his shoulder as if she were a feather weight. Her midsection slammed into his shoulder, almost knocking the air out of her. She sucked for wind, inhaling a torrent of vile smells in the process.

This couldn't be happening. What would they do to her?

He patted her covered head as they moved out onto the harbor road. "You señoritas can rest easy. We're bringing your valises, too.

We'll make sure your valuables find their way into our pockets before we put you on the ship." His low, wicked laugh, echoed by his mate, made her want to chew nails and throw up at the same moment.

~

Six weeks on board the *Magdalena* were more like months for Marisol. Most of the time she and Carmela stayed in the cramped women's cabin to avoid the crew and the indentured male passengers.

But a greater concern gripped her than the crowded conditions. Every morning for the past week, she had thrown up in the chamber pot. *El mareo?* But she had never suffered sea sickness when sailing, nor had she experienced the ailment for the first five weeks of this voyage.

One day, after a difficult episode, Marisol wiped her mouth and sank onto the cot. Other women in the cabin had murmured when her vomiting started, then piled out the door as fast as they could.

Only Carmela remained. Concern ridged her face as she handed her mistress a damp cloth. She patted her hand, and whispered, "My lady, do you also have a tender bosom?"

Marisol hung her head. "Yes, dear friend." A tear slid down her cheek, one she was too weak to hold back. She had to face the truth. "I may be with child."

"How do you feel about that since..." Her maid lifted her brow.

Marisol faced her. "You think because I conceived a babe in violence, I would hate the little one?" She didn't expect her friend to answer. "The child had no choice in this matter. I would never be bitter against an innocent baby." She looked away as a fresh wave of hopelessness cloaked her. "But I wonder how we can ever handle this."

"Our God will care for you, milady, and the babe." Carmela spoke with confidence. A confidence Marisol craved.

But she shook her head. "The same One who protected me from

Diego and both of us from the kidnappers? Sorry to disappoint you, dear friend. But I have no such assurance."

A deafening boom sounded from the side of the ship, sending Marisol's heart into her throat. They both jumped to their feet. Another blast followed, and the cabin rocked, causing them to grab hold of the cot posts to keep from being thrown to the floor. The sound of splitting wood, running boots, and vulgar curses echoed from above.

What was happening? Marisol clung to her post, her mind churning as she eyed the wooden ceiling, trying to make sense of the noises. Then the acrid odor of smoke stung her nose, and her gaze darted to the door. Smoke was seeping into the room. As the stench wrapped around her, it seemed to press on her chest and clog her airways.

Carmela coughed and wrapped her arms around herself. "We're under attack, and they've hit us. May the Blessed Virgin have mercy on us."

A ruckus of footsteps sounded in the hallway, and the other women passengers flew into the cabin, their faces tight with fear. The last one in bolted the door as whispered murmurs surged among the women. Marisol strained to hear what was being said, but no one seemed to know what was happening. The only thing they knew for certain was the fear etched on each face.

Their voices ceased a few minutes later as loud knocking sounded on the door.

"Who is it?" Marisol called.

A hoarse, anxious voice answered from the passage. "The captain says tell ye, we're under attack by them English pirates and ye may have to fight for your lives."

The voice was slightly familiar. Marisol pushed toward the sound and unbolted the door, then opened it wide.

A short Spanish sailor stood there, pale under his dark tan. "He's sent a sword. Hope one of you can use it."

He thrust a rapier handle into Marisol's hands and scrambled back up the passage.

CHAPTER 2

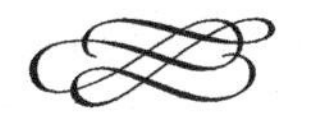

Moans from the women filled the cabin. An older woman named Jezebel marched forward and slammed and bolted the door.

Marisol checked the sharpness of the blade with her finger tip. It would do. She moved away from the other cringing occupants. Swinging the weapon, testing its weight in her grip, she found pleasure in how fast it whistled through the air. Just the familiar grip of a weapon settled the nerves tightening her shoulders. This one was similar to the sword Papa had trained her with.

She could feel the weight of the other women's gazes as they followed her every movement, even though she could still hear sniffles and sighs from some of them.

The middle-aged, hardened woman they called Jez for short, her red hair streaked with silver, cackled out as she watched Marisol test the sword. "*Hola chiquitas,* we have us here a noble lady and she's got fighting skills to defend our lives."

Barely muffled yells, curses, and cannon blasts still filtered down to them from the passageway. The indentured women screamed almost with one voice every time the ship rocked, as charges from the enemy hit home. Smoke still seeped through the ceiling and under the door. Marisol worked to control her own fear, but the solid feel of the sword hilt in her grip helped steady her nerves.

Carmela wrapped her trembling arms together and moved to stand closer to Marisol. "Thank God the cannons fire on the other side of the vessel."

At last, the deafening shots and shudders of the vessel ceased. The winners would likely board the losing vessel now. Which side was the *Magdalena* on?

A whistle sounded overhead, which must be the grappling hooks. The crack of timbers splintering surely confirmed it. Heavy boots stomped across the upper level. Invaders boarding their ship? *God, no!*

The women huddled tighter as muffled sounds drifted from above—cutlasses connecting and clanging, the growls, grunts, and death wails of victims.

Marisol's heart pounded as she turned to her maid. "When they force the door, try to keep the women as far back as possible so I can deal with whatever pirate comes for us."

Trembling from her head to her feet, Carmela nodded.

Marisol had to fight the panic that threatened to choke off her own breath. An enemy of Spain was now boarding the *Magdalena.* She shook away sickening stories she'd heard of what pirates did to captives, and swung her thick tresses behind her. Stiffening her spine, she flexed the sword and sliced the air back and forth to gain complete mastery of the weapon.

Terrible curses, stomping, clashing of steel and death cries continued to filter down from above. Then, a tomblike silence settled over the ship. The women clutched each other and rolled wide eyes from Jezebel to Marisol.

The red-haired grandmother put her hands on her hips. "You girls, quit your moaning and fainting away. Whoever has taken this ship should be glad to have pretty ones like you to sell. So lighten up."

Heavy boots hit the deck steps and thundered down the passageway. They stopped at the bolted cabin entrance.

Marisol hid the weapon behind her.

A loud knock pounded the door. "Open up, ladies. We've mastered your vessel but we won't harm you." Chuckles followed the throaty speaker, and a different voice sounded. "Not much, that is."

Jezebel shrugged her shoulders and unbolted the door. The rest of the women cowered against the rear wall in Marisol's shadow.

A large man in English clothing, with two pistols and a sword swinging from his leather baldric, stood in the passage grinning. He wore a scarlet scarf under a purple-plumed hat that sat jauntily upon curly red hair pulled into a queue. Blood splattered his shirt.

He sized up Jezebel and frowned, then stomped inside the cabin. Another grin split his swarthy face when his eyes lit on Marisol. He strode closer. "I'm an officer of Captain Becket's, here to take charge of you...ladies."

He emphasized the last word, standing in front of Marisol. "You, most lovely one, may come with me. I will protect you with my life." He reached a hairy arm the size of a beefsteak toward her and licked his thick lips.

She stepped back, swung the sword from behind, and cut a stripe on that same limb.

The man stopped and stared at his arm as blood began to seep from the wound. Then he laughed, swiped the red drops on his clothing, and whipped out his own blade. "By the gods, lads, we've got one tiger in the brood. Get the rest of them. I'll take care of this one's claws." The men behind him herded the other women out into the passage, including an unwilling Carmela.

Marisol moved into fighting stance and struck swords with the pirate. Blows bounced and clanged and sparks flew from the steel blades as the two moved in a macabre dance, clashing, colliding, and then lunging away. Each movement she'd learned so meticulously now came back to her like a familiar habit. The man's dark eyes widened and his growls grew louder as she met his every advance with a precise defense.

She bared her teeth in what might pass as a smile. She was too agile and accurate for the larger man. Before all the women were out in the passage, she whacked a strike on his chest, slashing into his baldric. He snarled and plunged toward her, but she sidestepped his thrust.

"What are you doing, Patrick? Trying to destroy our bounty?" A new voice boomed across the room from the doorway, but Marisol didn't take her eyes from her opponent.

The man attacking her stopped short, moved aside, and sheathed his weapon. He beamed at the newcomer.

Marisol straightened and shifted so she could see both men, but kept her sword aimed to kill. Her breath came in spurts. Her hair, hot and heavy, blanketed her tense shoulders like heavy wool. Who was this member of the enemy crew who drew such respect from her attacker?

Dressed in a smart, gray ruffled shirt and white cravat, this Englishman didn't appear to have been part of the ship battle except for a few red splatters on his neck piece.

He looked at her, and a smile flashed across his tanned face. "You can also put up your blade, milady. None of my men will accost you." He spoke in excellent Castilian.

She stepped back and regarded him, but did not lower her weapon.

He laughed—a pleasant sound—showing even white teeth. "Come now, good swordswoman, whoever you are, you've earned my protection by getting two hits on my proud officer. No one has ever accomplished that as far as I know." He continued smiling at her and the other pirate.

Patrick's red face darkened for a moment, as if trying to decipher the Spanish, then he threw his head back and guffawed. "Captain, I was giving the lady some leeway, seeing as how I didn't want to hurt her." He swiped his mouth on his sleeve. "No sirrah. She'll bring a good price at the market with that proud look of hers and pitch black mane down her back. You ever seen hair like that, sir?" He winked, strode into the passage, and slapped another pirate on the shoulder. "Git these women aboard the *Dryade* before I tear your hide off."

The man in the entrance focused his gaze on Marisol. "I am Captain Ethan Becket at your service, milady." He swept off his white-plumed hat and bowed. A scarlet sash, holding a shining Toledo rapier, circled his narrow waist.

Marisol would know that type of sword anywhere. She brushed damp ringlets from her perspiring forehead, sighed, and lowered her weapon.

He strode forward and took it from her hand.

Her maid hurried back into the cabin and rushed to Marisol's side. "My lady, thank God you're all right."

Captain Becket glanced at her and motioned for Marisol to precede him up the corridor. Carmela grabbed both their small valises from the corner and followed her.

They proceeded up the steps to the deck, strewn with bodies and streaked with blood. The man behind them spoke. "I want to see you at my table tonight, sword lady who cut my lieutenant. What shall I call you?"

Anger surged inside her at his impertinence. At all the unknowns of this horrid capture. She stamped her foot, twisted around, and spat on his boots.

Carmela gasped.

The man grabbed Marisol's shoulders with a strong grip, then used a hand to turn her face up to him. Before speaking, he brushed a strand of hair from her cheek. "If you value your life, my pretty one, never do that again. Not that I would hurt you, but my men might." His gray eyes studied hers and he smiled. A dimple creased his bearded chin.

Her heart jolted and her pulse pounded as she met that confident gaze. She tried to move from under his hands, but he held on.

"And you *will* attend my table." He released her and spun on his heel, striding toward his crew.

Marisol forced air into her lungs, and glared after him.

A voice called out, "Captain, look at the plunder we've pulled from the hold."

Within minutes, she and Carmella had been forced onto the pirate ship with its English flag flying on the top mast. Marisol questioned their escort when he led them to a cabin separate from the other indentured women.

"Captain's orders, ma'm. You orter be happy to have yo own space." With that he left.

Marisol gritted her teeth. What exactly did the arrogant English captain have in mind?

When the door closed behind him and a lock clicked, Carmela's brown eyes darkened and her lips tightened. "What do you make of this, milady? Why did they separate us from the other women?"

Marisol flung herself down on a cot and stared up at the ceiling. She sighed, then looked at her friend. "The captain may think he can have his way with me, but not as long as I have this." She bent and pulled out the small sword still hidden in her boot. She'd been assaulted once, but she'd die before it happened again.

An hour later, a key turned in the lock and a boy of about twelve or thirteen placed a bucket of water inside. He doffed his crumpled hat and pink flowed into his cheeks when he glanced at Marisol sitting on the cot with her arms folded. "The captain sez both ye are to come to dinner in his cabin in about two hours. There's clean dresses and stuff in that trunk yonder." He gestured to a chest in the far corner. "I'll be back for ye."

The draw of a bath and clean clothes was more than she could resist. She and Carmela had found precious few opportunities to wash themselves or their clothing after being forced aboard the Spanish ship on its way to the West Indies.

She chose a rose-colored silk dress from the trunk and encouraged her maid to wear a pale blue that looked well on her.

"Will we accept the pirate's invitation?" Carmela asked.

"We will go to his dinner. I can learn a lot at a captain's table."

In the captain's quarters that night, Marisol sat with Carmela in the two vacant chairs near Captain Becket. Ignoring the winks and grins from the men around the oak sideboard, she feasted her eyes on the generous platters of food. The various dishes and fruits made her mouth water. The *Magdalena* had served nothing like this spread.

"Please help yourselves to all you like, ladies. After we bless it, that is." Captain Becket nodded to an older gray-headed man at the other end of the large table. The man stood and spoke a prayer over the food.

Carmela poked Marisol with her elbow. She ignored it, but she couldn't stop her mind from spinning. What kind of pirate ship prayed over their meals before partaking?

The captain reached for a wooden platter and drew a succulent, roasted chicken quarter onto his plate. He bit into the juicy meat with gusto, wiping his chin with a shiny cloth. He pulled a chunk of brown bread from one of the many loaves on the table and pushed it into his mouth after each portion of poultry.

Marisol fingered the blue napkin beside her plate before placing it on her lap. What kind of pirate ship had silk napkins and china?

Carmela, smiling with anticipation, lifted a platter of chicken, helped herself, and passed the dish to Marisol.

From her initial bite, Marisol forgot everything around her but the succulent meat—the first she'd had since leaving Spain. She made short work of the fowl, a thick portion of bread, and a sizable helping of steamed cabbage, interspersed with long drinks from a goblet of water. Perhaps she shouldn't relish these extravagances her captors offered, but she and Carmela needed to keep their strength up. And she wasn't sure she could have resisted the tantalizing smells of this meal.

As she touched her napkin to her lips, she looked up and found the captain staring at her with that infuriating smile of his.

So it entertained him to see hungry ladies dine on his generous fare? Resistance surged inside her again, and she dropped her hands into her lap, determined not to take another bite or drink. A serving boy poured wine into a gold-rimmed glass beside her plate, but she ignored it. Carmela partook of hers and poked her lady's arm. Marisol shook her head. Never would she entertain a low-down pirate.

Everyone stood when the captain rose to offer a toast, but Marisol stayed seated. Carmela came to her feet, but sat again when Marisol didn't move.

Captain Becket held up his wine challis. "To His Britannic Majesty, the King of England."

All the men shouted their approval and drank the tribute.

Once again, he poured wine and took up his goblet. He nodded toward Marisol and Carmela. "We have two Spanish ladies at our table tonight, and we will not forget their loyalties." He hoisted his cup. "To His Most Catholic Majesty, the King of Spain."

Marisol gasped, fumbled with her skirt and petticoats, and stood with Carmela beside her. They both raised their wine goblets.

Some of the men muttered until the captain continued his salute. "May the good king continue to supply England with great wealth."

Jovial laughs erupted, and the toast was drunk.

Marisol did not drink. She plunked her cup down and marched to the door with her gown swishing behind her. She could hear the hurried footsteps of her maid behind her, but she didn't turn to look.

The young crewman who had escorted them fell into step beside them in the passageway. "That's our Commander. Always got a cheerful laugh up his sleeve, 'specially after we've won a battle."

Marisol glared at him and clenched her jaw.

~

The next morning the captain sent for her and Carmela. They entered his cabin and found him sitting in a large chair behind his desk, feet propped on the corner of the furniture.

He studied a map held in his hands. When he saw them, he folded the map and moved his feet to the floor.

"Please sit and relax, ladies. I just want information, and I've something to share with you."

Marisol sat on the edge of a wooden bench and her maid slipped down beside her.

He leaned forward. "What were you two doing on a Spanish ship for indentured servants?" His eyes sought Marisol's, then moved down from her lace mantilla to her ruffled pink skirt.

His steady gaze was hard to meet, but she held his look, even though heat rose up her neck.

He glanced at Carmela, but the maid lowered her head.

He looked back at Marisol. "We seldom find ladies with their maids traveling on a ship as indentured servants."

Marisol squeezed her fists in her lap and took a deep breath. "We planned to buy passage to my aunt's estate in Cartagena, but ruffians accosted us, stole our funds, and we had no choice but to sign indenture papers to travel to the West Indies."

A frown creased the man's tanned forehead. His thick brows almost met in the middle. "But why did two women leave Spain alone? Were you not aware of the great risks without an escort?"

Lying did not come easy to Marisol. She lowered her eyes and searched for the best answer. "We had an escort. My husband."

A muffled gasp sounded from Carmela. Hopefully the captain didn't hear it.

"The attackers killed him when he tried to protect us." Marisol lifted her head and forced herself to look the captain in the eye. The man may soon know of her pregnancy. This small lie would take care of that, wouldn't it?

Captain Becket leaned back in his chair. His piercing gray eyes moved from one to the other under his furrowed brow. "I am sorry to hear of your misfortune, both of you." Then his gaze came to rest on Marisol. "And for the loss of your husband."

He sounded sincere, but could a pirate have compassion or sympathy? She cast that idea aside.

The man looked away. "But your situation poses a problem for me as far as trying to assist you...which you would deserve." He searched Marisol's face again, and heat stained her cheeks.

Did he doubt her story? She took a deep breath and plunged in with her request. "Can you help us get to Cartagena? My aunt will reward you."

He toyed with a feather quill on his desk. "The problem is that my crew is expecting something from the sale of all the indenture papers, yours included."

She sighed. "Of course. Pirates must all have their share."

The captain stiffened and his nostrils flared. "Madam...Señora, I am no pirate and this is not a pirate ship. I am a privateer with a Letter of Marque from His Majesty, the King of England, with full authority to attack enemy vessels."

She stared at him. He must believe what he was saying, but he was deluding himself. She swallowed hard, lifted her chin, and regarded him with coldness. "We both know there is no real difference between pirates and privateers these days."

He threw the quill down on the desk. "Whether or not you understand this, Señora, I have to inform you that you"—he glanced at Carmela—"and your maid will have to be offered as indentured servants when we get to the port of Charles Town."

Marisol stood. Every part of her wanted to defy him. To slap that handsome face. "That's fine. Just house us with the rest of the slaves." She turned and flew from the cabin. Or would have, except her dress caught on the door handle. She jerked it free and heard the fabric rip. A sob escaped her lips before she could clamp her jaw tight enough to hold it in. She swiped her eyes and hurried to her cabin, her maid trailing behind her.

Carmela locked their door and came to sit by her. "My lady, why did you let this man upset you so?"

Marisol swallowed the lump in her throat and shook her head. "I have no reason to allow him to cause me any kind of displeasure. He's the captain of this terrible ship and we have no choice but to obey whatever he says."

Carmela sighed and nodded.

But the man did disturb her. More than anyone she could remember, other than Diego that last evening. She pushed that horrid scene from her mind. This was a different kind of...unease. Clenching her eyes, she couldn't force the captain's handsome face away, with its look of sympathy when he spoke about the loss of her husband. But he was a man, wasn't he? And she'd never trust another.

She sighed remembering her lie to him. She fell back on the cot and placed her hand on her abdomen. *For you, little one. You must have a father. I must have a husband, even a dead one.* Yet another word echoed across her heart. *Murderer.* She pushed her face into the pillow to cover a sob. Surely things couldn't get worse than this.

But the following week, Carmela came down with a fever.

CHAPTER 3

Captain Ethan Becket walked down the *Dryade's* gang plank onto the Charles Town dock and groaned. A crowd of jostling men blocked his way. They pushed, spat, and cursed around the platform of indentured servants from his ship and others in the harbor.

His loyal lieutenant and navigator, Tim Cullen, strode beside him. "Wonder what's drawn so many buyers today?" He gestured to the brigantine bobbing in the dark water beside Ethan's. "And for that ship's folk, no less. God bless the poor souls that survived the crossing with that captain."

Ethan hated to see people herded across a platform and bid for like animals. The throng blocked their way, but he scanned the men and women lined up from the neighboring vessel.

A couple holding the hand of a young daughter clung to each other. An older male trudged up, hunched over until the seller prodded him in the back. Three almost-grown boys stood with their chests out and shoulders high. Confidence and daring shouted from the firm limbs of their bodies. Two painted women, past their first spring, twirled fans and smiled at the men near the raised dais. All the people wore dirty, ragged clothing.

These poor from Europe had flocked to the New World and a new beginning. And soon they would walk away with their masters for the next seven years.

The indentured servants from Ethan's ship filed onto the platform. He couldn't leave until he saw what would happen to one in particular. He searched the female faces for the young woman who had invaded his dreams on the voyage back to Charles Town.

Ethan found the Spanish lady he knew only as Marisol at the far end of the row. His heart lurched, and a band tightened around his middle. He had no choice but to let her papers be offered for sale because of the ship's articles of agreement.

He'd tried to befriend her on the way to Charles Town, but she refused his efforts, especially after her maid died of the fever. From that day on, she had all but locked herself away in her cabin for the rest of the trip. Ethan insisted she take the trays of food inside, and he sent a woman named Jezebel to attend her.

Although in a ragged Spanish dress and a torn mantilla covering most of her black hair, she stood now with her head high. Her stoic, lovely, face stalled his breathing.

Tim turned to glance at him. "You've noticed her, too, sir? Wonder why she kept to herself most of the trip?"

Ethan's lips pressed, and he shook his head. "Let's stand here and see what happens to her." He refused to acknowledge his hammering heart and the way his throat had grown dry. No woman could interest him again. His Olivia would forever hold his heart, though never again his hand, this side of eternity.

Within the hour, the señora stood alone on the platform. All others had walked away with their new masters. Several better-dressed men still waited, smoking cigars and pipes.

"Now we've saved the best for last, gentlemen." The hawker's voice shouted across the heads of the men present. "Here's a real Spanish noblewoman. She speaks three languages and can sword fight like a sailor." He spit a glob of tobacco juice off the side of the platform.

"You shoulda seen this slip of a lady handle a blade when the

Dryade overtook her galleon. I've heard she sliced into Captain Becket's best swordsman. This here woman will make a great governess for your children—girls, *and boys*." He walked toward her and looked her up and down. "She's a mite weak-looking from the crossing, but sirs, you feed her well, and I promise she'll perk up and make you a good tutor for your younguns." Then he grinned and winked at his audience. "Or a warm mistress for your bed."

The woman's cheeks drained of color, and she trembled as if about to faint.

Ethan gritted his teeth and swallowed the bile rising in his throat.

Tim kicked the dock post and glanced his way. "Captain, I just got me an idea. Think about it. This could be just like your sister the Spanish devils captured. You rescue this woman, give her a safe home, and maybe the good Lord will do the same for Miss Grace."

The thought blasted into Ethan's mind and took root. Dear sweet Grace. Was she still alive somewhere on the Spanish Main? Was she in safe hands? One day he would find and rescue her. Soon.

Tim continued, "Don't you see? You know that's the way you taught us God works when you still was a pastor. Think of the great governess this lady could make for your boy and helper for your housekeeper."

Yes, Joshua was almost too much for Mrs. Piper now. The bands around Ethan's chest loosened, and he inhaled a deep breath. Though he doubted God cared about Ethan's concern over his sister, still, his son would need a good tutor. He looked at Marisol again. Even needing a bath and clean clothing, her natural beauty shined through.

He shook that notion from his head. He would help her, that was all.

A pompously dressed, overweight gentleman at the front dumped his pipe on the edge of the platform and announced in a loud, authoritative voicc. "I'll give you twenty-five pounds for her indenture paper."

Eduardo Talley. The owner of Charles Town's main tavern and other nefarious businesses made Ethan's skin crawl.

He pushed through the crowd, stopped at the podium, and looked straight at the perspiring man. "I bid fifty pounds."

Marisol staggered back when she recognized Ethan, but something akin to fire glinted in her blue eyes before they darkened to indigo. She lowered thick black lashes and dropped her chin almost to her chest.

The hawker beamed at the captain and the tavern owner and licked his lips. "Well, sirs, nothing like a little competition, is there?"

Talley's corpulent face set into stiff lines, and he mopped his damp brow with a soiled handkerchief. "I'll give seventy-five pounds." As if that ended the bidding, he pulled out a thick purse.

Ethan fixed his gaze on the tavern owner and gritted his teeth. No way would he allow the woman to end up in the man's soiled hands.

Eduardo Talley shifted away from Ethan's smoldering look, but he clamped down on his pipe and started counting out notes.

Ethan turned to the hawker. "I'll give you one hundred pounds in gold." His incredible bid drew gasps across the dock.

Even Marisol now stared at him, her eyes wide and full lips parted.

He pulled a leather pouch from his sash and laid it on the platform.

Tim Cullen, looking on, whistled under his breath and rocked back on his heels, grinning.

Talley swore, then gathered up his notes. "Only a fool would pay that kind of money for a woman, sirrah. Even if she was the Queen of England." He ground out the words, then spat at Ethan's feet and slung his heavy body away.

~

Marisol couldn't bear to look into the captain's face—the same one she had tried to block out of her mind the past month sailing to Charles Town. Never had she dreamed she would end up sold like a commodity that others called indentured servanthood. She stooped and picked up her bag, then went to stand before him, her head bowed.

He'd paid an unbelievable amount of gold. What were his plans for her? She moistened her tight, dry lips.

He spoke to her in his perfect Castilian. "Marisol, you have nothing to fear." His deep voice sounded kind. But so had Diego's the weeks before his attack.

The lieutenant who Marisol knew as Tim Cullen doffed his hat and grinned. His red hair gleamed in the midday sun. "No, ma'am. We mean you no harm. Can't say the same about that other feller." He reached for her valise, and she let him have it.

She looked into Ethan's bearded, tanned face, defined by the sunlight washing over the dock. Never had she seen such eyes—clear as smoke from a holy fire, but tinged with sadness. She took a deep breath and responded in English. "My full name is Doña Marisol Valentin. Thank you for saving me from that other señor." Or had she now ended up in worse hands? On no account would she trust any man again, no matter how smooth his words, or startling his glance.

He smiled and motioned for her to accompany them. "Come, I've a carriage waiting." As they walked away from the dock, he spoke to her again. "Doña Marisol Valentin, when you're settled in, I would like to know more about you."

The *more* she could never share. She placed her hand across her middle. But she would have to tell him *something more* soon.

The captain helped her into the carriage, and Tim placed her bag next to her feet. The captain turned to him. "You will see to the unloading of the rest of our cargo as soon as possible?"

"Yes, sir. Have no worry about that. Just as you instructed." He saluted his superior and walked back toward the *Dryade*, whistling.

The captain climbed in beside her and did not speak again as the carriage, driven by the ship's cabin boy, passed through Charles Town streets. She was unwashed, with her hair hopelessly knotted and her dress near rags, which surely made her an unpleasant companion.

But that was hardly her fault. Nor was she eager to impress this man.

Marisol turned her attention to the three-story mansions they passed along the bay. Each had a widow's watch at the top level with a protective railing.

After riding in silence for a while, she glanced sideways at Captain Becket. His handsome bronzed face no longer carried the imprint of a smile. His brows drew downward in a frown and a muscle quivered in his jaw. Was her odor that bad? Or did he regret the gold he laid down for her? Heat spread over her cheeks and moisture gathered in her eyes. She blinked it away, locking her jaw.

The houses became smaller as they arrived at the outskirts of the colony. At a bridge over a fast-flowing river, the horse stopped and snorted. The boy spoke to the animal, "All right, Dolly girl. You know this here bridge, so get on over it and take us home." Tossing her head, she finally stepped forward onto the wooden slats. Her hoof beats sounded loud in the evening air until they reached the other side.

They passed a church and graveyard, and arrived at a small, two-story frame house with a barn and fence behind it. The carriage stopped at a walkway.

Captain Becket stepped down, reached for her valise, and then extended his hand to help her alight. His strong hand swallowed hers and sent a tingle up her arm. She released him as soon as her feet touched the ground.

"Hope you like your new home, Doña Marisol. And I've two people I want you to meet. Mrs. Piper and my son Joshua." His somber air lifted and his lips softened as he spoke his son's name.

So he was married. Good. But why did that news nip at her heart?

The man turned to the young driver and touched his shoulder. "Danny, rub the mare down and feed her, and thank you for being a great cabin boy this trip. I'll be taking you again on the next one—and soon."

The boy's face lit in a smile that reached his ears. "Yessir, Capt'n. I wanna go." His visage, too, carried the mark of southern winds and sunshine.

The captain led her up a stone-laid path with daisies growing on both sides. He stepped onto the porch, and opened the door. "Mrs. Piper, I'm home. Joshua, my boy, where are you?"

As Marisol entered the hall behind him, a blue-clothed ball of energy flew from a side room and latched onto Señor Becket's knees. "Daddee!"

The man set the valise on the floor, scooped up the boy, and kissed his cheek. "Son, I want you to meet a new friend of ours who will be here with you and Mrs. Piper. Say hello to Doña Valentin." He turned to Marisol as his mouth curved into tenderness. "This is Joshua. He's just turned a big two."

The child muttered, "Hullo," and pressed his face into his father's broad shoulder.

A smile tugged at Marisol's cheeks as she looked at the small boy with thick brown hair like his father's. "Hola, *joven hombre*."

The youngster raised his tousled head and turned wide eyes toward her, his father's same startling gray ones.

She spoke again quickly. "Joshua, that was in the Spanish language. Here's my greeting in English. Hello, young man."

The captain offered her a brief, arresting grin. Then he turned to a woman dressed in a blue house dress and spotless apron who stood in a side doorway. A small lace headpiece lay on top of her smooth gray hair, pulled into a low bun at the back of her head.

"Mrs. Piper, I want you to meet Doña Marisol Valentin. She will be your helper and a governess, if you please, to Joshua. She's fresh off the indenture platform."

So that's what he had in mind. Governess. Marisol breathed a sigh of relief.

"This is Mrs. Piper, the best housekeeper and cook in Charles Town." The captain nodded toward the older woman.

The housekeeper smiled at him, then turned her attention to Marisol. Her wide, blue eyes examined her and beamed a warm welcome. "Well, I do say this is good news, Ethan. Welcome, my dear, and praises be to God for another soul rescued from the indentured block." She reached for the valise and sniffed. "I believe you can use some food and we'll see what else." She motioned for Marisol to follow her.

Did her words mean Captain Becket had rescued others?

They sat down for the midday meal at the kitchen table, a far cry from the long dining table she'd been accustomed to at their Cadiz estate. After the captain and Joshua finished eating, the two of them moved into the front room. Marisol took the opportunity for a second helping of the savory shepherd pie and fresh bread. It'd been so long since she'd let herself enjoy such fare.

The housekeeper smiled. "Would you like a bath after you finish, my dear?"

Marisol swallowed her mouthful. Her unwashed presence had to be offensive to this woman, especially here in her spotless kitchen. "I'd love to, and a change of clothes." She looked down at her plate and sighed. Her other dresses in the valise were as dirty as the one she wore. Never had she been in such a plight.

"Good. I'll heat the water and we'll wash all your clothes, too. I'll find something you can wear meantime." The housekeeper poured water into a large pot hanging in the fireplace.

Captain Becket stuck his head into the kitchen. "Do you think the room upstairs will do for Marisol, Mrs. Piper? It's fine to move my old sea chest to the hall corner."

"Count it done, sir."

"I'm going to take a walk with Joshua, so help our new *governess* get settled." Ethan emphasized the word, then left with his son in tow.

"To the cemetery, is my bet," the woman mumbled, shaking her head.

"Pardon?" Marisol studied the housekeeper, who was stacking more logs on the fire, her face pink from the heat. The clean smell of burning pine filled the kitchen.

"I said he's probably gonna go see his wife's grave, he is. That's where he goes every time he comes back from his sea ventures."

He was a widower then.

Marisol tried to keep her features composed, but her smile wavered. Did that news make her safer or more at risk in his house?

The older woman stopped her busy activities for a moment. "His wife died pert near a year ago and the wee one she was trying to birth went with her. He's not gotten over it."

"How terrible." Perhaps that had been grief shadowing the captain's countenance as they drove home from the dock, not her odor or regret at having purchased her indenture paper at a dear price. She helped herself to another spoonful of the tasty shepherd pie.

The woman dusted off her hands. "You might as well know, too, that's when Reverend Ethan Becket became a captain instead. Threw him bad. Said he couldn't understand why God would take his precious wife and wee one. He left the little Presbyterian church down the road and went back to sea. He was a fine preacher and everybody loved him and his Olivia. But enough of that. Come with me."

The man had been clergy? Marisol shivered. She wanted nothing to do with clergy. Tales of the monstrous acts of the Dominican priests who presided over the Spanish Inquisition had reached her ears through Carmela. She even wondered if they had something to do with the strange death of her English mother.

Marisol had been twelve years old at the time. One day her beautiful, laughing mother was with them, the next day she disappeared. Her father brought Marisol into his large study and told her, with tears streaming down his face, that her mother had died. Then Carmela came to live with them. No one ever explained why there was never a funeral for Mama.

She took a deep breath and stood to follow the housekeeper.

Mrs. Piper led her upstairs to an attic room under the eaves of the cottage. A lovely chamber. The single window faced east so she would be able to see the sun rise. A cot and a small table holding a lantern lined one wall, a trunk, chifforobe, and chair the other side. A braided rug warmed the room with its splashes of red, orange, and yellow.

Marisol helped Mrs. Piper move the trunk to the hall and transport a wooden tub downstairs. The thought of a real bath delighted her more than she would admit to the housekeeper.

Upstairs preparing, Marisol pulled her most precious possession from her bodice, the Valentin family rose-cut ruby brooch—the only jewelry she'd managed to hide from the kidnappers, the ships' crews, and passengers.

On the Spanish ship, they had stolen everything else of value she and her maid had hidden. Dear Carmela. She blinked at the moisture forming in her eyes. How she missed her friend. A tear slid past her defenses, edging down Marisol's cheek. Why had God let her precious maid succumb to the fever on the ship? If He was all-knowing, He must have been aware of how much she'd loved and needed her friend.

She pressed the pin with its golden V filigree to her lips, then looked around the room for a good hiding place. The lowest drawer in the chifforobe seemed best. She removed her boots and the hidden short sword, then replaced the blade in one shoe before pushing the pair under the cot. Undressing down to her chemise, she padded down the stairs when Mrs. Piper called her.

In the kitchen, Marisol slid down into the tub until she submerged to her chin. She closed her eyes in delight and relished the warm water enveloping her. Finally rousing herself, she ducked her head and scrubbed her hair and body with the special soap given her. Mrs. Piper had been adamant about using the soap.

"Good for lice," she said. "But I added some lavender to it, too."

The woman took Marisol's clothes to the back yard to boil them in a pot.

A thought of the captain fluttered across Marisol's mind as she enjoyed the exquisite pleasure of her first real bath since leaving Spain. Mrs. Piper had assured her he wouldn't return for another hour or more. Which meant she didn't have to think about him or any man.

She sank low again, savoring the warm water on her skin. She owed Ethan Becket one hearty thanks at least. Whatever reason caused him to save her from that horrible other señor, Marisol would forever be grateful and do her best to please him as governess of his son.

After stepping out of the tub, she wrapped herself in the drying sheet Mrs. Piper left for her. Hearing the joyful cries of Joshua and the deeper voice of Ethan Becket approaching from the road, she darted up the stairs to her room.

She slipped on the under clothing and ruffled yellow dress Mrs. Piper had laid out on the cot for her. Being clean had never felt so wonderful. She glanced in the chifforobe door mirror, scrunching her nose at her black hair, even darker when wet, that hung in long waves down her back. The ivory skin of her face, now rid of its layer of grime, glistened with cleanness. She'd inherited her light complexion from her English mother, her thick dark tresses from her Spanish father. But then something else caught Marisol's attention in the looking glass.

Her thickening waist. How long would the full-skirted dresses hide her secret? Thank God the morning sickness had almost ceased. She dried her locks as best she could, then plaited them and wound them around her head. As she worked with her hair, the fragrance of lavender lingered in the room and refreshed her spirit, even as concern over the pregnancy weighed on her heart.

After readying herself, she headed downstairs to see where she could be helpful. After Mrs. Piper's kindness, it was time she set to work helping the woman. Marisol stood in the kitchen cleaning and peeling vegetables for the evening meal when Ethan and Joshua walked in from the porch swing.

The child ran to a wooden crate of toy soldiers and cannons in the corner. Ethan started to follow, but when he looked in Marisol's direction, he stopped short, his mouth falling open as his face grew pale.

Heat rushed into her cheeks when she met his pained eyes.

The housekeeper laid her paring knife aside. "I loaned her the dress, sir, since all of hers needed care. I hoped you wouldn't mind."

Captain Becket turned to the woman. "No, of course not. She would need clothing. She can use whatever fits her." He ducked his head and left the kitchen.

Marisol looked down at her frock and frowned. She should've guessed the dress belonged to his wife, since Mrs. Piper was much plumper. She pressed her lips together and chided herself for at first thinking the man was so taken by her fresh appearance. Besides, why should she care what he thought?

As they readied the food, Marisol apologized to Mrs. Piper several times for needing to ask so many questions about the meal's preparation. She'd never felt so inept. The housekeeper, no doubt, now knew she had never prepared a meal. But the woman didn't chide her for her ignorance. Not once.

The evening meal was an interesting affair, with Ethan stuffing bread and cheese into his mouth, followed by spoonfuls of thick cabbage soup. Sitting across from the man, attempting to ignore him, was no easy thing. His physical prowess, vitality, and attitude of self-command intrigued her. Unlike any man she had ever met, she was both attracted and warned. Diego Vargas had once appeared self-confident, attractive, and even kind at times.

Instead, she focused her attention on Joshua and his charming chatter. The boy had a good appetite like his father.

Later, when Captain Becket retired to the study with his pipe, Marisol read a story to Joshua, lying in his trundle bed in Mrs. Piper's bedroom. When his eyes closed with contentment, she pulled the cover up to his little chin, kissed his rosy cheek, and slipped upstairs to her bedchamber.

After unpinning and brushing her hair loose to hang down her back, she undressed to her chemise, put on a borrowed gown, and dropped onto the cot. With her full stomach, bathed body, and the lavender scent still lingering in the air, her eyes drifted shut the moment her head rested on the bed.

She was in the stable corridor again, scrambling backward away from Diego Vargas. One glance at the lust in his eyes as he advanced on her made fear claw in her chest. He reached out and she tried to duck away, but his massive hand grabbed her bodice, then knocked her to the floor. The breath left her in a fell swoop, and she scrambled for air. Only when she inhaled her first gasp did she see him casting off his sword, unbuttoning his clothing. He advanced on her, and for a second, fear held her immobile. He bent down, and a scream welled up in her throat.

A bang sounded, jerking her into confusion. Her bedroom door pushed open, and Ethan stood there holding a lantern, dressed only in his trousers. Mrs. Piper huffed up the stairs behind him.

No. Marisol struggled to push the remnants of the dream away as she stared at the concerned faces. She sat up and pulled the blanket to her chin, glad the dim light hid her warm cheeks. "I'm sorry. I was having a nightmare." She looked into the two faces peering at her. She couldn't let them know the reason for her torment. "I'm so sorry, please go back to bed. It will be all right now. Did I disturb Joshua?"

Mrs. Piper approached and sat on the edge of the cot, then patted Marisol's hand. "No, you didn't and you *will* be fine, lamb. No doubt you lived a nightmare on that Spanish ship. But things will be better for you here. Would you like me to stay a wee bit?"

Ethan moved toward the stand. "Would you prefer I leave this lamp on the table?" His strong, tanned physique glistened in the beaming light.

Marisol forced her eyes away and turned to Mrs. Piper. "No, to both of you. Thank you so much, but I think I will be fine. I was just so tired." She yawned and forced herself to relax on the cot, wishing she could crawl under it.

"If you're sure." Mrs. Piper seemed reluctant to leave, but

finally stood and padded toward the door, following the captain into the hall. He pulled the door closed behind them.

Marisol sighed and shut her eyes, but the whispered words of Mrs. Piper outside the room infiltrated her sleepy mind.

"Wonder who the man was she screamed about? She sure hollered out his name loud enough, like he was about to do her harm."

Captain Becket's strong voice didn't adjust well to a whisper. "Who knows what the poor girl went through on board the Spanish ship before we rescued her. We can only make her feel safe now."

"Yes, sir. We'll do our best." Footsteps descended the stairs, Mrs. Piper's softer steps following the captain's heavier tread.

Captain Becket wanted her to feel out of harm's way? The best way to do that would be to leave her alone.

~

Ethan strode into his bedchamber and closed the door. The vision of the woman upstairs, sitting up in her bed, her thick raven hair fanning out from her pale, lovely countenance, wouldn't leave his mind.

He sat on the edge of the mattress with his face in his hands. Why did his breath still come so fast? He needed something to steady himself. Something to clear his mind of what he'd just witnessed.

He stood and walked to the mantel, then picked up the small framed image of Olivia and pressed it to his cheek. His dear, sweet wife. As usual, a glimpse of her gentle face eased the raw edges of his nerves.

Driving back through Charles Town toward home earlier, the pain of knowing Olivia wouldn't be there to throw open the door to him had been as strong as ever. Would it ever lessen?

He replaced the small picture and balled his fist, wishing he could slam it into the wall. And he would have if he'd been on the *Dryade,* but he had to control himself here at home. Why would a good God take a sweet, wonderful wife like Olivia and an innocent babe? His heart seethed and his nostrils flared as he paced across his bedroom. One thing was sure. No woman could ever replace Olivia.

He stretched out on his bed and let thoughts of her, memories of the love they had shared, lull him to sleep. Before he slept, Marisol's striking face flashed across his mind and the words she had screamed out. *No, Diego Vargas!* A male Spanish name. Who was he and what part had he played in the life of the young woman who would live in Ethan's house for the next seven years?

What secrets did she conceal behind that exquisite face and brooding eyes?

CHAPTER 4

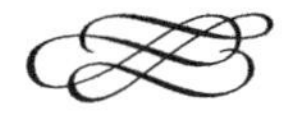

The next morning, a knock sounded at Marisol's door. She arose from bed and reached for her robe. Had she overslept? "Buenos días. Who is it?"

"It's me, lamb. I have something to show you." Mrs. Piper's voice exuded kindness.

Marisol opened the door. "Come in."

The housekeeper, in her starched apron and cap, entered and sat on the cot, then patted the space beside her for Marisol.

"This is a book I'd love to loan you, my dear. I received my copy at a George Whitefield meeting in a field outside town last year, and Captain Becket received a copy, too. I'm loaning you his copy from his library, since I read mine every night and every morning." The woman held out a thick volume. "Have you ever seen a Holy Bible like this?"

"No, I don't think so." Marisol took the tome and opened it. English leaped up from the page, and a memory fluttered across her mind. She looked up at Mrs. Piper. "In Spain, the Church fathers banned this book. The Inquisition judges arrested anyone found with it in their possession." How could she read something so forbidden? But she didn't hand it back to the housekeeper.

"I thought this might be the case with you, child. But I suggest you read it and decide for yourself if it's a worthy book. Many scholars labored years, and some even died getting this Bible to us in English." The woman smiled. "It might help relieve more nightmares. Especially read Psalm 23." She stood. "And keep the Bible as long as you like."

"I will. Gracias. But won't Captain Becket miss his book?"

The housekeeper clasped her work-hardened hands in front of her and sighed. "I'm sad to say Ethan doesn't have much use for it now. Not since he lost his two loved ones. And besides, he said this morning he was preparing for another trip to who knows where on the *Dryade*. Him and the boy, Danny." She turned and left the room.

Marisol sat for a moment as the woman's words sank in. Captain Ethan Becket still grieved the loss of his wife. And he escaped to the sea for relief. Would to God she could break away from her past the way he was doing. Maybe if she could get to Cartagena, she could start a new life there.

Ruined for life. Murderess. So far, she hadn't escaped the voice that rolled around her mind.

She shuddered and laid the Bible on the table. After splashing water on her face, she dressed in a gown of pale blue muslin from the trunk Mrs. Piper had placed in her room, then headed downstairs.

After the morning meal, Marisol drew Joshua to the back yard and told him she wanted to show him something. From her window she'd seen a bird's nest on a low branch in the oak tree near the barn. And unless she was mistaken, baby birds filled it. She could use the nest to teach him Spanish vocabulary.

They tromped over the grassy plot to the tree, then she pulled the limb down just enough for Joshua to see inside.

"Birdies!" he exclaimed when he saw the small birds with their mouths all open and crying. He reached toward them.

Marisol grabbed his hand. "No, we must not touch them. Their mother is probably searching for food for her babies and will soon be back."

She pulled the child away and explained as they walked. "They're robins. Can you say *robins?*"

He repeated the new word.

"And they live in a *nest*."

The two-year-old echoed the word, and she patted his hand.

After she taught him how to say nest in Spanish, he went to play in a sand pile in the middle of the yard. She heard him muttering *nest* and *el nido* over and over. He would be a joy to teach. She sat on a nearby bench and watched him dig in the sand as the sun grew warmer.

The frantic flying of the mother bird around the tree drew Marisol's attention. Whatever was wrong? Joshua noticed, too, and stopped playing. He stood and started toward the nest.

Fear gripped Marisol's chest as she saw a long, slithering shape moving in the grass.

"Joshua, come back. Right now!" She ran toward him, scanning the yard for anything to stop the intruder. Not even a rock protruded from the ground.

The boy saw the serpent, stumbled, then plopped down on the ground, crying. The black striped snake lifted its head and flicked its tongue into the air.

Madre de Dios, help.

Marisol reached Joshua, her heart racing as she pulled him away. She'd only have one chance to step on the head of the reptile without being bitten. Pulling her skirt out of the way, she waited until the animal recoiled, then stomped as hard as she could.

Her boot landed squarely on the snake, and she pressed down with all her might as it writhed and whipped the ground. Joshua toddled closer and clutched at Marisol's skirt.

"No." Pressing harder on the snake's head, she scooped up the boy, away from the twisting animal's body. Her breath was coming in short gasps as she clutched the lad to her, but she struggled to rein in her rampant emotions.

She'd almost lost her charge on her first full day as governess. She patted Joshua's shoulder with a trembling hand and tried to swallow, still keeping her foot pressed down. How long could she hold the snake with her boot? *Dear God, send help.*

She'd just drawn a breath to call for help when a man raced from the barn, brandishing a shovel. "Step aside, ma'am, and I'll take care of 'im."

She eased her foot aside, and the man struck quickly, chopping off the head.

With the danger gone, he looked at Marisol with wonder on his face. "Ma'am, I ain't never seen a woman do what you jist did." He took off his hat, put the hoe handle under his arm, and wiped his brow.

Joshua looked up from Marisol's shoulder. "Snake gone?" He pointed at the still writhing body.

She patted his thick curls. "Yes, it's gone, even though it might keep moving for a while. Let's tell our helper we appreciate his aid." As she turned to the man, something about his thin, tanned jaw, deep set dark eyes, and prominent nose looked familiar. "I'm Marisol Valentin, the new governess. We thank you for your help."

"Yes'm, I knows who ye are. My son tol' me. Danny's my boy what drove you here from the dock yestidy and was on the ship, too." He still stared at her.

Ah, yes. The man was an older version of the boy's same countenance. He spoke again. "Sorry, I dun forgot me manners. I'm Nate, and I keep the garden and flowers here for Captain Becket."

"Glad to meet you, señor." She inhaled a steadying breath to force her mind back to normal affairs. "I love the daisies at the front walk. Now we'd best go inside and prepare for the noon meal." Marisol turned to carry Joshua toward the house. When she reached the steps, she glanced back. The man still stared.

Then he shook his head and headed toward the barn.

~

As they sat down to the meal that evening, Captain Becket looked first at Joshua, then Marisol. "I've heard an amazing tale from my carriage driver. A tale it seems he got from an eye witness. His pa. It's about a snake."

Heat rose in Marisol's cheeks.

The child stopped a spoon in midair. "Ole snake gone. Head off." He sputtered and porridge spilled over his chin.

"Governess, do you know anything about this snake tale?" The captain stared at Marisol with lifted brows.

Mrs. Piper wiped Joshua's face with a napkin. "She saved your son with naught but her boot. I saw it out the kitchen window. Wouldn't have believed it, if I hadn't seen it."

Marisol cleared her throat. "It was nothing to brag about, I assure you. I grew up around an estate—that is, stables, and we often dealt with snakes. I'm sorry if you think I was not...taking good care of your son. We had looked at a bird nest and..."

Ethan shook his head and passed the roasted beef and vegetables. "I just want to thank you, Doña Marisol Valentin, for dealing with this intruder until Nate could get there with his hoe. You're a brave woman."

Joshua swallowed a mouthful and repeated, "B'ave, woman," in the same tone as his father's.

Marisol could only breathe out a sigh of relief.

After the meal, Ethan glanced at Mrs. Piper. "I have work to do at my dock office." He nodded at Marisol, then kissed his son's cheek and left. A few minutes later when they were tidying the kitchen, his carriage rumbled down the drive.

Marisol put the boy to bed and wandered out to the front porch with the Bible Mrs. Piper had given her. She sank into a rocker. The twilight of this southern hemisphere was something to behold. The previous night she'd been too tired to enjoy it, but tonight she'd bask in it.

A pinkish golden light permeated the grounds and trees as the sun slipped farther toward the horizon. Crickets strummed in chorus in the warm evening air, laced with the fragrance of Nate's flowers.

She opened the Bible to the middle as Mrs. Piper had shown her and found the Psalms, then the twenty-third chapter. *The Lord is my shepherd. I shall not want.*

The thought of having nothing to want for—of having Someone care for her needs as a shepherd did his sheep—seemed too wonderful. How did one go about making the Lord her shepherd? And was it even possible for a murderer? Probably not.

She leaned her head back on the rocker and closed her eyes. The sleepy sound of the cicadas filled her ears and blocked her thoughts.

~

In his merchant office above the dock, Ethan checked off all the cargo goods on his accounting sheet that Tim had left for him. The buyers had vied for the sugar, tobacco, cacao, and casks of rum from Jamaica. He'd made a neat profit on this merchant trip.

Not to mention the gold they'd plundered from the captured Spanish galleon that carried Marisol and the other indentured servants. He'd added quite a few pieces of eight and nuggets to his strongbox, left after the coin he paid for Marisol's indenture paper. As usual, when the Spaniards ran up the white flag and surrendered under his cannons, he'd ordered the crew to take the gold and let the ship go free. Indentured servants aboard the ship had been a surprise.

While Ethan worked with the figures in his accounting book and stashed the strongbox in its secret place, one thought kept flittering across his mind. What woman would have the courage or the know-how to stop a snake with her boot? What other secrets did she have under that mane of shining black hair?

He looked over his instructions for his solicitor once again—the usual things he asked him to take care of before he went to sea. But there was a new item. Marisol Valentin. He wrote a note instructing the lawyer to grant extra funds to Mrs. Piper for cloth, so suitable clothing could be made for the new member of his household.

He closed the books, locked the office, and walked to his carriage while the rays of the setting sun filtered across the harbor in golden, red, and purple hues.

Driving to the house, he stiffened as he drew near the Presbyterian Church he'd once pastored. Reverend Dobbins stood on the steps, and Ethan stopped the carriage to greet the minister, although he stayed seated. The pastor walked toward him with a lively step.

"Hello, my man, are you back for good?" The elderly minister's eyes lit with expectancy.

Ethan ducked his head, then shook it. "No, I will sail again soon, sir."

The light in the man's face faded. "For a moment I had a sudden thought I might be able to return to England before another hot, humid summer here in Charles Town. But if you're not coming back to pastor...."

"Sorry, sir." Ethan's lips tightened, and he blinked his eyes to dispel the memory of the wonderful times he'd stood behind the sturdy oak lectern in the little church. His lovely Olivia had sat in the front row, her eyes on him, baptizing him with her look of love. He cleared his throat and fixed his glance on the minister. "Don't you like your ministry here, other than the weather, sir?"

"Well, it'll pass for better than the backwoods of Carolina, for sure. But my wife has longings to see our grandchildren. Has anyone told you we have three in England?"

"No, I didn't know." Ethan needed to go before his recollections sank his soul in the familiar drought. He picked up the reins. "Sir, I need to be getting home before dark. I wish you and your family the best. And drop by to see the new governess I found for Joshua. I believe you'll like her."

Ethan clucked his tongue, and the mare started down the road at a brisk pace. Maybe when he returned home, if Marisol had not retired, they could talk. He wanted to know more about her.

She'd had her own personal maid when they boarded the Spanish ship, so she must be a lady used to having servants. Mrs. Piper confirmed it to him when she mentioned how little Marisol knew about preparing food. Then there were the three languages he understood she spoke. Add to that the snake episode and her amazing courage. Who *was* his new governess?

~

"Hello."

Marisol sat up, startled. Had she dozed off? The last golden hues of sunset faded into twilight across the yard. A tall, dark figure stepped from the shadows to the porch edge.

"Do you mind if I join you?" Captain Becket's deep voice rolled over her.

"No, of course not." How could she object? It was his house. She struggled to pull herself from the ties of sleep so she could speak coherently. It didn't help that his captivating presence and tantalizing smell of sea and leather threw her insides into tumult.

"I've been waiting to hear your story, Marisol. Can you share with me where you're from in Spain and how things were with you and your family?"

She stiffened, grateful for the falling darkness, for her face had surely gone pale. She moistened her dry lips. *What* could she tell this man?

He stepped away. "If you're not ready, that's all right. We can talk tomorrow." Before she could answer, he bounded up the steps into the house.

Marisol started to call him back, but didn't. She would have to get her story together. He would ask again.

Leaving the porch, she walked upstairs to her room and sat on her cot. She opened the Bible again and read the dedication page title—*Epistle Dedicatory to King James of Great Britain, France, and*

Ireland. The notes revealed that the work on the translation he authorized began in 1604 and was completed in 1611.Then she read the entire twenty-third Psalm.

The words touched her heart in a way no written language ever had. But where was this good shepherd when Diego Vargas ruined her for life and left her branded a murderess? She laid her hand across her belly. She must take care of herself and the little one. Whatever story she told of her past must, above all, protect the babe, the innocent person in her sad tale. She closed the book and laid it back on the table, changed into her gown, and climbed into bed.

~

As she relaxed on the backyard bench the next morning, watching Joshua playing in his sand pile, Captain Becket strode across the sparkling, dew-drenched grass and sat beside her. His strong, masculine presence and spicy scent brought all her senses to life. What was it about him that drew her?

She wanted nothing to do with another man. They couldn't be trusted. She'd learned her lesson well with Diego. He had visited in their home and seemed harmless until the dreadful night he showed his true colors.

She glanced into the captain's bearded face. His question of the night before hung heavy in the air between them, although he didn't speak. He gazed at her with clear gray eyes that seemed to see into her soul.

She lowered her chin and blurted out the words she'd planned. "I...my husband and I were from the northern part of Spain. We decided to travel to my aunt's sugar estate in Cartagena and start a new life. As I told you, ruffians sat upon us that early morning at the Cadiz harbor. My husband gave his life trying to defend us. Carmela and I lost our funds and had no choice but to sign indenture papers to sail to the West Indies." She swallowed and glanced at Ethan's face.

"What a terrible thing to have happen to you." Ethan's sincere voice made her wince.

Moisture pressed against her eyelids. She hated lying. But some of it was true. "Then I had the pain of watching my dear Carmela die of the fever on your ship." She spat out the last three words and clenched her fingers in her lap. Tears overflowed, but she swiped them away.

Captain Becket covered her tight fists with his wide calloused hand. "I'm sorry for your losses, Marisol. And I hope you feel assured of your safety here with us. Thank you for sharing your story."

His brief touch and kind words caused a flutter in the pit of her stomach. She pulled her hands away.

He turned to watch his son at play. "I have something to tell you and Mrs. Piper. I am leaving next week for a long trip."

She looked up at his strong, rigid profile and the way his beard came to a point below his chin. His features were perfect, symmetrical, but lines about his mouth and eyes spoke of pain. "Where will you be sailing this time, Captain?" She hated that something seemed to be wrong with her breathing, and she cleared her throat to steady herself.

"To England to see my parents and take care of other business." He stood, walked to his son, and lifted him to his shoulders for a ride. The boy laughed with joy and patted his father's thick curly brown hair as they sauntered toward the house.

~

The next morning, Marisol awoke with the nausea she thought had ceased. She threw up so hard and long in the chamber pot, Mrs. Piper knocked at the door.

"Marisol, are you all right? Can I help?" The woman came into the room, concern lining her features.

When the vomiting faded, Marisol stood and splashed cool water from the basin on her face. She dried her cheeks and dropped onto the cot. She had no strength left to keep up any pretense.

The housekeeper sat beside her. "Do you have anything to tell me, lamb?"

Moisture gathered in Marisol's eyes and she looked away from the kind face. "I'm with child."

The woman patted her hand. "Well, don't you worry, dear girl. Was it one of the Spanish soldiers who took advantage of you?"

"Oh, no, that's not what happened." Marisol lowered her chin. Lying to Ethan Becket was one thing, but it would be much harder to give her embroidered story to the gentle housekeeper.

"So what happened, child?"

Marisol clasped her hands in her lap and looked down at them as she repeated what she had told Ethan. When she glanced into Mrs. Piper's face, she saw kindness and understanding, and it made her own chin tremble. She hated not being able to tell the truth.

"So you lost a husband? Bless you, my dear." The woman patted Marisol's hands. "And never you fear about this pregnancy. Captain Becket will not take it mean-spirited, like some indentured masters do. No sirree. He's got the biggest heart of any man in Charles Town. You'll see. God will work all this out, for you, my dear. Would you like for me to tell him of the pregnancy?"

Marisol nodded and sighed, glad to have that weight lifted from her shoulders. Was God or the captain's heart big enough to help her get to Cartagena to her aunt before the birth of the baby? Her indenture paper specified seven long years of servitude in Charles Town. The West Indies Spanish city of her dreams might as well be on the other side of the world.

Mrs. Piper touched Marisol's shoulder. "How far along are you, dear?"

Marisol placed her hand on her stomach. "I think between three and four months." She looked into Mrs. Piper's soft face and spoke in a tremulous voice. "I believe I felt the baby shift last night. It was like a little flutter. Could that be a movement?"

A wide smile creased the woman's lined features. "Absolutely, and that puts you closer to four months." She clucked her tongue. "And, if Ethan goes to England, he will be gone his usual six to eight months, and your child will be born while he is away. So you can relax about that."

"Oh. You mean he'll be away that long?"

Mrs. Piper nodded.

Marisol's dream of sailing to Cartagena for the birth of her child shattered like a piece of fine porcelain clattering to the floor. She lowered her chin and forced back moisture from the corner of her eyes.

After the woman left, Marisol wiped a tear escaping down her cheek and clenched her teeth. One thought struggled to the front of her mind, bringing a measure of peace. Though her baby would be born in Charles Town, not Cartagena, at least she wouldn't have to worry about facing Captain Ethan Becket through its birth and first weeks. That counted for something.

Later that day, when Joshua took his nap, Mrs. Piper asked Marisol to go to the market near the dock for a few needed items.

She drove the buggy in the warm sunshine to the dock area and past the many stalls, enjoying the smells of flowers and the savory scent of fresh baked bread. After finding the spices Mrs. Piper needed, she headed back the way she'd come. She'd forgotten about the slaughterhouse area up ahead, but the moment she heard the sounds of cattle mooing, pigs squealing, chickens squawking, and the smell of animal droppings and blood wafting through the air, she turned the carriage around. She would find a different way home.

A few streets over, two figures appeared in the road ahead of her, one much larger than the other. As she neared, anger pulsed through her as she made out the details of a man beating a child. A young girl.

She stopped the horse, climbed out, and marched toward the red-faced, heavy-set man. "Why are you beating the child?"

He stopped and turned toward her, weaving a little as he did.

"This ain't none of yo bus'ness, lady. Git back in your buggy." He gestured to his victim. "She's nothin but a thief and I'm teachin' her a lesson she won't soon forget."

The thin girl of about twelve crouched in a corner against the wall, clutching a half-eaten apple in a dirty hand, tears streaking her cheeks. The look she sent Marisol pressed hard on her chest. She couldn't let this beating continue.

The man raised a stick to swing against the girl's thin shoulders. Marisol bent and retrieved the sword from her boot. Inhaling a breath for courage, she lunged toward the drunken abuser before he could hit the child again. With every bit of strength she possessed, she slammed the flat side of the blade into his head. He stood still, blinking as if surprised, then collapsed like a sack of potatoes.

Marisol turned to the girl, who'd curled into a ball, but peered up through frightened eyes. "Thank ye. I was so hungry. Ain't ate in days, so I took the apple."

"Where are your parents?"

"I ain't got none, ma'am. I just live wherever I kin find a place."

Marisol pursed her lips, then smiled. "Would you like to come with me? I think I can help you find a safe place where I live."

"Yes, ma'am." The child's voice filled with tentative hope.

Marisol took the girl's thin hand, helped her stand, and led her to the carriage. Marisol's breath came in spurts, not from the stunning blow she'd delivered the man, but from the pure outrage that still raced through her body. "Let's get you away from here."

Surely Mrs. Piper wouldn't turn the youngster away.

~

Ethan whistled on the quarterdeck, drew his cloak closer, and gazed out over the dark Atlantic waves boiling up the sides of the *Dryade* as they headed toward England. After two months of hard sailing, he expected to soon see flocks of birds flying south and other signs of the English port of Bristol. The powerful sails of his vessel, full of a good fall wind and snapping, couldn't drive the ship fast enough to suit him.

He loved this French East Indiaman he'd captured after six months at sea in the small brigantine he still owned, now dry docked in Charles Town. This Indiaman boasted 950 tons, eight nine-pounder guns, and 22 six-pounders. Plus enough space for cargo and passengers to fit well on the vessel.

The French captain and his frightened crew had done all they could in battle, but Ethan's brigantine had sailed circles around them, getting in multiple cannon shots. Yet always careful not to cripple the craft, since they intended to take it, not sink it. They boarded without having to kill a single man, just the way Ethan preferred. After dropping the crew off in longboats near French Martinique in the Windward Islands, he and his men had sailed to a secluded island for repairs.

And now, soon they'd reach England.

Thoughts of his parents and the Bristol home where he'd grown up brought a quickened beat to his heart. He planned to spend the winter there with them on this trip. No quick visit like the last one, trying to get back to Olivia. The whistle dried on his lips as her sweet face rose up in his mind. He shook away the memory, squeezing his eyes shut against it.

But then another lovely face drifted through his thoughts. Marisol Valentin.

Mrs. Piper told him about the young woman's pregnancy just before he left Charles Town. Marisol had shared her story with him, but had she told him all of it? Who knew what she had gone through besides losing her husband? He'd assured Mrs. Piper he planned to take care of the woman and her child, but he had no desire to be in town when her time came.

His lips hardened into a thin line. The birthing would dredge up terrible memories of his own Olivia's last day—hers and the babe she was trying to birth. He wanted to breathe a prayer for Marisol and her baby's safety, but the words refused to form. His prayers hadn't helped his wife. He took a deep breath.

Mrs. Piper had assured him she knew of a wonderful new midwife who had come to Charles Town. Her eyes had brightened when she spoke. "The woman has not lost a mother or babe since arriving in the colony."

A movement on the quarterdeck steps brought his mind to the present. Lieutenant Tim Cullen approached, then leaned on the railing. "Sir, sure good to hear you whistling again." He pulled a pouch of tobacco from his pocket and placed a pinch in the corner of his right cheek. "Where will you be heading once we dock in Bristol and sell our goods?"

Ethan's face relaxed. "I'll be going home to visit my parents once we unload our cargo. Our sugar, tobacco, rum, rice, and cotton will have buyers haggling to get them, so we should get a good price. After we settle, can you take care of paying the crew, and make sure we don't miss too many of them when we start back in the spring? They'll have a good down time in port with their pockets lined with a little gold. Can you get an account of them at least once a week?"

"Sure. I know which taverns to check, and I'll be sure to keep a good eye on the ship, too. I'll stay on board most nights with the assigned guards." Tim spat tobacco juice over the side of the ship.

"That's fine, my man. Knew I could count on you."

~

Three days later, they docked in Bristol, England. As he'd hoped, Ethan received a good price for their shipment of goods. The next day around noon, he rented a wagon for the trip to his parents' small estate, about ten miles northeast of town. The conveyance was necessary for the trunk of gifts he was bringing for his parents and the house servants.

He arrived at the gate at tea time. Although far from wealthy, Ethan's father earned a good salary as a professor at Bristol College, and the house came with the position. Ethan had grown up on the estate and loved every nook and cranny.

The elderly gatekeeper looked up at the driver of the wagon and swiped his hat from his head. "Why, Captain, it's you. Welcome home, sir." He swung the oak gate wide.

"Thank you, John. Good to see you again, too." Ethan drove the wagon through.

Two black and white collies barked as they sprinted toward him from the porch of the house. The horse snorted, but didn't rear as the dogs came close.

"Hey, boys." Ethan looked down at them as they raced alongside the wagon. His own beloved Thunder had passed before Ethan's last visit home five years earlier. These two had to be Thunder's grown pups.

Ethan parked the wagon in front of the main entrance and alighted to pet the dogs. They wagged their tails as if they knew him, and their happy barks echoed across the lawn. A house servant came running down the steps. He bowed and helped Ethan unload the trunk and carry it inside, then a stable hand led the horse and wagon toward the barn.

"Oh, Ethan, welcome home, my son. And you made it in time for tea." Ethan's gray-haired, but still regal, mother held up her arms to him. Ethan walked into them, wrapping himself around her tiny body, almost lifting her off the floor. He breathed in the lavender scent he knew and loved. So many memories this scent stirred. Bedtime stories. Hugs when she tended his scrapes. If only he'd appreciated her as much then as he should have.

His father stood beyond, a pipe in his hand. He, too, hugged Ethan, and it still seemed strange to be taller than the man he'd always looked up to. "My boy. So happy to see you. Come into the parlor."

A young woman sat at the tea table, ready to pour from the silver pot. She looked up and smiled as Ethan came near. "Hello, cousin. Do you remember me?" Her silky voice matched her golden curls and glistening, yellow satin dress.

He stared. It couldn't be Emma. That second cousin had been a nervous fifteen-year-old with an unmanageable blond mane the last time he'd seen her.

The girl smiled and Ethan's mother took charge. "Ethan, this is Emma. She grew up, married, and had her first child since your last visit."

Ethan took Emma's hand and bowed over it. "I would have never guessed it was you, cousin."

A rosy glow lit Emma's cheeks. She looked up into his eyes, but a shadow crossed her brow. "Married, but also widowed, Ethan. I lost my dear John just six months after we wed. He served in the Royal Navy."

"I'm sorry to hear it, Emma." He released her hand.

Ethan's mother motioned for him and his father to take a seat around the tea table. Ethan sat, never taking his eyes away from the angelic face of the young woman before him.

Mrs. Becket smiled and clasped her hands in her lap. "Ethan, I am sure you and Emma will have lots to talk about concerning the twin tragedies you've both faced. But for now, let's have tea before it grows cold."

He grinned at his mother. Always practical.

He eyed his pretty cousin and the graceful way she poured and served the fragrant, steaming tea. He did want to talk more with Emma. The three months of winter he planned to spend in England would allow plenty of time for that.

As he took the cup she offered, their fingers touched. She gazed at him and smiled, a look that stirred something in his chest.

CHAPTER 5

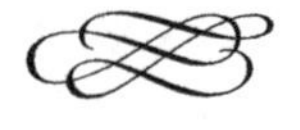

A sharp pain crossed Marisol's back, pulling her from a fitful sleep. She sat up, laid her hand across her large abdomen, and attempted to arise. Another pain wrapped from her back around her midsection, raising a cry to her lips. She'd had so many aches and miseries lately, but this was definitely more intense. The moment the pain loosened, she sank back on the bed.

Perspiration popped out on her forehead. She gripped the edge of the cot and called out, "Mrs. Piper."

Hurried steps sounded on the stairs, then the woman came huffing into the bedroom. "What is it, my girl? Has your time come?" She pushed a strand of gray hair back under her mob cap. "I was just at the bottom of the steps when I heard you call."

Marisol pressed her lips together to stifle a groan as another pain shot across her lower abdomen. "I don't know, but something is really hurting. Help me get to the wash stand. I would so love to cool my face."

"Now don't worry, I'll bring the bowl to you. I wouldn't have you fall on the floor for any man's gold." She walked to the stand, picked up the basin and a cloth and brought them back to Marisol.

"I was thinking last night it was about time. When you came to us, I think, from what you told me, you were already about four months. Then you were here for the month before Ethan left for England and he's been gone four months, so that makes nine months. This little one is right on time, unless this be false labor. And I think it's a boy by the way you've carried him so high. What will you name him if it's a lad?"

Marisol bit back a groan. "He will be named Samuel...Perez." After dear Carmelo. She took a deep breath and looked up at the housekeeper. One more lie. "That was my...husband's name. We were only married two weeks when he died, so I took back my maiden name Valentin."

Mrs. Piper cocked her chin but her bushy brows rose. "I see."

By noon, Marisol knew for sure she was in labor, nothing false about it. Beads of sweat continued to slip down her forehead, and it was all she could do not to cry out when the pains came.

"I've already sent for the midwife, and I've got hot water heating and lots of linens standing by." Mrs. Piper stood over her with a cool cloth to swipe Marisol's hot face. "You know it's the custom to bleed new mothers during birthing, but I hate the idea. I plan to tell the midwife not to bleed you, although I think she might not plan to anyway. I was told she refused to bleed Mary Stafford on Bay Street, even though her mother-in-law and husband were insisting. Mary did very well and gave them a fine boy in just five hours."

"Five hours?" Marisol groaned. "Why should it take so long?" She arched her back to find relief from the next pain building across her middle.

"Well, I'm going to be praying it won't take that much time, dear girl." A knock sounded below on the front door. "That's probably the midwife, Eliza Rubens. Let me go and bring her up. Thank God we have Amy taking good care of Joshua."

Marisol caught Mrs. Piper's hand as she turned to go. She licked her dry lips before speaking. "Please, if I start...screaming, have Amy take Joshua for a walk. I would hate for him to be frightened."

Mrs. Piper squeezed her hand. "Oh, don't you worry about that, little mother. I've done sent the two of them over to the minster's house for the duration. Mrs. Dobbins loves to pet that boy. Misses her grandchildren in England, she does." The woman hurried out of the room.

Soon she was back. "Here's the midwife. I told her you were very brave, dear girl."

Marisol watched as a simple-clad woman followed the housekeeper into the room. The short, stout, midwife hung her bonnet and wrap on the door, scrubbed her hands in the bowl, dried them, and pulled a clean white apron from her satchel. She tied it around her waist.

Her brisk steps sounded across the floor as she walked to the bedside and laid a cool hand on Marisol's forehead. "How is it going, dearie?" Her bright brown eyes exuded kindness.

Marisol bit her lower lip and groaned as another hard pain convulsed her. When she got her breath, she tried to speak, but no words came. Yet something about the woman's manner comforted her, and she let her eyelids drift low to enjoy the moment's peace.

"That's fine. Don't worry about talking. Conserve your strength." She turned to Mrs. Piper. "Can you bring me some melted butter?"

The housekeeper's brow lifted. "Melted butter? Yes. But...what for?"

"I am just going to make sure the baby's head is turned in the right direction and the butter will grease the pathway."

The woman walked to the window and opened it. "And she needs fresh air and sunshine in this room."

Mrs. Piper smiled. "You're not going to bleed her either, I hope."

"Absolutely not. She needs all the strength of her life to birth a child. The Bible tells us the life is in the blood."

Gracias, Dio. God had sent her an angel to help her with the birthing.

Within minutes, Mrs. Piper returned with the requested bowl of melted fat.

Eliza rubbed the golden oil on her hands and performed her

inspection on Marisol. "Good, the baby is headed the right way. You can do this, dear one. I can help you."

The next three hours crept by in a blur of pain for Marisol, attempting to push when the midwife said to and trying not to scream when the pains became unbearable. Twice, the midwife gave her a sip of wine with saffron and aniseed to offer relief.

Finally, when Marisol was certain she could stand no more pain, one very large cramp enveloped her like an ocean tide.

"There." The midwife's happy exclamation broke through her agony. "Here comes a fine baby...and it's a boy, little mother."

~

Ethan traversed the garden path of the estate with Emma at his side, both of them wearing cloaks against the spring breeze. Crocus and daffodils lined the way, offering a beautiful relief from the long winter months they'd endured.

He glanced into Emma's face. "Are you sure it's warm enough for you to be walking outside? Your cheeks are a bright pink." He smiled at her.

She patted his arm where her hand lay. "I'm warm enough, and I'm enjoying this bracing air and spring blossoms. Aren't you?"

"Yes, but it's having a pulling effect on me."

"A pulling effect? What do you mean?" She stopped and turned to face him.

"Spring is calling me back to Charles Town."

"Oh." Her voice dropped and a frown flitted across her brow. She ducked her head. "Of course, I knew you would be going back eventually. When will you leave Bristol?"

"Just as soon as I can get my crew together and load the ship's supplies for the journey south." Ethan looked into her blue eyes searching his, and his glance hesitated on her parted lips.

For one moment, he wondered how it would feel to kiss her, but he turned away instead. He could never love another woman besides Olivia, not even one as beautiful as Emma.

They finished the walk with scarcely another word, then Emma parted from him in the front hall.

His father met them. "Son, come into the parlor. Your mother and I have something to tell you."

Ethan cast his cloak off and followed his father inside, then took a seat near his mother, who had a look on her face like before his boyhood birthdays. She knew how to keep a secret to the last moment, but this must be one she was eager to tell.

His father cleared his throat. "Ethan, we've decided to immigrate to Charles Town at the end of this school term in June."

Ethan's mouth fell open. He looked from his father to his mother. So this was the news they'd held onto all the time he'd been in England.

She reached over to pat his hand. "Yes, son. We've thought about it for over two years. It's time to go. Your father's teaching contract runs out this term, and the school has already indicated they won't be renewing it. We Protestant dissenters will never enjoy legal equality with the Anglicans in England."

His father leaned toward him. "We believe we'll have much more freedom in the Carolinas. Don't you agree?"

Ethan smiled. "I do. I'm just surprised you've come to this decision without my help."

Emma stepped into the room. "I've decided to come, too, Ethan. My son and I. Would you mind?"

Ethan turned to look into her lovely, questioning face. "Mind? Not at all." He stood. "Well, this is big news for sure. And it's just the impetus I need to get back home and prepare a house for you in Charles Town." He looked around at their faces. "You do want to settle in Charles Town, don't you?"

Mrs. Becket wiped a tear from her eye. "Yes, dear son, we plan to settle in Charles Town. I want to be very near my grandson, Joshua, whom I've not even seen."

Ethan grabbed up his cloak. "And that you shall. I'll take care of it." He stopped at the door. "I'll get the *Dryade* ready to sail in two weeks." He grinned at Emma. "If I can round up all my crew that quick."

~

THREE MONTHS LATER

Hidden in the early morning shadows of the cemetery, Marisol silently watched Captain Becket place flowers on his wife's grave. He had finally returned the night before from his long trip to England, and the welcome sight of him caused her heart to hammer so hard she feared he might hear.

His bronzed face, thick arms, and broad chest certainly befitted a seaman's demeanor. Nothing remained to hint he'd once been the minister of the small rock church beyond the graveyard. How had a man of the clergy become what some might call a pirate?

Ethan turned, and she shrank behind a monument. She hadn't meant for him to find her watching him.

"Marisol." His deep voice rooted her bare feet in the dew-laden grass. He strode toward her. His heavy booted step, and the jangling of his sword and pistols startled a nearby cluster of birds into flight. He stopped a yard from her. "I'm glad you followed me. I have some good news to tell you."

She fought to keep from trembling as she looked up into his bearded face and startling grey eyes.

"You must know how much I appreciate your care for Joshua these many months." A smile tugged at his thin lips beneath his mustache. "And now you have a fine son of your own. Samuel, I believe Mrs. Piper said you named him?"

She nodded, and heat climbed her neck at his closeness. A scent of sea, leather, and spice tantalized her senses.

"My parents will be immigrating to Charles Town, along with my cousin, Emma. They will take over Joshua's care. My cousin even has a boy of her own about Joshua's age."

She stiffened and the blood drained from her cheeks. What was he saying? Would he be selling her indenture paper?

He searched her countenance and laid a broad, warm hand on her shoulder. "But in no wise are you to fret about your future." He smiled. "I'm going to arrange your freedom from any indentured obligation, and I'll help return you and your son to your home and family. Wherever that is."

Marisol averted her face and tried to swallow, but her mouth had dried up like a potsherd. She could never return home to Spain. But at least she could finally reach Cartagena and find her aunt.

"Does that make you happy?" He stood tall and straight like the mainmast on a ship.

Marisol forced a smile. "Yes, of course," she whispered.

"You may also be interested to know I'm planning a special voyage soon. I've heard news of my captured sister's possible location on the Spanish Main, and I'm going to search for her. But keep this mum for now. I don't want to disappoint my parents again if it's a false lead. "

She took a quick, sharp breath and raised her eyes to his. "That's...wonderful, sir. If it is good information." His eyes had shuttered, his mouth pinched shut as though he was done with the conversation.

And it was time she return to her duties. She curtsied. "I need to get back to the house and my responsibilities now." She turned and darted back up the path toward the cottage before he could stop her. The Spanish Main. Those three words echoed in her heart with every footstep. How close would he sail to Cartagena?

After dinner that evening, Mrs. Piper retired with Joshua in her charge. Marisol carried three-month old Samuel upstairs and tucked him in his small bed next to hers. She kissed his rosy cheek and hummed a lullaby until his striking hazel eyes closed in slumber.

A glance at the corner bed showed the young servant girl, Amy, was asleep, so she tiptoed into the hallway to the top of the stairwell landing. Concealed behind the large elephant ear plant, she picked up the lively voices of Captain Becket and Benjamin Thompson, an older acquaintance and neighbor of the captain who had once been a seaman himself.

As she sat and listened, the two talked for hours in the room below. As sleepy as she was, she lost count of the many adventures Ethan shared with Mr. Thompson, until he started talking about a new mission.

"Here's the big news, my friend. I ran across a sailor in England who had escaped from Spanish captivity. He had been on the same ship with Grace, my sister, when the Spanish took it. He tells me he thinks Grace is working as a tutor to a don's children in Cartagena." Ethan's excited voice ascended the stairs and jolted Marisol fully awake.

Cartagena de Indias? The city in which her aunt lived. Could Mrs. Piper's God be working out a way for her to get to her aunt's estate, which was located in the busiest trading center on the Spanish Main?

"I've got a pretty good crew, Ben. Not perfect by any means, but experienced seamen, and a ship flying a French flag will have no trouble docking at Cartagena. I plan to go ashore as a priest. Did you know I once studied for the priesthood before the new light of Lutheran's gospel flowed into my heart and family?"

Benjamin Thomas' deep voice responded. "I never knew that."

"Yes, and I even have the robe and other necessary items for a priest in my old trunk upstairs."

His deep, confident voice warmed Marisol like a trade wind full of promise. She fell back against the wall as an idea ignited all her senses. Why shouldn't she and Samuel accompany Captain Becket?

Her deceased father had been Spanish, and his sister, Marisol's aunt, still lived in Cartagena, as far as Marisol knew. Aunt Lucia might well be of help in locating and rescuing Grace Becket if she were in the sprawling city. Perhaps Marisol could pay back Ethan for her own rescue from the servant's block.

She closed her eyes as another thought turned her cheeks pink. She would see Ethan Becket every day aboard ship. But a cloud of distrust and shame snuffed out the leap of joy in her heart. She never wanted to have anything to do with another man, and what man would be interested in a wanted murderess?

But Ethan was talking again, his voice full of invitation. "Come with me, Ben. Don't you miss the smell of the sea and the wind in your hair? I could use another experienced seaman aboard and the good prayers I know you'll pray. What could stop you from going on this adventure with me?"

The man expelled a long breath. "I wondered when you would get around to asking me. Yes, I think this might be just what old Doc Blake would advise."

"Are you having health problems, old friend?" Ethan's voice expressed concern.

"Nothing a voyage like this can't take care of, son."

Marisol peeked around the plant. The two men below stood.

Ethan spoke again. "Oh, and sir, I don't plan to tell my parents I'm going after my sister. It would be too much for them if I came back without her. So keep our plan to yourself, if you don't mind."

~

The next morning, Marisol sent Amy to the garden to gather vegetables for lunch, then sat on the rug in the nursery with Joshua, Samuel, and some toy soldiers. She shook her head as Ethan's son pulled all the little men into his space. Samuel squealed, and Marisol returned a few soldiers to his reach. A warm breeze flowed through the curtains at the open windows, bringing the scent of the freshly plowed fields of the neighboring plantation. Marisol breathed deeply as the boys played.

Mrs. Piper came into the sitting room. "How are you three this lovely day?" She stooped down and lifted Samuel into her arms. "Oh, he smells of his fresh bath." She hugged the child and kissed his rosy cheek.

The boy touched her face with two wet fingers, and then sucked them back into his mouth. He wiggled to be put back on the floor with the wooden soldiers and Joshua, so she sat him down.

"We're fine, ma'am."

The woman hesitated. "Marisol, we're so happy to have had you with us these many months, and finally your precious boy. I've appreciated you so much. I understand Ethan's folk will take over Joshua's care after they arrive, and Ethan is going to release you and help you get back to wherever your family is. I will miss you sorely, dear girl, and your precious boy."

Family. Marisol struggled to stop moisture gathering in her eyes. What wouldn't she give to have her own sweet Mama and Papa back? Would she ever have a kind, loving family like Ethan had to surround and support him and his son? She blinked and swallowed. "I've been blessed to be able to help Captain Becket...and you and Joshua." She couldn't trust her voice to continue over the huge lump in her throat.

Mrs. Piper pulled up a chair and patted Marisol's arm. "Of course, none of this will happen any time soon. Ethan's parents and cousin will have to sail from England and get settled here. I understand they've started on their journey, but it could take even more time if they encounter bad weather."

Marisol ducked her head. "Of course. Everything will work out fine." Looking up at the housekeeper, she forced cheer into her voice and a smile onto her lips. Would the woman understand if she shared her secret plan of sailing with Ethan to the Spanish Main?

~

Ethan's parents and Cousin Emma arrived six weeks later from England.

The day following their arrival, Marisol, holding Samuel in the carriage, accompanied Captain Becket, Mrs. Piper, and Joshua to the house in Charles Town that Ethan had let for his family. When the buggy reached the cobblestone streets of the town, the clip clop of the horses' hooves seemed to echo the excited beat of Marisol's heart. Now that his family had arrived, Ethan would soon set sail for the Spanish Main.

She hugged Samuel and tried not to think how the two of them would manage during her stowaway on Ethan's ship. Amy, she must also take Amy. She would be a blessing. The girl loved to help with Samuel. Besides, Marisol cared for her like the little sister she never had. She settled it in her mind. The three of them would sail to Cartagena.

Ethan held the reins and kept the mare encouraged at a brisk trot. "It will take a few days for my family to get settled, Marisol, so Joshua will continue with us for at least the next week or two. And while I'm outfitting the *Dryade*."

"Yes, sir." Marisol managed a smile. "I'll be glad to help your family in any way I can."

Mrs. Piper reached over and patted her hand. "I understand they have servants to assist them unpacking their trunks and in the care of the household, so you just enjoy your time with the boys, lamb."

As the carriage pulled to a stop in front of the house, an elderly couple and an attractive young woman came out to meet them. A man working on the weeds at the side of the property stopped and stared.

After they exited the carriage, Marisol stood behind Ethan and Mrs. Piper, her son in her arms.

"Ho there, family." Ethan greeted his mother with a hug and his father with a handshake. He offered his cousin a wide smile. "Mother, Father, and Cousin Emma, may I introduce Mrs. Piper, my housekeeper, and Marisol Valentin, who has been Joshua's governess." He turned back to Marisol and Mrs. Piper. "This is my family. John and Mary Becket, my parents, fresh from England." Then he reached out and took Emma's hand. "And Emma Ducworth, my lovely cousin, who also decided to immigrate." Pink rose in the young woman's cheeks as she looked into Ethan's eyes.

One happy family indeed.

Mrs. Piper sat Joshua down and curtseyed. Marisol followed her lead as best she could while holding Samuel.

"Daddee." Joshua exclaimed and stretched his hands toward his father. Ethan swung the boy up in his strong arms.

"Mother, Father, this is my big boy, Joshua." Ethan turned the child toward his parents.

"Oh, he's a fine grandson, Ethan." Mrs. Wentworth bent and kissed Joshua's cheek.

Ethan glanced back at Marisol. "Marisol, a widow herself, has been a blessing to our household and to my son in several ways, and she has a boy of her own, Samuel."

Widow. If only her story was so simple. Marisol willed her heart to stop twirling at Ethan's kind words, and smiled at his parents. She dared not look in the face of Emma Ducworth a second time. The first time had caused her stomach to sink and made her wish she'd chosen a better dress to wear today.

She couldn't remember ever experiencing such a feeling. As a Valentin she always felt superior to other women in Cadiz. But this lady was almost too striking to be real, with her long, thick blond curls upswept in combs at the sides. Not to mention her sweetheart-shaped face with its flawless skin and soft pink lips. Ethan would see that face every day until he sailed. Even now, Emma lifted adoring blue eyes toward him.

The group headed to the front door, held open by a servant woman who curtseyed to Ethan's mother and his cousin.

Emma preceded the group into the house, her blue satin dress rustling with every movement of her trim body. She stopped at the sitting room door and clasped her slender white hands in a fetching, apologetic way. "I'm sorry you'll see quite a bit of disarray. We haven't finished our unpacking."

Ethan walked to her side and touched her arm. "Don't worry, Emma. We all understand and won't worry about a little disorder."

She turned to him, her face shining. "Thank you."

"Of course not," Mrs. Piper assured Emma as she walked up to them.

Ethan handed Joshua back to the housekeeper and followed his father into the study across the hall. His mother led the way to the parlor.

Marisol attempted to move past the two women in the doorway, but Emma laid her hand on Marisol's arm. "What a fine boy Joshua is, and I'm sure you've been a great help to him." Emma turned toward Mrs. Piper and patted the boy's sailor jacket. Joshua looked at her. "Oh, my, and he has his father's amazing gray eyes, doesn't he?"

Marisol stiffened. Emma was beautiful and probably looking for a husband. Did she have her sights on Captain Becket? After all, they were only second cousins, not close relatives. It wasn't her business though. She'd best keep far away from thoughts like that. Whatever happened between Captain Becket and Emma held no significance for her own life. Her driving hope and only ambition lay in getting to Cartagena. Somehow.

In the sitting room, Marisol placed Samuel on a rug near another small boy, with several toys spread around him. Mrs. Piper set Joshua down next to him. The two boys each reached for a toy, while eyeing the other child on the blanket.

Emma walked over to the play area. "And this is my son, James. I'll bet these three will have a great time together while we get to know each other."

As they all sat, Marisol chose a chair at the edge of the play mat with Samuel at her feet.

Mrs. Piper turned to Ethan's mother. "How was your crossing, Mrs. Becket? Many storms?"

The elder woman leaned back on the sofa. "We were blessed, I have to admit. It was a pleasant sailing, and we had a fair wind for the most part. But I'm happy to be on land again, and I daresay Emma feels the same."

"Oh, yes. I'm so glad we've arrived timely and without incident at sea." Emma wrinkled her nose. "I'm particularly glad we didn't run into any pirates."

Marisol held back a smile. Did the woman have any idea Ethan

Becket might be a pirate, at least part of the time he was at sea?

Mrs. Piper looked at the children and changed the subject. "How old is your son, Emma? Joshua is two, and Samuel will soon be five months."

Emma's eyes turned to her son and her shoulders drooped. "James is eighteen months old. His father didn't live to see his birth. He died in the King's navy from a battle at sea a few months after we married."

Mrs. Becket took Emma's hand in hers. "And what a great loss, but we are so glad you decided to come to Charles Town with us, dear. You and James will have a wonderful new beginning here."

Marisol ducked her head. Did that hope for a new beginning include Ethan in the picture?

Mrs. Piper nodded at Emma. "Most of us immigrated for similar reasons, lamb. We can all do with a new start at times. And I daresay your James will love having another boy to play with, as will Joshua and Samuel."

Mrs. Becket nodded. "Oh, I'm sure he'll enjoy having playmates, and I will love having my grandson with us. He looks so much like Ethan at that age."

An exasperated squeal came from Samuel, and Marisol bent to divide the toys between the three boys more equally.

Emma stood. "Will you please excuse me while I see about a pot of tea?" She swished out of the room gracefully, with her curls bouncing around her shoulders.

Marisol's lips tightened. The woman was the perfect hostess, in addition to being fine-looking. A ball rolled off the mat, and Marisol reached for it, handing it back to Joshua.

In a few minutes, the housekeeper entered with a full tea tray. Emma followed, but stopped in the doorway, carrying another tray. "I'll take this into Ethan and his father in the study and be right back, ladies."

Marisol sighed and lowered her eyes. Of course Emma, not the housekeeper, would have to take the tray to Ethan. But why did that matter to her?

CHAPTER 6

Hidden in the dark hold of the *Dryade,* Marisol awoke with a violent start. Her breath came in gasps and her pulse thundered in her neck. She sat up and first checked Samuel, curled up in his bedding beside her. His even breathing in sleep calmed her racing heartbeat.

She peered beyond her son in the darkness to the sleeping servant girl, Amy. Looking around the packed belly of the vessel, she listened for a long minute to the waves slapping against the ship's hull. A sudden clucking of a chicken jerked her attention toward the noise. She pulled the Toledo blade from her boot and moved off the firm bed she'd made among the grain sacks.

Without a sound, she wedged herself around the bins of vegetables, water barrels, and leather trunks to the chicken crates. But she saw nothing in the musty shadows of the hot, airless cargo area.

After looking once more, she crept back to her cramped spot. What had awakened her? Could a rat have run across her legs? She shuddered, adjusted Samuel's blanket closer around him, and sank onto her hastily-made cot.

After pushing the knife back into her boot, she pulled her knees up to her chin. It had delighted Amy to come with Marisol and

Samuel. If they could only keep their presence secret for a few more hours until the third day dawned. Once they were well out to sea, surely the captain wouldn't turn back to Charles Town. He would continue toward the Spanish Main and Cartagena.

Captain Ethan Becket. What would he say when he discovered them stowing away on his ship? How did he react when he was furious? She would soon find out.

Shaking aside her troubled thoughts, Marisol smiled as the servant girl stirred and sat up. "Did you rest well, Amy?" she whispered. "The ship's rocking and the waves lapping the hull make sleep easier, do they not? I think we've slept a great while." Without windows in the hold, Marisol could only guess if it were day or night by the sounds on the deck above.

She looked upward. A minuscule of light filtered down around the bolted hatch. She thought they'd been on the ship two days and nights since stowing away early the day it sailed out of port. But the time seemed longer from the way their food store had diminished.

Amy brushed the hair from her face and stretched. "Are we ready to have something more to eat, ma'am? And may I light the candle?"

Marisol nodded and reached for the basket of food they'd brought with them. The thin, growing girl never missed a meal if she could help it. And she loved using the tinderbox Mrs. Piper had given them to light the candle. Marisol had confided in the housekeeper the day before the ship sailed. At first Mrs. Piper tried her best to talk her out of stowing away, but finally gave in and helped pack a food basket and a water skin. She also agreed to keep the plan secret.

Then she had hugged Marisol and wiped a tear from her cheek. Her farewell words warmed Marisol's heart. "I will surely miss you and your boy, Marisol, and Amy, too."

The food container held the last of the bread and cheese, and they had one more flagon of milk and a few apples left. Amy didn't hesitate to say a quick prayer and start on the food.

Marisol's stomach twitched like it was full of butterflies. Until Captain Becket discovered them, she would have no peace. She forced down a piece of bread and a small wedge of cheese. She would need all the strength she could muster to face him.

Samuel awoke and reached toward the candlelight with a happy chortle. Marisol took him in her arms and nursed him back to sleep. He'd been such a good boy. The rocking of the ship and darkness lulled him into more rest than usual.

Afterwards, Amy snuffed out the candle and fell back to sleep on the pallet beside Samuel.

As Marisol sat in the darkness, her mind drifted back to her conversation with Mrs. Piper as Marisol had struggled to convince her of her need to take this voyage. "Milady," she'd said to her, "don't you think my Spanish heritage can be of use when Captain Becket goes for his sister held by the Spanish dons? I have an aunt living on her own large estate in Cartagena. She is the only family I have left, and Captain Becket has told me he wants to return me to my family. I believe Aunt Lucia will know if an English woman is serving as a tutor in the city, and may help with the rescue." This reasoning had finally won over the nervous housekeeper.

The rocking of the ship finally lulled Marisol to sleep again.

A piercing scream jolted her awake. Amy struggled in a nightmare, and her terrible shrieks bounced off the sides of the ship's interior.

Marisol's own heart raced as she shook the girl awake. Amy's cries ceased, yet the damage was done. Samuel stirred and let out his own loud cry.

"Sshh..." Marisol picked him up and held him to her chest, doing her best to comfort and silence him.

In the next moment, boots crashed on the steps from the deck above. Voices filtered down to them. Every muscle in Marisol's body strained as she and Amy looked up toward the hatch. Samuel stopped crying, plopped three fingers into his mouth, and turned his head up toward the sounds, too.

"I know I heared something. Sounded like a young-un," a rough voice intoned.

"Nay, Samson. Maybe it's a seagull trapped below." That voice, with its depth and authority, Marisol knew well. Her breath stopped in her throat, and her palms grew clammy.

Now was to be her reckoning, it seemed. What would Captain Ethan Becket think of their stowing away? Would he turn the ship back to Charles Town?

The hatch above them opened and light poured down, chasing the shadows out of the hold. Marisol looked into the astounded face of Ethan Becket, then to the crewmember with him, a dark man with a terrible scar crossing his cheek and down into his thick, black beard.

"Marisol. What in tarnation?" Captain Becket stomped down the steps and, in two strides, stood before her, his nostrils flaring, his brow like a thundercloud.

The other man dropped into the hold and came to stand beside the captain. The two of them made quite a picture of brawny strength—one white, one black. But Marisol had never seen Ethan's face so smoldering and harsh, his lips flattened into a tight line.

She swallowed and hoped her voice served her without breaking. "Sir, you know I'm from Spanish descent. I think I can be of help when you go for your sister in Cartagena. I have an aunt living there who could assist—"

Samuel squealed a happy holler and reached his little hands toward the captain.

Captain Becket's face softened, but his gray eyes still blazed. He took Samuel into his arms and spoke in a low, controlled tone to not upset the boy. "That's the most ridiculous thing I've ever heard from you, Marisol."

Then he glanced at Amy clinging to Marisol's arm, and shook his head. "What in the world did you think I could do with two women *and a baby* aboard ship?" He expelled a long, audible breath and turned to the man beside him. "Samson, bring them up and find a cabin for them. After we sup, I'll decide what to do with them."

Samuel patted Ethan's beard, and the captain looked into the boy's happy face, blinked, then placed him back in Marisol's arms.

After dinner he would decide? So Captain Becket wasn't turning the ship back toward Charles Town at the moment? Marisol breathed a little easier.

"Aye, sir." Samson gathered up Marisol's and Amy's belongings as Captain Becket scrambled up the steps two at a time, then disappeared above. The man helped Marisol and Amy climb out of the hold and escorted them up another floor to a deck with state rooms.

He stopped at a heavy oak door, turned, and cast dark, but friendly eyes on them. "This should work for you ship hoppers til Capt'n decides what to do with you." His English surprised Marisol, because he looked like the African Moors who had worked on her father's Spanish estate. How did he get the terrible scar that ran from his temple down into his beard? He opened the door and set their baggage inside, then stood back for them to enter.

Marisol liked the spacious compartment at once. Three cots lined the far wall and a port hole in the ship's side poured a stream of light into the room. Holding Samuel tight, she moved to the window and looked out. How wonderful it was to see daylight again, and a setting sun that painted the sky in shades of deep pink, orange, and purple.

The sound of the sails snapping in the brisk wind seemed to take a weight off her heart. The ship was moving fast across the turquoise sea.

Toward the Spanish Main.

She took a deep breath of salty air, hugged the child, and sat with him on a cot. Amy moved beside her and poked her with an elbow, nodding at the man standing in the doorway.

Marisol turned her attention to the man Captain Becket called Samson. He stood with his arms crossed over his chest. The name fit the character, Samson, she'd read about in the Bible Mrs. Piper had loaned her. He stood over six feet tall and muscles bulged on his arms, his thick chest and legs encased in black knee boots to his thighs like Ethan's. His curly, obsidian hair hung in braids to his shoulders. Her gaze caught once again on his scar.

He tilted the injured side away. "I will come back in an hour to take you to the captain's table." His strong voice vibrated through the cabin.

"Thank you for your help, but we would much prefer to dine here, if we may." Marisol rested her chin atop Samuel's curly head as he sat in her lap and smiled. "It's almost Samuel's bedtime."

The man's dark eyes fastened on the boy and softened for a moment. "No, the captain will want you at his table. I will be back." With those short words, he bowed, turned on his heel and left, closing the door behind him.

About five minutes after Marisol finished nursing Samuel, a light knock sounded at the door. Amy flew to Marisol, her eyes wide.

"Who is it?" Marisol called with her best noblewoman voice.

"It's jist me with some water for you ladies to wash up 'fore supper at the captain's table." It was the voice of a lad. A familiar voice. Amy's brows lifted.

Marisol pushed her toward the door and she opened it. Danny, the son of Ethan's gardener, stood with a sheepish grin. He and Amy were almost the same age, but the boy was taller.

"So it's you, little miss," he said with a smirk, and set two buckets of water inside the door, then doffed his cap.

Amy jutted out her jaw. "Yes, it's me, Danny, and what's it to you?"

Two spots of pink lit his cheeks as he glanced around her into the room at Marisol and Samuel. "It ain't nothin to me, but I can't believe all you stowed away. The Capt'n is fit to be tied, but he sent this water for your clean up." He gestured to a corner. "There's a trunk of clothing, if you need any." He clamped his hat on his head. "I best be getting back." He turned and scrambled down the passageway.

Amy closed the door, picked up the buckets, and brought them to a table that held wash cloths and soap.

"How thoughtful of the captain." Marisol laid the sleeping Samuel down on a cot, propped a pillow between him and the edge, then shed the clothes she'd worn for two days. She and Amy bathed, then Marisol opened the trunk of clothing. Lovely dresses and frothy petticoats popped up out of the intricate carved trunk. They even found combs and a lace mantilla among the contents. Had Ethan stolen this ladies baggage from a Spanish ship he plundered?

Next to her skin, Marisol donned a delicate white chemise, then frothy petticoats trimmed with lace. A gorgeous, rose-colored satin dress with full sleeves, sashed with green, accented her small waist. The voluminous skirt swished as she moved. She pulled on her boots, rather than the silk slippers, and pushed her small sword inside the one on the right. She found a pretty, smaller dress of blue muslin, trimmed in white lace that fit Amy well. Had it belonged to someone's younger sister?

Amy helped Marisol plait part of her hair and wind it around the top of her head, leaving thick strands to flow to her shoulders in the back. Would Ethan Becket still be as angry as he was when he found them stowing away? Somehow she must convince him she could be of real help to rescue his sister.

They'd barely finished dressing when a firm knock sounded at the cabin door.

Marisol opened it and gasped. Ethan Becket stood there in a ruffled white shirt, black trousers, and dark, shining boots. A red sash circled his waist and crossed one shoulder, but held no guns. His cup-hilt rapier swung by his left side.

The captain's mouth dropped open, his gray eyes widened, and his face softened. He gaped from her hair to her rosy bouffant skirt, just clearing the floor. "My God, Marisol. You look like an upper class Spanish lady. Is that who you are?"

Her heart surged at the force of his presence. Or maybe it was his deep voice that rumbled through her. Warmth flowed over her cheeks. That was her true identity. But was this the time to reveal it?

She smiled, gestured in the room toward the sleeping child, and willed her voice to sound normal. "Samuel is asleep after his evening feeding. Would you mind my leaving Amy here to care for him, Captain?"

He glanced from her into the room. "I will have the cook send her food here." When he turned back to Marisol, his eyes regained their earlier glacial look and his jaw once again turned to granite. "It's best, Marisol, for her to remain here, because you and I must have a serious talk about what you've done." He extended his stiff arm to her and guided her down the corridor toward his cabin and dinner.

~

Ethan ground his teeth at the thought of what to do with the beautiful woman walking beside him. Her elegant gown salvaged from his latest adventure swished against his boots. And a young female and a baby to protect besides her. How could he subject his crew to two women on board when they believed a woman on ship was bad luck?

And how could he keep them safe, not only from his crew, but what if pirate ships attacked? Pirates abounded on the Spanish Main, hoping to plunder a treasure ship. One thing he knew for sure. He *could not* waste time going back to Charles Town. Not with his sister possibly living a life of danger and hopelessness ahead of his ship.

He glanced down at the small, but firm, hand lying on his forearm, then to her pale, proud face. Both delicacy and strength molded her countenance. Her nose was straight, short and charming, her mouth full and soft. His pulse leaped again, just as it had when she opened the door. What a beauty. Why had he not seen it before?

As if feeling his perusal, she lifted her chin and turned sapphire blue eyes to him.

"If you're Spanish, Marisol, where did the blue eyes come from?"

"From my mother who was English. Only my father was Spanish." She averted her glance.

Why had she never mentioned this? His lips tightened more. What other secrets did this woman hide?

~

The fine Spanish plate adorning the captain's table did not surprise Marisol after seeing the contents of the trunk in her cabin. Plunder from her countrymen's ships, no doubt.

Captain Becket pulled out a chair for her beside him as the men around the table rose in deference to her. She sat, and the others followed her lead. She glanced around and recognized the one with whom she'd crossed swords. But he was busy buttering a large slab of bread. A blond-haired man dressed in a blue silk shirt and waistcoat eyed her with a grin spread across his handsome face. She turned from his bold look and invitation as the captain stood.

Ethan tapped on his glass with a spoon. All movement stopped around the table. "Men, this is Marisol Valentin. I am sad to say, she, her little son, and her maid, have been stowaways from Charles Town. She was my son Joshua's governess."

At least, he didn't mention she was his indentured servant.

His face turned hard. "Trust me. I am as unhappy about this as any of you. I will decide what we do with these three. Meanwhile, I want my entire crew alerted that I will hang and quarter any man who accosts them or treats them with anything but respect."

Marisol covered a gasp with the back of her hand. She glanced around at the men. All gave rapt attention to their captain. This was an Ethan Becket she had never met.

She stole a look back at him, but he avoided her glance and introduced those seated around the table. "You'll recognize my lieutenant, Tim Cullen." The red-headed Irishman doffed his cap and smiled at her. "And I think you know Benjamin Thomas." The older man nodded at Marisol. His thick gray brows rose as he looked from her to the captain.

Ethan indicated a thin wisp of a man, almost bald, dwarfed by the large form of Samson next to him. "This is George Johnson our ship surgeon, and you've met my boatswain, Samson." The dark head of the African tilted a fraction toward her, but the shining black eyes never left his captain's face.

"And in the doorway is Kurt, our good cook, who has prepared what we are about to partake of." The man, missing his left leg at the knee and leaning on a crutch, grunted and turned away.

Ethan gestured toward the one other sailor Marisol recognized. "And the first of our crew you met and sword fought to his dismay, Patrick McKinney, my second mate." The crewmember threw his head back and laughed.

The blond man beside him stood and bowed with a flourish of his lacy cuffed hand toward Marisol. "Don't forget to introduce me, dear *Capitaine*." Long blond curls of a wig swung back to his shoulders when he straightened up.

"Bonjour, charmant demoiselle."

She averted her face from his too warm acknowledgement.

Ethan affected a mock bow. "Oh, yes, who could forget his highness aboard ship? Marisol, this French peacock is Gabriel Legrand, my first mate. He likes to brag he's a gentleman who prefers sailing the seas to estate managing. More likely he was a court jester."

The crew guffawed, and on that more pleasant note, Ben spoke a blessing over the food. Then Marisol took a relaxed breath as the men's attention turned to the platters of food and drink being served by Danny and another young sailor. Lively talk and jesting from the crew, even with their mouths packed full, flowed around the table.

Marisol placed small portions of food on her plate and was surprised at how agreeable the ship's fare was. But sitting next to Ethan kept her body taut, her dining uneasy. How could she convince him she could help rescue his sister? Would he change his mind about turning the ship to deposit her back in Charles Town?

She glanced at him as he attacked the chicken, potatoes, and vegetables piled on his plate. One of the young men refilled his wine glass each time he drank. He never spoke a word to her. Most of the crew finished the meal in short order and left the table, one by one.

When Ethan wiped his chin and shooed the waiter away from pouring him more wine, Marisol laid her fork down and placed her hands in her lap.

He stood, cast his napkin on the table, and motioned for her to follow him. "I have something I need to say to you, Marisol."

He escorted her up the corridor and to the main deck. Crew members scattered in all directions as they approached. The sun cast its final purple and pink arms of light across the ocean, and shadows clung to the quarterdeck where he led her. Marisol shivered, not for the cooler evening trade wind, but because Ethan seemed different, stiff, angry.

He stopped and turned to face her, his legs planted wide, confirming his long experience keeping balance on a ship's deck. Even in the partial light, Marisol could discern the tightness of his face.

She grasped the railing and held on tight as the ship crested a wave.

Ethan crossed his arms in front of him. His eyes flashed in the falling darkness. "Rule number one, Marisol. You are never to come onto this deck without an escort I appoint. Rule number two, you are not to converse with my crew, but stay out of sight as much as possible. Samson, Danny, or Lieutenant Cullen will check on you daily to see about your needs or the children's. Do you understand? Will you abide by these rules until I can decide what to do with you?"

In Charles Town, she had never known his voice to sound so harsh. The breeze lifted her mantilla, and she raised a hand to hold it, aware that Ethan watched her, alert. "Yes, of course, sir."

"Now I'm waiting to hear why you've done this, and your reason had better be good." He faced the sea and rested his hands on the railing, as if looking at her made him angrier. His voice, though low, held an ominous quality.

Marisol swallowed and took a deep breath. "Sir, I overheard your talk with Mr. Thompson when you shared what you had learned about your sister possibly being in Cartagena."

"So you listen at doors, too?" He turned to glare at her, then looked back at the sea.

She ignored his remark. "My father's sister lives in that city."

He stiffened, then moved toward her. A raw urgency seemed to take hold of him, and he placed thick, tanned hands on her shoulders. "What? You have an aunt living in Cartagena? Are you telling me the truth?"

Her heart jolted and her pulse pounded. His scent of sea, spice, and man sent a dizzying current through her. She tried to step back, but he held her firm. She swallowed with difficulty and found her voice. "Yes, I believe Aunt Lucia will know if an English woman works as a tutor in the city. She'll help us."

"Us? Why should you care about my sister you've never met? What is going on in that head of yours, Marisol, to bring your baby and Amy aboard my ship, upsetting all my crew?" He gave her a little shake and looked at her with such a derisive expression, her temper flared.

She stomped her booted foot and, to her surprise, smashed down on his. Hard.

He growled and pulled her to him, scrunching her bouffant skirt against his body. His tight, bearded face came within inches of hers. Manly, warm breath feathered across her cheek. "Now that kind of attack will never do, my Spanish lady. Maybe for a snake, never for a captain. Did you mean to do that?" His compelling eyes held her captive as much as his arms.

Her knees threatened to fold, and she couldn't breathe. She tried in vain to pull away from the warmth of his encircling arms and firm chest. "No, I promise I didn't, Ethan. Please let me go." Her voice held a tremor she couldn't control.

He did as she asked and her knees buckled. He caught her elbows to steady her as a chuckle escaped his lips. New strength flowed to her limbs, and she pushed away from him. "Let me go back to my cabin, sir. I have a plan to help you, but we can talk about it tomorrow."

In the daylight.

She turned back the way they had come, and he followed her down the deck steps. Tim Cullen's whistle reached them before he appeared in the corridor. He glanced in their faces, and the music drowned on his lips. He squeezed against the wall for them to pass and continued up the passageway, shaking his head.

At Marisol's door, Ethan bowed, but stood in the way of her entering. "Tomorrow then, Marisol, and the plan you've concocted. I hope it's better than what you've planned so far."

She swished past him and entered, shutting the door behind her. Inside, she leaned against the door and took a ragged breath. Good thing Amy and Samuel were asleep.

Tonight she had seen two new sides of Captain Ethan Becket, former minister of Charles Town's Presbyterian Church. Had he really said he would hang and quarter someone? And the way he had shaken her and pulled her into his arms spoke more of a pirate than a former minister.

Marisol changed to her nightdress and lay on her cot, wondering about the terror and the thrill she'd experienced when pressed against him. How could opposite emotions flow through her at one time, and what did they mean? She turned to watch the moonlight tumbling from the port like fairy dust.

Warned. That's what the incident proved. She must remain on diligent guard whenever in the presence of the *Dryade's* captain.

CHAPTER 7

Ethan leaned on the quarterdeck railing the next morning, facing the early dawn. Pink streaks spread like glowing brush strokes across the eastern horizon. A cool breeze snapped the sails and the waves sloshing against the hull assured the ship's good speed.

Sleep had not come quickly after the incident with Marisol. What had he been thinking to take her into his arms? He breathed in the fresh salty air.

Yes, she was beautiful. And desirable. He clenched his eyes shut and tried to replace Marisol's face with his precious Olivia's. But for the first time her beloved image eluded him. He banged his fist on the railing.

"Got indigestion, Captain Ethan? In the form of three stowaways?"

Ethan turned as Benjamin Thompson joined him. The breeze lifted his mentor's gray hair as he laid a hand on Ethan's shoulder and smiled. Compassion flowed from Ben, as it had during the loss of Olivia. The man, an elder in the congregation, had been instrumental in Ethan coming as pastor to the Charles Town church six years earlier.

"You're right on target. I don't know how to handle—." Ethan stopped in mid-sentence. He'd almost confessed to his wise friend his attraction to Marisol. But voicing the feelings might give them more power.

Benjamin removed his hand and stared out to sea. "Two females and a baby on board. I have to agree, you have a problem. Did your governess tell you why she's done this?"

Relieved at the conversation going in a safe direction, Ethan straightened his shoulders and sucked in the sweet scent of the sea he loved. His demeanor of strong captain of the *Dryade* slipped back over him like a mantle. "She told me she has an aunt living in Cartagena who might help locate my sister."

"That's interesting. And it's something to think about."

"She says she has a plan of action she'll share with me today." Ethan glanced at the older man, his wrinkled countenance made golden by the rising sun moving into full view across the capping waves. The glorious pink shades of the sunrise had almost faded away, leaving warmth, promising a hot day of sailing.

Benjamin turned to face Ethan. "Listen to her idea, Captain. This may be the breakthrough you need, and all part of God's plan to rescue your sister."

"You think so?"

"Yes, I believe it's possible." He continued to regard Ethan a moment longer. "And I know you will do everything in your power to protect the children and her while they're guests on your ship."

Ethan's brow furrowed. "Of course I plan to, but you, a former captain, can imagine how much trouble that will be."

"Yes. But maybe I can help. Send me when they need to come on deck. That's a fine boy she has." He smiled. "And you, dear *Dryade* Captain, must remember Marisol is a vulnerable woman." He walked to the quarterdeck steps and turned to glance once more at Ethan. "Maybe even to your charms, my man." His voice had lowered so much, Ethan almost missed those last words.

His charms? Had Benjamin seen him take Marisol in his arms

last night? Heat flowed up his neck. She hadn't seemed vulnerable or defenseless. He flexed the still painful toe she'd stomped and reminded himself of the snake incident and her sword fighting with Patrick. Marisol Valentin was the least helpless woman he had ever met.

But he would be much more careful. He exhaled a deep, annoyed breath, and forced his mind to shipboard matters. He strode to the helm and spoke to the helmsman. "How is it going, my man?"

"We're making good time, sir. If this wind holds."

He walked among the crew on deck as they managed the sails and rigging to get the best wind under the boatswain's direction. Samson nodded at Ethan, and his men moved with more gusto when they saw the captain coming.

The cabin boy, Danny, came to stand at attention before Ethan, who nodded to him, giving him permission to speak.

He doffed his sailor's hat. "Sir, Miss—Señora Marisol sends word she is ready to talk with you." Pink spread across the boy's face.

"Yes, Señora is the right title for her, Danny. Bring her to my cabin."

The boy turned to leave, but Ethan stopped him. "But first, Danny, find Mr. Thompson and ask him to come to my cabin. Then go for Señora Valentin." He smiled at the way the young man saluted, his chest pushed out with importance. "Yes, sir, Captain. Right away."

~

Marisol walked into the captain's cabin and glanced around. At dinner on her first evening aboard, too many male eyes of the officer crew had stared at her, preventing her inspection of the room.

Now, the captain's quarters with its low ceiling didn't seem as big as she remembered. Large windows across the end filled the area with light. A bunk built into the wall, a chifforobe, a hefty trunk, and the large table at which Ethan and Benjamin Thompson sat completed the fixtures in the room. Maps nailed to the dark oak paneling lightened the wall that had no windows. Rows of leather-bound books filled shelving built in the few spare spaces.

She glanced first at the captain, then at his elderly friend. Mr. Thompson's presence would be good. Ethan stood and pulled out a chair for her next to the older man.

Marisol sat and adjusted her azure silk skirt. She didn't miss Ethan's appreciative glance, and was glad she had dressed as a proper Spanish lady, including a blue-on-ivory silk mantilla. She pushed one side of the long lace covering across one shoulder.

Mr. Thompson expelled a breath and shook his head. "My dear, you look like a noble Spanish lady this morning instead of a governess. How's that fine boy of yours?"

She turned to face him. "Samuel is fine and I've dressed like this for a reason." She cut her eyes back to Ethan, then lowered her lashes from his intense gaze and looked back to Benjamin. "I have a plan to help the captain walk onto the Cartagena dock with no questions asked." The man's brows rose, and he nodded her encouragement.

"Let's hear it. Time's a-wasting." Ethan's deep voice rolled over the room, tripping Marisol's heart. Yet skepticism poured through his words.

She hesitated, hating to admit she'd eavesdropped on the two men's earlier conversation before the ship sailed. She forced herself to look straight into Ethan's face. "I overheard your plan, Captain, to go ashore as a priest."

Ethan chuckled, the sound sending a pleasant ripple through her. "So you've mentioned. Have you no compunction about listening at doors, Marisol?"

Heat warmed her cheeks. But she kept her eyes focused on his. "If you arrive as a priest escorting a Spanish widow, with her child and maid, to her aunt's estate, you will have little trouble with customs." She had both men's attention now. "Also you will not be required to stay in the priest's community. I am sure my aunt will invite you to stay at the estate."

Benjamin Thompson struck the table with his hand. "By heavens, Captain Becket, that's most interesting. I'm glad to hear there might be a way for you to get through customs and avoid other priests."

Ethan looked at her, his face now serious. He leaned back in his chair and cocked his chin. "Tell me about your aunt, Marisol, who you say lives in Cartagena. How long has it been since you've seen her?"

Marisol inhaled a breath. *Lord, I pray nothing has happened and Tía Lucia is still alive and well at her estate.*

"Her name is Doña Lucia Valentin Chavez. She lives at her Blue Mountain Sugar Plantation outside the city, but also has a house in Cartagena. I was about ten the last time I saw her."

Ethan frowned. "That's quite a long time ago. Would she recognize you as an adult, if she still lives, that is?"

Marisol lowered her eyes and tried to calm her thoughts. The two men stared at her, awaiting her answer. How could she convince them her aunt would most surely know who she was? Would it be wise to tell these two men of her family jewel? She'd never shared it with anyone since leaving Spain, not even Amy or Mrs. Piper.

She made up her mind and took a deep breath. "I believe she would recognize me, but I also have proof of who I am, a family heirloom." Marisol pulled a ribbon from around her neck. Both men stared as she loosened the large ruby brooch with a filigreed "V" across its shining face, then passed it to Ethan.

He examined the thick gold band and large red stone encased, then expelled his breath. "Beautiful and valuable jewelry, Marisol. How have you kept it from thieves? And I assume the 'V' stands for Valentin?" He held the pin up for Ben to see, then passed it back to her.

"Yes, the letter stands for my father's family name, Valentin. Tía Lucia is his sister and she'll know this family heirloom right away.

My father gave it to my mother on their wedding day. After she died, he pressed it into my hand and told me to guard it with care."

Ethan leaned forward. "Marisol, never show this brooch to anyone on this ship. Who else knows about it? Does your little maid?"

"No, I've been diligent to hide it."

"Good." Ethan turned to Benjamin Thomas. "What do you think about my becoming Marisol's priest escort?"

Benjamin nodded. "I think it's a commendable idea and might be just what you need to disembark at Cartagena without a lot of questions. Will the dock authorities know the Chavez name?"

Marisol turned toward Ben. "Yes, sir, I'm sure they will. It carries great authority in Spain, and should at Cartagena as well."

Marisol ducked her head. She could tell them the name Valentin also carried power in many Spanish ports...but now with *murder* attached to it.

Ethan's brows knit together again. "But there's danger and risk in all of this, Marisol, and there's Samuel. How would you live or keep your child safe if we find things very different when we land —not to mention what could happen aboard this ship before we get there?" His frown deepened.

Marisol rubbed the back of her stiff neck. She must have a reasonable answer. "Sir, you promised to return me and my son to my family. This is your chance. Doña Lucia is all the family I have left. If we find things different when we land, I won't hold you responsible. I'll go to the Cartagena Monastery and ask asylum. The good Franciscans will take in a mother and child."

Benjamin Thompson drummed his fingers on the table and nodded again.

Ethan exhaled a long breath and stood. He clenched his fists and opened them before speaking. "All right, Marisol. We'll plan this thing the best way we can and go for it, but I tell you again, while on my ship, never walk around alone. You must have an escort. Ben here has offered to escort you on deck once a day, and I guess you can bring Samuel and Amy. But have no other contact with my crew, other than to send messages through Danny or Tim Cullen." He leaned over the table and looked straight into her face.

His pewter grey eyes searched hers, and his proximity made her breath catch in her throat. Not even a hint of a smile crossed his thin lips. "Do you understand and agree with what I am requiring, Marisol?"

She ducked her head from his intense stare. "Yes, I do, sir."

~

Marisol meant to obey those orders, and she kept them for a while. But one day, fast-growing Samuel cried for more after she nursed him. She knew she should offer some kind of porridge or curds like she'd seen Mrs. Piper do for Joshua. Danny had already been around for the morning, and wouldn't be back for several hours. She'd have to find the ship's galley, or Samuel's fussing wouldn't stop.

"It's all right, son. I'll find more for you to eat." She placed him in Amy's lap. Samuel loved the girl, and she had a way with him.

Marisol slipped out the cabin door, looked both ways, and turned right down the corridor. That was the direction she'd seen Danny come with their trays. She walked fast, her skirts swishing behind her. A whiff of what smelled like stew cooking drifted across her nose and she smiled. This was the right direction.

Around the next corner, she ran headlong into Gabriel Legrand. Delight lit up his amber eyes as he wrapped his arms around her and staggered backwards. His strong, too-sweet scent stirred nausea in her middle.

He licked his lips and murmured in her ear, "*Dame magnifique!* Not in my wildest dreams did I imagine you'd ever run into my arms like this."

She pushed away from him. "I didn't mean to, sir. Please forgive me."

"Don't think a thing about it, *belle* Spanish lady. I love having women run into my arms." He pulled her back into his grasp, then leaned closer. He was trying to kiss her.

She fought against him, twisting away as memories of another man slipped through her mind. Diego Vargas. Every muscle in her body stiffened in response. She pushed at the Frenchman with all her strength and fell back against the wall, out of his grasp.

But she hit the wall so hard, her breath swooshed out of her lungs. He reached for her again and she kicked out at him, lost her balance and fell to her knees.

She scrambled to her feet. How much farther could the kitchen be? No sounds came from the deserted corridor in either direction.

But before she could turn and run, he swooped on her like a bird of prey.

She gritted her teeth and plunged an elbow in his side. "Move away, sir, and let me pass, or you'll be sorry." If she had to, she'd scream for help. But the last thing she wanted was for Captain Becket to know of her disobedience.

He slackened his grasp, threw his head back, and laughed, a guttural sound that sent shivers down Marisol's back.

In a flash, she jerked her skirt aside and retrieved her small sword from the top of her boot. She stepped sideways from him, and pointed the sharp steel at his chest.

"Oh my, the belle-fleur has a hidden weapon." Excitement heightened the man's voice. "Well, I like to play a little *difficile*, too, sometimes." He whisked his sword from its sheath and leveled the tip under her chin.

CHAPTER 8

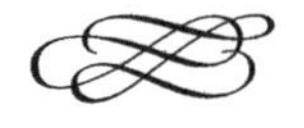

Marisol knocked his sword from her chin with her rapier and flicked her blade across his wrist, bringing blood.

"*Mon Dieu*, belle dame. Where did you learn to use a sword like that?" Gabriel withdrew a step and licked the cut on his wrist. The next second, he engaged again, determined, by the set of his jaw, to knock the smaller sword out of her hand with one strong thrust.

But Marisol was ready. All the hours she'd spent training with her Spanish instructor at her father's insistence came to her rescue. Even though hampered by her full skirt, she parried his every move. Her blood rushed through her body, filling her limbs with extra strength. The sharp clang of metal striking metal echoed down the corridor.

Gabriel breathed hard, and Marisol gasped for air, but she held her own, sidestepping his thrusts, and getting in a few of her own.

"What in tarnation is going on?"

Marisol almost lost her grip on her weapon as the familiar voice boomed down the hallway. Gabriel lowered his sword and turned around, his heaving breaths loud between them. Ethan stood in the upper corridor, staring at them, his face dark as a winter storm.

Gabriel sheathed his blade, wiped the sweat from his upper lip, and smiled at the Captain. "Just a little game of swords, sire. Didn't know this governess of yours could handle a rapier. She's one surprising lady." He made to walk away, but Ethan moved in front of him.

"Gabriel, await me in my cabin." The Captain's taut voice brooked no discussion.

"Yes, sire." The man ducked his head and swaggered up the corridor.

Ethan turned gray eyes hard as flint on Marisol. "What were you doing out of your cabin alone, Marisol?" He stood in front of her and crossed his thick arms.

She bent, slipped her sword back into the top of her boot, and tried to catch her breath. The last thing she wanted was to face this man, but she had to. Straightening to look at him, she pushed strands of hair back from her hot face with one hand and flexed the one that had grasped her rapier. She wiped the dampness in her palm on her skirt. "Sir, I can explain. I needed some—"

"Marisol, I don't care what you needed. You promised to obey my rule of never leaving your cabin unescorted. Do you see what can happen? And what might have happened if I hadn't intervened?" His voice was low, but hard as steel.

She lowered her eyes and nodded her head. She wanted to tell him she could take care of herself and that Gabriel would have never bested her with a sword, but she didn't dare.

"Go to your cabin. I'll send Danny to you for whatever you need."

"Yes, sir." Without looking at him again, she strode past him and back up the corridor.

~

Ethan stood looking after her, trying to digest the scene he'd walked up on. Marisol was giving Gabriel a real fight, an amazing display of swordsmanship, and with the shorter blade that she pushed back in her boot.

Her earlier sword fight with Patrick had been one thing, but no man aboard ship, other than himself, could hold his own against the Frenchman's skill with a rapier. And she did it with a short sword. No wonder she was flexing her hand after such a match. He shook his head. How many more surprises did she have waiting for discovery?

He strode on deck and motioned for Samson to follow him. As they walked to Ethan's cabin, he explained what had transpired and that he planned to lock the Frenchman in the hold.

Gabriel, sitting at the big table, looked up at both of them when they entered and threw his hands up. "I swear, Capitaine, nothing happened to the belle dame."

Ethan stood over him. "And I told you what would happen if any member of the crew accosted our guests." He nodded to Samson, and the huge African clapped a chain around Gabriel's wrists and yanked the surprised man's sword from its scabbard.

Gabriel's face paled. "Now, Captain, you're surely not going to..."

"Lock him up in the hold, Samson. We'll think awhile about the hanging and quartering."

"Yes, sir." Samson jerked Gabriel to his feet and the two marched out. Gabriel's cursing in French colored the air behind them.

Ethan sat at the table and pondered. His governess was a woman of many talents...and secrets.

He went on deck, found Danny, and sent him to the women's cabin. Why did she disobey his order? He grimaced. He'd not given her an opportunity to tell him what big need prompted her to leave the cabin unescorted.

Before bed that evening, Ethan opened the trunk and pulled out his Franciscan priest's robe and hood. He touched the rough fabric and fingered the rope belt. Then he lifted the leather strap holding the crucifix he would need to wear at all times in Cartagena.

He touched the wooden rosary beads and pouch—all necessary items he'd bought years earlier in England. He had started out to be a priest, after a harsh tour in the British navy, and was in training when he and his parents saw Luther's light and became part of what some now called the Protestant Reformation. Then Ethan met and married his Scottish Olivia, and he answered a call into the ministry. They'd become part of the Presbyterian Church and later sailed to Charles Town to pastor that church when its minister had died.

He replaced all the items in the trunk and closed it with a thud. How difficult it was to imagine he'd once thought of becoming a priest. He undressed and stretched out on his bunk. Once, he preached that God could use anything in one's past when one converted—that nothing was ever wasted in God's economy. His priest training would now help in the rescue of his sister from her Spanish captors. He'd been mulling around new names he might use as a priest, and Father Garcia de Berlanga seemed right. He could only hope it would be.

~

A few weeks later the *Dryade,* flying its French flag, sailed into Cartagena Bay, striking her colors and topsails as a sign of nonaggression to the Spanish authorities.

In her Spanish noblewoman's clothing of widow's black and gold, Marisol stood on a corner deck, with Amy alongside holding Samuel. The child had three fingers plopped in his mouth and he twisted back and forth in the girl's arms, delighted at all the sounds and sights as their ship glided into the dock.

Marisol perused the other tall-masted ships along the busy wharf. Many Spanish galleons bobbed alongside each other, and also smaller brigantines and sloops, with an occasional East Indiaman. Porters rushed about, hauling casks of wine, wooden crates of squealing pigs and squawking chickens, iron-hooped bales of cotton, and large bags of sugar onto awaiting ships.

Other porters, scurrying off the vessels, carried stores of rice, rum, bolts of cloth, and household goods to waiting wagons. The noise of the clanging chains, pulleys, and voices yelling commands filled the air. Smells of fruit, onions, and cooking food on the quay vied with the odor of the *Dryade* crew's unwashed bodies, now crowded on the deck to see their new port.

Marisol looked forward to a real bath herself after the weeks of sailing.

As they stood on the deck, a terrible smell drifted from a sloop pulling into dock to their left. Moans of human misery rose over the port clatter.

Amy grimaced. "What could make that dreadful smell, ma'am, and that sound?"

Marisol raised a lace handkerchief to her nose. The horrible odor of human waste, sweat, and death could only mean one thing. A slaver. The thought sent a shudder through her. Cartagena, purported to be Spanish America's biggest slave port, now had a new haul of pitiful slaves to work the sugar plantations.

"It's a slave ship, Amy, bringing a fresh load of people, and it's a terrible plight those poor souls are in, hence the moaning."

But something else, besides the horror aboard the nearby ship, contributed to a spasmodic trembling within Marisol that made even her hand shake as she reached up to keep her mantilla in place in the breeze. Was her aunt still alive and owner of the Blue Mountain Sugar Plantation? Or would her entire plan fail before it could begin?

~

In his cabin, in his priest's full regalia, Ethan gave last orders to his top officers. "Tim, you'll be in charge in my absence."

After Tim nodded, Ethan turned to Samson, whom the crew feared. "I know you can keep the men out of bad trouble in port and the taverns, and make sure they make it back to the ship each evening." He smiled at his boatswain. "One thing in favor of their good behavior is fear of the Inquisition spies. Feel free to remind them they are everywhere."

Samson saluted the captain and all three left the cabin.

Ethan came on deck with his monk's hood pulled up and strode near Marisol and Amy. "Here I am as Father Garcia. You two must remember that name and forget any other." He glanced around, keeping his voice low. "Are you ready?"

"Yes." The cold knot in Marisol's stomach tightened. What if her aunt had passed away? What if the Chavezes no longer owned the plantation? It had been ten years since the visit with her father to see his sister. Why hadn't she worried more about this earlier?

She shook herself, took a deep breath, and followed Ethan down the gangway onto the dock and toward the custom official's table. Amy carried Samuel behind her.

The small, squat man looked at them and narrowed his eyes at Marisol in her widow's black gown. She raised her fan to her nose as if the smells of the wharf offended her.

Ethan spoke in perfect Castilian. "Sir, I am Father Garcia. I have escorted this widow, her child, and maid, from Spain to her aunt's estate here in Cartagena."

"Who's the aunt?" The man spat tobacco juice on the dock beside him.

Marisol lowered her fan enough to speak. "Her name is Doña Lucia Valentin Chavez."

He stiffened and squinted up at her. "*Pareces un Chávez.*"

She threw up her chin and stamped her foot to confirm the man's idea that she looked like a Chavez. "Do not detain us, sir, or my aunt will have words with the authorities."

He scratched his beard, slid a paper from the pile on the table, signed it, and handed it to Ethan.

They followed Ethan down the dock, then waited as he found a porter and instructed him to bring their trunks. He located a coach awaiting passengers. When he asked the man if he could take them to the Blue Mountain Plantation, the driver nodded and gave a big smile. "Sí, sí, I take you there fast to the Chavez estate with my good horses." Ethan pressed money into his hand and the man jumped up to the driver's seat and spoke harsh Spanish words to the porters, who loaded the trunks faster.

Marisol breathed easier. The plantation and Chavez name were still valid and carried import. All was well so far.

The three entered the carriage with Samuel chortling over the horses as they stamped and tossed their heads at the added weight loading behind them. Then the prancing hooves clip-clopped down cobbled streets. As they transitioned onto a hard dirt road outside of town, Samuel dropped his head to Amy's shoulder and fell asleep.

Marisol took him into her arms, leaned her head back on the leather seat, and closed her own eyes. It seemed but a few moments later when Ethan's voice roused her.

"We're pulling into a long tree-lined drive. Do you recognize it?" His deep voice rolled over her, alerting all her senses.

Marisol moved Samuel from her shoulder to her lap and looked out the coach window. "Oh, yes. I could never forget this lovely entrance."

Flowering and fruit-bearing trees cast welcome shadows over them as the carriage wheels crunched down the seashell-paved drive. Magnolias towered above African tulip trees, mango, and palms loaded with coconuts. Shrubs and flowers graced the ground below—red and yellow helicon, pink bromeliads, and one white, crimson-centered orchid she spied in their midst. Her father had loved the flora of Columbia, and she thrilled at remembering names he taught her when they'd walked around the grounds of her aunt's home.

She breathed in the wonderful fragrances and lifted her eyes beyond the drive to acres of sugar cane waving in the warm trade wind. The rows of green stalks stretched for what seemed miles toward the ridge of mountains, gowned in their blue haze.

Their coach slowed as they rolled by a column of slaves carrying farm tools, followed by a white man on horseback close behind them. He lifted his whip to the tip of his hat to acknowledge the carriage as they passed.

Soon the expansive, walled hacienda came into view. Just as she remembered. Her heart leapt at the sight, but the hard knot churned in her stomach. Was her aunt still alive and in charge of this beautiful plantation? Out buildings, including stables and a mill, garrisoned around the sides of the plantation house.

The coach driver pulled up to a large, carved black metal gate between orange brick columns, flanked by two guards in green and silver livery. He spoke to one of the armed servants who moved to halt the carriage.

The driver spoke again, and the young guard stiffened to attention at the name of Chavez, coupled with Valentin. He motioned to the second guard, who opened the gate wide, then mounted a horse, and galloped down the drive toward the house.

The first man came to Marisol's side of the vehicle, took off his silver plumed helmet, and bowed, gesturing toward the entrance. She acknowledged the servant's attention with a slight lowering of her chin and rapped on the ceiling for the driver to proceed.

The coach passed through the gate and down the wide, lovely drive banked on both sides by fragrant pimento trees and beds of flowers in every color and shape. A sweet lavender scent flowed through the windows. The driver slowed the horses, as if to give the servant entering the house ahead of them time to alert the owners of visitors.

By the time the coach reached the steps at the front of the house, a mulatto woman in a bright blue dress and head wrap stood at the top, smiling a welcome.

Marisol alighted with Samuel in her arms, then started up the steps. Amy and Ethan followed at a polite distance. The woman curtsied and gestured to the open doorway, so Marisol entered the foyer. Thick walls and colorful tiled floors repelled the heat, while high arched ceilings and long windows allowed cool breezes to circulate. Heavy shutters hung at the sides for protection against winds and rains.

A woman came down the steps of the great staircase, in a lovely brown silk gown, edged with silver lace. Doña Lucia Valentin Chavez.

She still walked with her proud shoulders erect, much the way Marisol remembered her. She was the most magnificent elderly lady Marisol had ever seen, with hair now turned silver in delicate coils under her mantilla, and a back as straight as a ramrod. Her nose might be a shade too long and her eyes a little hooded, yet the remnant of unmistakable beauty still graced her pale face. Her dark-eyed glance perused Marisol's face, then stopped on Samuel, who turned toward her and plopped three fingers into his mouth.

"*Tía* Lucia." Marisol hurried forward.

Her aunt lifted a thin hand to her chest, and a wide smile creased her cheeks. "Yes, I can see in you the little girl of ten years ago. Marisol, my dear, I'm delighted you've come."

Still holding her son, Marisol blinked back moisture. Samuel pulled his fingers from his mouth, gave a happy squeal, and lifted his arms toward Tía Lucia.

The woman's intelligent eyes swept down to the child, then flew up to Marisol's face.

"This is my son, Samuel." Marisol could only pray her aunt didn't ask about the lad's father. Not right now, anyway.

The boy leaned toward the older woman. She took a deep breath, then extended her arms for him.

Marisol handed him to her, and couldn't stop tears from stinging her eyes. Children had a way of breaking down stiffness and formality, and Samuel was fast proving he never met a stranger.

"His eyes are so startling, Marisol." She bent toward him to get a closer look. "Tawny, with a streak of green. My old nurse called these tiger eyes. You seldom see them in Spanish territory."

Marisol stiffened. Diego had such eyes.

Her aunt hugged the boy and kissed his smooth pink cheek, then passed him back to Marisol. She gazed at Ethan and extended her hand to him. "Lucia Valentin Chavez, good sir."

He took her hand and pressed it. "Father Garcia, my lady. So happy to meet Señora Marisol's aunt."

"Father, I assume you accompanied my niece here, and I welcome you." She glanced back at Marisol. "Come, you and your party must be famished and tired. First, some tea, and then we'll have your rooms ready." Lucia clapped her hands, and the servant who had greeted them at the door appeared at her side. She gave several orders, and the woman hurried away.

Tía Lucia led the way to a lavish sitting room. Lemon oil emitted a pungent scent, and heated candle wax flowed in the air as they entered.

In the middle of the room, a maid stabilized a small ladder while a footman stood on it to light the candles of a magnificent golden chandelier. Soft light flooded the room and dispelled the afternoon shadows dancing on the rich wood paneling, polished furniture, and tiled fireplace. The two bowed to Doña Lucia and her guests, then hurried away.

Marisol sank onto the deep green silk settee when her aunt motioned for her to sit next to her. Ethan, in his priest's robe, and Amy sat nearby in carved upholstered chairs. Samuel squirmed to be placed on the thick Oriental rug at Marisol's feet, but she hesitated.

"My dear, let me send for my niece's child, a girl just the age to play with and care for your son while we talk." Doña Lucia rose and pulled a cord near the mantle. She spoke quick Spanish to the servant who appeared.

A few minutes later, a stout girl of nine or ten with thick black hair plaited down her back came into the room. She curtsied to Doña Lucia, Marisol, and Father Garcia, and dropped to her knees on the floor beside Samuel. She pulled a carved wooden soldier from a pocket in her shift, and Samuel squealed and reached for it.

"Take him into the hall, Francisca, and teach him the colors of the tiles." Doña Lucia spoke, and the girl lifted the lad into her arms, clutching the toy.

Marisol sent a pointed glance to Amy, who followed them into the hall. She breathed in a relieved breath. Her son loved people, but Amy knew how to care for him.

Her aunt turned back to Marisol. "Tell me how you arrived here, Marisol, grown up, and with a child. And does your black gown indicate the usual meaning?"

Over the next hour, tea, biscuits, and thin slices of coconut cream cake disappeared, consumed on gold-embossed porcelain. Marisol shared her planned story, hoping it would be the last time she would have to do so.

"Marisol Valentin Perez is a brave woman, Doña Lucia." Ethan's strong voice calmed Marisol's nerves after she told how kind he had been to escort her to Cartagena.

"Father Garcia, I owe you and our Lord for protection, good sir, of my niece and her child on the voyage. Please stay with us and rest for as long as you need before you return to Spain." Doña Lucia now sat with her hands crossed on her lap as a servant removed all the tea things, and another waited at the door.

Lucia pressed Marisol's hand. "I was so sorry to hear about your father passing last year. Please consider staying here as long as you like. With our Spanish laws, the next male cousin in Spain will inherit your father's estate when your uncle dies. One day you will need another place to live. Will you think about this? I would love to have you with me."

Marisol blinked back moisture. This was exactly what she'd been hoping for. Was she to have a family again? She cleared her throat. "Aunt Lucia, I will be happy to talk about this." Her voice cracked, and she swallowed hard.

Samuel's chortles in the hallway sounded more like fussing now, so Marisol stood. "Thank you so much for your warm welcome, this delicious tea, and your kind offer. I think we would like to go to our rooms now. Might Amy and Samuel bed in my room?"

"Of course, my dear. And we have comfortable quarters for visiting priests next to our upstairs chapel." She smiled at Ethan and gestured with her hand. The servant at the door watching her every move entered, bowed, and led the way to the grand staircase that curved up to the second floor.

Lucia's voice followed them. "Dinner will be at eight, Marisol. I look forward to having your company. Yours, too, Father Garcia. Please join us."

Ethan turned and bowed.

Marisol followed the servant with Samuel in her arms, Ethan and Amy following behind. Halfway up the stairs, Marisol glanced back at Ethan and whispered, "Has all gone well so far?"

Ethan smiled and responded in a low voice. "I thank God how easy this has been. I like your aunt and believe she will be a help."

As she settled into her room, Marisol thought on his words. They were the first reference to God and prayer she'd heard from Ethan. Was he coming out of his grief and anger over his wife and child's untimely death? And how could she tell her aunt about Father Garcia's *other* purpose for coming to Cartagena without revealing his true identity?

CHAPTER 9

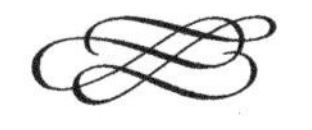

After feeding Samuel and rocking him to sleep, Marisol prepared for her first real bath since boarding the *Dryade* in Charles Town. Sponge baths were better than nothing, but a real bath was a luxury she no longer took for granted. Her aunt sent servants with a large tub and buckets of heated water, and Marisol sank into a soothing bath scented with lavender soap.

Afterwards, she dressed with care for dinner. Discarding her black widow's garb, she chose a gray silk dress with white lace. When her hair dried, Amy helped comb the thick locks and pull them up with the prongs of a large silver comb. Then the girl attached the white lace mantilla to the comb over Marisol's thick black hair, leaving a few soft curls cascading near her cheeks.

She sent Amy down to the kitchen to ask for her own meal to eat in the room. As soon as the girl returned, Marisol kissed the sleeping Samuel's cheek, then inhaled a deep breath for courage and swished out the door.

Midway down the stairs, she realized someone stood at the bottom looking up at her. Ethan. He pushed his priest's head piece back on his shoulders to reveal his tanned face and beard.

"Good evening, Señora Perez." He bowed, and a grin stretched over his thin lips. When their eyes met, new and unexpected warmth surged through her.

"Good evening, Father." She didn't dare let a smile touch her face. Who might be watching or listening?

As if in response to that thought, a livery-clad servant appeared, bowed, and gestured for them to follow.

He led them to a large dining room painted in pale yellow. Gold damask curtains hung over three long windows, through which rays of the setting sun beamed. A huge table dominated the room, covered in a white cloth with china settings under a magnificent chandelier. The candles on the fixture and the table exuded the fragrance of citrus.

Marisol's aunt sat at the head of the table. She stood and welcomed them, motioning for her and Ethan to sit on either side of her. As servants seated them, a centerpiece arrangement of white gardenias with their glossy dark green leaves wafted out their heady scent.

A young woman dressed in red satin sailed into the room, and a male servant seated her beside Marisol.

"Marisol, this is my niece, your cousin, Adriana Cortez. I don't think you two have ever met. Her husband sails with the King's navy. The girl I sent for to play with Samuel is her daughter. Adriana, this is Marisol Valentin Perez and Father Garcia, who has been so kind to escort her and her son to Cartagena from Spain, as I told you."

The young woman's dark eyes darted from Marisol to Father Garcia, then back to Marisol. "How do you do?"

"Well, thank you." Marisol looked into the hard eyes of the woman greeting her. No warmth or welcome lived in those deep orbs. What did she have against Marisol at this very first meeting?

Father Garcia nodded, acknowledging the introduction.

"Father, would you bless the food before we partake?" Lucia smiled at him and he bowed his head to comply.

Marisol couldn't help wondering how long it had been since he'd spoken such a prayer.

~

Two evenings later after dinner, Marisol sat beside her aunt in the courtyard, somewhat cooler after the sunset bathed it in pink and golden hues. Many flowers emitted their fragrances, and the hum of crickets filled the twilight falling around them.

Finally, they were alone. Father Garcia had gone into Cartagena —in a ragged sailor disguise—to visit the taverns and seek information about his sister. This might be a good time to speak to her aunt, though she hated to embroider any kind of story to the woman. In her mind, she went back over the way she had decided to tell about Ethan's need to rescue a captive in Cartagena. She clasped her hands in her lap and took a deep breath. "Aunt Lucia, may I share something with you?"

Her aunt turned to her, then reached and patted Marisol's hands. "Of course. What's on your mind?"

"Father Garcia has a dual purpose for coming to Cartagena. He did come to escort me, but he has another reason, too."

Her aunt raised her brows in interest. "Really?"

She could only hope her story sounded plausible. "He's traveled a lot and makes friends wherever he goes. One friend in France had a sister of his English wife who was captured by one of our Spanish ships at sea. The man learned that someone might be holding her in Cartagena, forcing her to work as a tutor for his children. Father Garcia promised to look into it."

Lucia pursed her lips. "How old would this sister be and do you have a description of her?"

Marisol's heart jumped. Her aunt's interest was good.

"I think he said she would be about twenty-eight now. She was taken five years ago, and I understand she resembles her English mother with blond hair and blue eyes."

Lucia clicked her tongue. "Let me think about this, Marisol. That kind of coloring would be rare among us and, therefore, easy to find, if such a person is in Cartagena."

Her aunt stood. "Meanwhile, I have news for you. I've decided to host a celebration for your arrival, for your coming to live with me."

"Oh, Aunt, how exciting. What do you plan?"

"We will dine and dance and introduce you to Cartagena."

Her aunt's face turned pensive. "Tell me, have you discovered our stables yet? I have an Andalusian stallion we've recently bought. He can follow a dancer in the Flamenco. If I remember correctly, even as a child you determined to learn the steps of the Flamenco."

Marisol took a quick breath. "Yes. I love horses and I learned the dance. I miss my mare that we trained to follow me."

Her aunt smiled. "Go see my prized horse tomorrow, Marisol. He's a pure Spanish breed. I'm sure he can do all the fancy airs you've seen in Spain. Perhaps you and he can become friends."

~

The next morning, after feeding Samuel and settling him with Amy and Francisca, Marisol padded down the stairs to the back entrance and made her way through the plantation grounds to the stables.

She walked the cool, hay-strewn corridor and peeked into numerous roomy stalls at the silky coats and shining eyes of well-cared for animals. The Blue Mountain Sugar Plantation possessed no lack of good horse flesh.

A yearning for the horse she had left in Spain tightened inside her the more she strolled through the barn. Were Jada and her latest foal well cared for? But she had to cast that worry aside. The purebred Andalusian and any colt from her were worth far too much for anyone to ignore their needs. Besides, her uncle may have sold them both to pay gambling debts.

A rumbling neigh blasted from further down the corridor. When she arrived at the stall and looked through the planks at the horse within, her mouth fell open and her eyes widened. A magnificent creature with a glistening dappled gray coat and a thick black mane stood near the far wall. His ears pricked as he eyed her.

She spoke in a soothing tone. "Hello there, big boy. I see your name above the door. Ambrosia's Dream. It fits."

The stallion nickered, threw his tail up, and paced the perimeter of the large stall.

"Hello, Señora. I see you like our Ambrosia and he seems to like you, from the way he shows off."

Marisol turned to a short, wiry man wearing the Chavez green livery. His tanned, wrinkled face gave evidence of some age. He whipped off his sombrero and bowed to her. "I am Pedro Rodriguez Martinez, chief stable hand."

"I am Marisol Valentin Perez. This must be Aunt Lucia's prize horse she suggested I get to know."

"That is good. I don't have enough time to exercise him much with all the other horses. You like to ride, Señora?"

"Yes, I...had an Andalusian back in Spain which I miss. Could we saddle him and see if he will take to me?"

"Certainly, Señora." Pedro reached for a bridle and entered the stall. The stallion came up to him with a nicker, then took the bridle and bit without hesitation.

He led the prancing animal into the corridor and toward a saddle rack. "Ambrosia has spirit, but he is mild-tempered, true to his breed." He placed a blanket and side saddle on the shiny back.

Marisol stopped him. "I prefer a regular saddle. Sorry, I only ride side saddle when I must. I am wearing a simple riding skirt for that type of saddle." She pointed to a small leather one on the rack with silver insets.

The man smiled and changed to the seat she mentioned. He tightened the girth, tested it, and turned back to Marisol. "Would you prefer I ride him around the enclosure first?" He was uncertain of her expertise with horses, but he would soon be at ease.

"No, I believe I can handle him. I've ridden since a child." She patted the strong neck and whispered to the stallion. "We'll be fine, won't we, Ambrosia?"

The horse tossed his head, touched her with his nose, and sniffed, as if to get her scent.

Pedro offered to help her up into the saddle, but she gathered the reins, put her boot into the wooden stirrup, and swung up without his assistance. As she settled in her seat, he adjusted the stirrup straps for the length of her legs, then tested them to make sure they held firm.

Marisol gave him a quick smile. "*Muchas gracias*."

The man touched the brim of his sombrero and stood back with watchful eyes.

The stallion pawed the earth as Marisol gathered her reins. She patted his thick neck, then turned him toward the doorway and clicked her tongue.

He responded at once and entered the enclosure with his neck arched and hooves stepping high, but landing without jarring his rider. As if he knew he had special cargo on board.

She touched his rippling shoulder with her crop and he performed a dancing gait around the perimeter. A familiar thrill ran through her. Could he already have training in the special airs above ground she had taught her own horse?

One by one, she tested him with the commands and praised him with every new movement he flowed into with enthusiasm. Riding him was like heaven regained. Happy tears overflowed her eyes. Too many months had passed since she'd been able to experience such a horse.

Pedro leaned against the barn and grinned. Once he even clapped.

After a while, she rode back to the entrance, breathless after many rounds of the enclosure.

The man looked up at her with honest respect. "Ah, Señora, I've never been able to get him to do all that. You are expert. Yes, expert horsewoman. Señora Chavez will be delighted. People from all over would love to see what I've just beheld."

Marisol smiled and swung down from the horse's back. She

patted the steaming neck. "You are the expert, Ambrosia. You and I are going to be great friends."

After handing the stallion over to Pedro to unsaddle and return to his stall, she made her way back to the house. She even found herself humming as she entered, but a figure ahead stilled her breathless song.

Ethan stood in the hallway, and something about his bearing tightened a knot in her middle.

He pulled her into a secluded corner before speaking. "I haven't learned anything in the taverns, Marisol. Have you spoken to your aunt?" His brows knit and his breath fanned her face as he spoke in a low voice.

Her heartbeat surged at his touch on her arm, and she breathed in his manly scent that made her chest flutter. Even in his priest's robe, he was the most handsome man she had known. Suppressing that thought, she met his gray eyes. "Yes, Aunt Lucia is working on it. And she's planning a celebration here to commemorate my arrival. We'll meet quite a few people, the kind who could have an educated tutor like your sister for their children."

His countenance lifted. "That may be a good opportunity to ask a few discreet questions." His eyes moved over her face and settled on her lips. For a moment, her breathing stilled.

Then he dropped his hand from her arm and turned away.

~

Ethan entered his priest's room next to the chapel. He jerked the sash away, shed the robe, and dropped onto the narrow cot. What was happening to him? He couldn't let his heart become involved with his former governess.

His attraction to her now must be because Marisol seemed so different since they arrived at her aunt's. She had a new peace and confidence. And where had she been this morning? Her cheeks were rosy, her lips...

He banged the headboard with his fist, and then sat up. He must concentrate on the main issue at hand. Was his sister in Cartagena? The coming celebration might be of help. He stood and paced the room.

If he found her, he must get her to the ship as soon as possible and leave this city. Tonight, he would put on a Spanish peon disguise and check on the *Dryade*. He'd told them he'd report back once a week. Had it been seven days yet?

He hoped his crew hadn't provoked censure from the port authorities. But their general rowdiness and appreciation for trim ankles may have resulted in arguments. Maybe even fights with outraged gentlemen demanding satisfaction on behalf of their insulted mistresses, wives, or daughters.

He gritted his teeth and lay back down on the cot. One consolation was that the man most likely to cause trouble was still locked in the hold of the *Dryade*. Gabriel Legrand.

He closed his eyes. He'd spent several nights searching taverns in the city for information, so a little rest might do him good.

The sound of a bell jerked him awake, and he strained to count the peals. Must be the signal for the midday meal. He sat up and shook his head to clear away the strange dream he'd had of Marisol. She was being chased by figures in dark robes, Dominican priests of the Inquisition, with soldiers accompanying them. That surely meant death, and in the dream he feared for her, but was powerless to help her.

He got up and sloshed tepid water from his wash bowl on the dresser over his face, head, and neck. But he couldn't dispel the edge of fear still surrounding her image. The sense of danger seemed to hang over him. Was she carrying some kind of secret that could destroy her?

CHAPTER 10

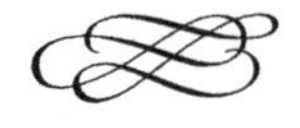

Two weeks later, Marisol granted Amy's request to help her dress for Aunt Lucia's celebration. Samuel kept himself busy playing on a rug beside them.

They didn't have much time left, for Lucia expected guests to arrive within the hour. She'd set the celebration for five o'clock in the afternoon because it would start with a horse and dancer presentation.

Earlier, Lucia had watched Marisol ride Ambrosia, and then Pedro rode as Marisol danced the Flamenco. Delighted, she insisted her niece do a dance presentation with the horse for their Cartagena guests. Later, the visitors would move from the stable arena to the house for dinner and dancing.

"Oh, ma'am, you'll charm everyone with this Flamenco outfit and your dance I saw earlier." Amy helped Marisol into a red silk dress with ruffles and veils to add movement in the Flamenco. She dressed her hair, leaving the back to float across her shoulders, then attached the lace mantilla with a bright comb.

"Amy, there's no one I wish to charm. But I hope to please Aunt Lucia." Marisol looked at her reflection in the chifforobe door mirror. Ethan's face flowed into her mind as if to deny her words. She tossed her head to dislodge that handsome visage.

Marisol pressed the comb tighter and touched the black, shining coils of her hair pinned on top.

"If you are testing the pins holding your hair, I guarantee my work will stay during your dance, milady."

Marisol smiled. "Of course they will, Amy, and thank you for all your help." She turned from the mirror to Samuel, who now watched her. He lifted his arms to be held, and she picked him up. "All right, my little man. I'll give you a good hug and kiss."

As she did, he pulled three fingers from his mouth and reached toward the shiny red and silver comb holding her mantilla in place. She grabbed the damp hand. "No. Let me find you another toy." Amy retrieved a toy soldier from the box in the corner and handed it to him. He clasped it to his chest, and Marisol set him back on the rug.

She picked up her riding crop and headed for the door. "Don't forget, Amy, you're welcome to bring him to see the flamenco, unless he falls asleep before."

Samuel gave a happy holler on his blanket, as if to announce to all he would not be sleeping when his mother danced the Flamenco. She couldn't help grinning at her son as the warmth of love swept through her. What had she ever done without him?

Marisol avoided the guests arriving at the main entrance by taking the back stairs. At the bottom, she met Adriana Cortez, the cousin she'd seen little of since her arrival. The young woman's hard glare from under her purple mantilla stopped Marisol in the hallway. She put a sincere, welcoming expression on her own face. "Hello, Adriana. I hope you've been well. I'm sorry we've seen so little of each other."

"Enough to know what you are planning, *Cousin.*" Her voice was hard and dry, and she emphasized the word *cousin* with a mocking tone. With both hands on her hips, she blocked the staircase.

Marisol stiffened and dropped the edge of her gown she'd been holding to descend the steps. "Forgive me, Adriana. I don't know what you're referring to."

"Don't you? I know you think you can get on Aunt Lucia's good side, even with this Flamenco dance, and maybe end up with half her estate. But I warn you, I'll fight for my rights. I've been here taking care of her all these years, not you."

Speechless and with her heart lurching, Marisol leaned against the wall. Her aunt was childless, but Marisol had never thought about who might inherit the estate. Nor had she cared. And Lucia Chavez was the last person she could imagine needing someone to look after her.

"Don't look so stunned, cousin dear. I'm on to your plan and will watch you every minute until I have something concrete to present to Aunt Lucia." She moved from blocking Marisol's passage.

Marisol opened her mouth to say she had no interest in her aunt's estate and Adriana was welcome to it, but the woman flounced past her up the steps, leaving a heavy scent of perfume trailing behind.

Taking a deep breath and willing her heart and breathing to return to normal, Marisol gripped the skirt of her red gown and proceeded toward the door. After exiting the hacienda, she crossed the grounds and entered the cool recesses of the stables. She stopped a moment to calm her emotions over the confrontation before heading for Ambrosia's stall. The horse would sense any loss of control by her or his rider, and it could mar the presentation.

Pedro already had the stallion out and saddled. His coat glistened like the silver adorning Pedro's new red livery and hat. He doffed the shining sombrero and bowed to Marisol. A wide smile creased his leathery face. "You approve the red bandings I've put on his legs to match your dress, Señora?"

"Oh, yes, Pedro. He looks wonderful. Let's hope he and I both do our best work this evening." She cocked her chin at him and smiled. "Pedro, are you a little nervous about all the guests coming to see us work today?"

"I'm too old to worry. But if I was younger, I might tremble a bit while our Viceroy is watching. He is an expert horseman himself and has fine horses at his plantations."

"Of whom are you speaking, Pedro?"

"Don Rafael Castillo, the Viceroy of New Granada." Pedro pulled a handkerchief from his pocket and wiped his damp forehead.

Strange, her aunt hadn't mentioned this important guest to her. Perhaps Lucia thought it might make her edgy to know such a notable person would watch her dance. But once Marisol began the flamenco, she always forgot everything but her steps and the horse with its rider flowing in the majestic dance around her.

She smiled at Pedro. "Don't worry, sir. Let's forget those who watch and concentrate on our work. All will be fine."

He nodded and placed the bright sombrero back on his head.

Voices of guests filling up the arena seating outside the fenced area filtered through the air. Would Ethan watch her dance the Flamenco? Just now, no one else in the group mattered. She frowned and tried to deny that thought. But it trailed her anyway.

At a quarter past five, a messenger from her aunt jogged into the barn to tell Marisol all was ready for them to begin. Despite her brave words minutes before, a flurry of butterflies clambered in her midsection as she, Pedro, and the horse made their way to the arena gate.

A drummer announced Marisol's entrance first. She glided into the pen as guitars began their heavy strumming. Stopping midway, she began her graceful moves and bends in time to the haunting Spanish music.

After a moment, the guitars paused and the audience seemed to draw a collective breath. She held her pose, careful not to look around. The drum started again, louder, and she turned to watch Ambrosia strut into the arena in timing with the instruments and their increased tempo.

Pedro sat straight as a sword in the saddle, with only one hand on the reins. The guests gave a unified *ah-h* sound like wind. Ambrosia danced up to Marisol, who bowed to welcome him. She flicked his muzzle with her veil and danced away as the crowd clapped.

The horse followed her steps, in time with the drums and guitar, and often did an air above the ground as they proceeded around the perimeter of the enclosure. Twice, Marisol came to the center to perform the most graceful bends and stretches while Ambrosia danced around her in a circle. Over and over, the crowd stood and cheered.

Marisol and the horse ended back in the center of the arena facing each other. Pedro touched the horse's shoulder and Ambrosia bowed low on one knee. Marisol bowed, and the people stood, their applause nearly deafening.

A tall man at the far right dressed in black and silver moved through the guests to the end of the fence and cried, "Bravo! Horse, rider, señorita."

The guests parted like the Red Sea for his passage, staring at him. Marisol glanced once in his direction before she took the rider's hand, put her foot in the stirrup, and mounted onto the horse's back behind Pedro. Her red gown's ruffled hem flowed across the rump of the stallion as he pranced back into the barn amid clapping and cheers.

~

Ethan stood behind the guests in his priest's robe and shook his head in disbelief. Who would have dreamed his governess, mother of Samuel, had this hidden talent—one that took years to perfect with special horses. Excellent with a sword, unbelievable as a Flamenco dancer. What other surprises did the woman possess?

The man who had yelled *bravo* so loud moments earlier claimed Ethan's attention. People gathered around him, but didn't crowd him, as if in awe or respect of him. He was tall and striking in his black taffeta suit, characteristic of Spanish nobility, with silver buttons, lace, and jewels. The golden hilt of a fine sword gleamed at his side. Who could he be?

Later, standing in a corner as the well-dressed guests poured into the dining room, Ethan stared at Marisol from a distance. So many people stopped to speak to her, to congratulate her on her performance. But even amid the throng, their eyes met, and she smiled at him. That smile stole his breath, as though she meant it only for him. He looked away without returning the greeting. Why could he not rejoice that she fit in so well in her new home?

He stood near the main door of the grand ballroom as the orchestra started a Spanish waltz. Courtiers young and old requested partners of women dressed in colorful silk and satin, standing about fanning their excited faces under lace mantillas. Candles in three chandeliers heated the room. No one took notice of him in his brown priest's robe. How soon could he interpose himself to ask a discreet question of some guests?

But no opportunity arose. Just as he was about to slip away to the quiet of his room above, Lucia brought the man in the black and silver suit toward Marisol. She stood against a wall, catching her breath after a dance set, but straightened as the pair approached.

He was older than Ethan first thought, maybe in his mid-forties. His granite features revealed an iron will, while his height and weight suggested a man of enormous physical strength. A scar slashed his tanned left cheek above a short pitch-black beard.

Marisol offered her hand as Lucia introduced her to Don Rafael Castillo, Viceroy of Granada.

So that's who he was. Ethan took a deep breath and tried not to frown.

The man bowed, took Marisol's hand, and kissed it. His eyes roved over her from the top of her piled black hair to her shining red heels and he smiled, still holding her hand. Ethan leaned forward to hear what he said.

"Señora Perez, I have never seen a better Flamenco, and believe me I've seen quite a few. Let me congratulate you." He spoke like a man used to people listening to his every word.

"Thank you, my lord." Marisol pulled her hand away and lowered her head.

The man bowed again. "May I have this dance?"

Lucia answered for Marisol. "I am sure my niece would be honored, sir."

Marisol, a frown on her lovely face, proffered her hand. He grasped it and led her to the dance floor. Other couples moved away to give them space, and Ethan soon saw why. The man danced with the flourish and energy of a dancing master. He led Marisol through intricate steps and twirls in time with the Spanish guitars, which changed their tune after the viceroy nodded to them.

Something in Ethan's gut stirred, flaring into a churning mass. Maybe it shouldn't matter to him, but he hated to see Marisol in the man's hands, like a doll on strings following his every lead. Twice, the viceroy bent to whisper something in her ear.

Other couples now stood on the sidelines and watched their leader dancing with such agility and grace. They clapped when the two finished the dance. The man held Marisol in his arms longer than necessary, and Marisol pushed away, but to no avail. When he released her and bowed, she turned and walked away without a backward glance, leaving the room by a side door.

Ethan followed, trying to diffuse the plethora of emotions racing through him. He caught up with her as she started up the stairs. "Marisol, wait. I want to talk to you."

She didn't look back, but nodded, and he followed up two more flights to a secluded landing near the chapel. When they were alone, with no sound of the dance below reaching their ears, she turned to face him. Shock rolled over him to see tears overflowing her lovely eyes. She lowered her head from his stare.

"What's wrong?" He took her by the shoulders and forced her to look up. "Did that viceroy say or do something improper to you?" Heat flushed through him at the thought.

~

Through tears she couldn't control, Marisol looked at Captain Ethan Becket, dressed as Father Garcia in his brown robe. His disguise didn't hide his muscular form or conceal his strong tanned hands, now gripping her.

She blinked, but still the salty flow gushed out. She couldn't speak, at least not what her heart wanted to admit—that the Flamenco dance was for him, and she hated he'd not been her partner on the dance floor moments earlier.

But all had gone awry. The Viceroy of Granada, a man her aunt had told her was the most powerful man on the Spanish Main, had somehow thought her flamboyant dance was for him. She never dreamed of attracting such a man, and she didn't know how to deal with the situation.

Worst of all, he reminded her of Diego Vargas.

She found her voice, though hoarse. "No, he did nothing." She looked into Ethan's intense gray eyes, filled with compassion for her—was it compassion or something else? A sudden desire possessed her to speak the truth to this man she so admired and respected. "I did the Flamenco for you, Ethan. Only you. Not this… this viceroy who seems to think I danced for him." Had she spoken the words or only thought them?

A light blazed in his eyes. He drew her to him and raised her chin with his thumb. His gaze perused her face, setting her heart afire. The way he looked at her…would he kiss her? Every part of her longed for him to.

He lowered his face to kiss away the tears from her cheeks, sending a tremble down the length of her. Then he bent, and his warm breath caressed her skin just before he brushed her lips with his own.

Sweet ecstasy. Her eyes closed of their own accord. The next instant he crushed her to him, his lips possessing hers with desire and urgency. Never had she known such a kiss. Fireworks exploded all the way down to her toes.

He ended the kiss, pulling back and gripping her shoulders. "Marisol." His eyes had darkened to an intense almost-black, still filled with the same longing that yearned within her.

But then he released her. Or tried to, but her legs gave way. Chuckling, he caught her.

His face turned serious. "I shouldn't have kissed you like that. I would never take advantage of you. Will you forgive me?"

He was an honorable man, Captain Ethan Becket. And that made her crave his touch even more. She whispered, "I don't regret it."

"You don't?" A smile tugged at the corners of his lips. Lips that had set hers aflame just seconds before.

She leaned against the wall, took a deep breath, and dared to look into his eyes, still smoldering in intensity. "Do you?"

A grin lit his tanned face, parted his beard, and revealed even white teeth. "I daresay every priest on the Spanish Main would *not regret it,* and wish to repeat that kiss." He reached for her again.

His words helped clear the haze from her mind. A good thing, for she needed to put some space between them. She forced a casual laugh and pushed him away. "I must go check on Samuel." Thank God for simple tasks that could suspend the crackling tension between them. She moved around him.

He encircled her again in his arms and whispered in her ear. "I will not forget this, or you, Marisol. One day..." He hesitated and drew in a ragged breath. "...things might be different for us, but for now, we must be careful to reveal no hint of what has happened here. Not by our faces or our words." He lifted her chin. "Do you understand?"

"Yes." She saw his eyes move to her lips, so she ducked under his arm and started back down the stairs. She held onto the railing, not yet trusting her legs to hold her. His whispered goodbye trailed her up the steps.

On the second floor, just before she reached her room, she noticed movement from the stairs below. She turned to see Adriana starting up the steps. Marisol ducked into her room, glad she hadn't had to face the woman—not with Ethan's kiss still heating her countenance. Amy and Samuel were asleep in their cots, the only sound in the room their even breathing.

Marisol closed the door and leaned against it. She couldn't seem to wipe the smile off her lips. She dropped into the stuffed chair near the dresser and pulled off her satin heels. What a day.

Exhaustion should be weighing her down, but something had happened when Ethan kissed her. Her body felt renewed with a fresh burst of energy, a feeling of well-being settling around her. Was this what love could do? Even thinking about the viceroy and how she must deflect or redirect his attentions seemed like a small problem now.

She removed the red silk dress and climbed into her bed. Sleep didn't come for a blissful hour as she remembered Ethan's arms around her, his manly voice, scent, and words carrying a promise. The consuming kiss, one like she had never known, still burned on her lips when she fell asleep.

~

Ethan entered his priest chamber next to the chapel with a grin still on his lips. He sat on the simple chair at the small desk and shook his head in wonder. His mind balked at all he needed to process.

Marisol dancing the flamenco. So talented. So beautiful. Who was she? Where did she come from? She must be from an estate similar to Blue Mountain with those special horses like the one that followed her in the dance.

Then Marisol with tears gushing from her eyes. Did she dance for him or the viceroy? Her soft lips had responded to his kiss. He closed his eyes, savoring the memory. His heart felt like singing—or praying and thanking God. Could he experience wonderful love again? Was God that good?

He flung off the robe and lay on his cot. Marisol's face replayed in his mind—her beauty, her energy. The love he saw in her eyes tonight flowed over him, filling, healing broken places he'd forgotten were there. With his spirit finally settled, he fell into a deep, restful sleep.

~

The viceroy called on Marisol the next day. Two servants came to get her, so she left Samuel with Amy and Francisca. Other servants bustled about downstairs as they descended.

Her aunt met her at the foot of the staircase, her face in tight lines. She leaned forward and whispered, "Marisol, I'm surprised the viceroy has come so soon. We must handle this situation with great skill and wisdom. Do you understand?"

"I think so. But I must tell you I'm not at all interested in him."

"But he is interested in you, dear. And he wields great power on the Spanish Main. Just be cordial and we'll discuss what next to do after he leaves."

Marisol sighed. "Yes, ma'am."

She walked into the parlor behind her aunt and looked at the man who stood up to greet them. In the clear morning light, he looked larger, more powerful, than he had in the evening's candlelight.

Probably in his forties, he was rugged and handsome, a man of physical strength still in his prime. Today he'd dressed in pale blue taffeta and silver, a perfect picture of nobility and wealth. When he bowed and came forward to take first her aunt's, and then her hand, Marisol again saw the scar that crossed his cheek, almost hidden by the well-groomed black beard.

"I am a busy man, dear Lucia, and hope I haven't surprised you with my quick return visit, nor you Señora Perez. But my responsibilities limit my time in Cartagena. I must soon return to my plantation and silver mine in Peru. Plus, the business of the vice royalty of Grenada keeps me on the run."

"I'm sure that's right, Viceroy." Lucia chose the silk sofa, and Marisol sat on the edge beside her.

The viceroy returned to the large king chair he had already chosen, which seemed to fit his grand bearing.

"Let me order tea." Lucia waved her hand and the servant at the door departed.

Lucia kept the conversation light as they indulged in the refreshments, but after the servants cleared the tray, she raised her gaze to the man. "To what do we owe the honor of this visit, sir?"

He beamed a warm smile at Marisol.

She stiffened and looked down at her folded hands.

He addressed her aunt. "I am not a man to mince words, Lucia. I would like your permission to court your niece." He flexed his broad hands. "As you know, I lost my wife last year and I'm a lonely man. See I have opened my heart to you." He smiled at Lucia and then again at Marisol.

The pompous oaf. Heat rose in Marisol's face and her breath strangled in her throat. She coughed, and Lucia patted her hand.

Her aunt affected a ladylike sigh of regret. "But, sir, Marisol has only arrived and her mind has not settled about her future at all. And I don't think you know, but she has a young child, a boy of about six months, she must consider. Also she has just changed from her widow garments."

The man's black eyes lit up. "A boy? I love children. I have three now grown. The child presents no problem at all." He stood, as if to close the subject.

Marisol fought nausea rising in her throat. Lucia offered the man a respectful smile. "Sir, can you give us a week to consider if...a courtship might be possible at this time?"

His dark brows drew together and his eyes hardened for a moment, then his mouth shifted into a smile. His face and voice resumed confidence. "Of course a courtship is possible, dear lady." He glanced at Marisol. "But I see you need time to think about it. I will come back in a week."

He bowed and strode to the door, his sword jangling at his side.

Servants scrambled ahead of him and flung open the heavy main entrance for him. They bent low as he departed.

Turmoil churned inside Marisol as the doors closed behind him. She had to get away. Somewhere she could vent her frustrations. She put her fist to her mouth and ran from the room.

CHAPTER 11

The next morning Marisol took a chair in the plantation breakfast room and awaited Lucia's arrival. Weight like a sack of rocks sat on her shoulders and she had no appetite, but her aunt would want to see her. She prayed Lucia could share a practical plan to deal with the viceroy's pursuit. One thing she had discerned about the man in her short acquaintance with him—he tolerated little disagreement with his wishes.

"Good morning, my dear." Her aunt's yellow morning dress and cheerful voice brought light into the room as she entered. She sat beside Marisol and patted her niece's hands clasped on the table in front of her. "Now, I don't want you to worry about the viceroy. We'll find a way to avoid any problem. Meanwhile, I have good news for Father Garcia. Do you think he'll be coming down for breakfast?"

"Did I hear my name? I am here and hungry, dear lady." Ethan entered in his priest's robe and smiled at both women before sitting down in his usual seat beside Lucia. She'd insisted he take that chair during his stay.

Lucia lifted her hand toward him. "You will have something extra to give thanks for in your blessing this morning, Father. I have news, possibly about the sister you are seeking for your friend. But first, please offer a prayer for our food."

"Indeed?" Ethan's eyes lit. "Let us pray."

After speaking the blessing, he sat forward, giving Lucia his full attention. "What have you found out, Señora?"

Marisol tried not to stare at him, less she reveal her inner turmoil. She couldn't deny the increased beat of her heart from being in his magnetic presence, hearing his deep, confident voice.

Lucia took a portion of scrambled eggs and bacon from the servant who appeared at her elbow. "I've heard a blond English woman works as a tutor at a plantation a few miles away. It's the Montevares' estate, owned by Don Pedro Montevares. He has a fleet of ships, too. I know the family, but not well. Enough, however, to announce a visit."

"That's great news, Doña Lucia." Ethan placed a large portion of the food on his plate. "How soon can we go?" A tremor in his voice gave hint of his excitement.

Just seeing him so pleased pushed away the melancholy that had settled over Marisol when she first awoke and remembered the viceroy's determination. She looked at Ethan and smiled. "I'm happy to hear this, Father Garcia. I know how much you'd like to find the sister...of your friend." She worked hard not to look into his warm eyes too long.

Her aunt took a deep breath and sat straighter. "I will send a note to Don Pedro this morning. We'll see. Perhaps I'll tell him of your arrival, Marisol, that I am introducing you, and of our eventual need of a tutor for Samuel. And that we heard he had a wonderful tutor for his daughter. I didn't think to invite him to the celebration, but a visit will make up for it." She turned to Father Garcia. "And, of course, you will accompany us."

Adriana Cortez entered the breakfast room, and all conversation about the coming visit ceased. She gave a big smile to her aunt and an obligatory nod to Father Garcia, then sat in her usual chair. The look she gave Marisol contained enough barely covered venom to send a shiver down her back.

~

After nightfall, Ethan slipped back to the dock and approached the *Dryade.*

"Who goes there?" Two guards stood shoulder to shoulder to bar access to the gangplank.

Ethan smiled. "I guess you lads don't know me well in this outfit."

The guards lowered their guns as recognition settled on their faces.

Tim Cullen, his lieutenant, hurried down from the quarterdeck. "Good to see you, Cap'n."

Ethan clapped him on the back and they walked to his cabin. Ben Thompson met them on the way and fell into step with them.

When they found seats around the table, Ethan eyed both men. "I've some good news. Marisol's aunt has discovered an English woman tutor on a plantation in south Cartagena. We'll visit her as soon as she can arrange it."

"That's great, sir." Tim Cullen leaned back in his chair and grinned.

Ben Thompson's face wreathed with smiles. "Ethan, I pray this will be your sister and you'll find her in health and well cared for. Have you any plan or idea yet how to rescue her, if it is Grace?"

A surge of determination washed through him. "No, but you can be sure I'll come up with one." If Grace was in this town, there was no way he'd leave without her.

~

The visit took place two days later. Marisol glanced out the window of her aunt's well-appointed coach, pulled by four white horses and driven by servants in green livery. The long pimento-lined drive of the Montevares estate was lovely, almost as beautiful as her aunt's home.

Tìa Lucia's voice interrupted her thoughts. "I have prayed for our God to guide our conversation here, especially if we meet the young woman you are looking for, Father Garcia. We must be very discreet."

Marisol smiled. She'd realized early on her aunt was not the expected Catholic. One evening, she'd found her reading an English Bible in a secluded corner of the large library upstairs.

Ethan nodded. "Yes, Señora. We'll depend on God to lead us in this venture." His voice ebbed with feeling.

They stopped and disembarked at the impressive entrance of the hacienda, with its steps guarded by carved bulls on either side.

Servants led them from a great marble entry into an elegant sitting room. Paintings and works of art from around the world lined the walls, probably a benefit from the man's shipping business.

They sat on matching silk sofas in front of the tiled fireplace as the servants fetched Don Pedro Montevares.

When he entered, Ethan stood in his priest's robes. Montevares nodded at him and took the extended hand of Lucia. "So glad to see you, Señora Chavez. Your note announcing your visit pleased me."

Lucia gestured to Marisol. "This is my niece I mentioned who's arrived from Spain. She's a widow with a young son."

He took Marisol's hand. "Yes, Señora, let me express my regret that one so young has become a widow."

"Thank you, sir. I appreciate your arranging this visit on such short notice." Marisol noted the man's kind face as she withdrew her hand.

Lucia motioned toward Ethan. "This is Father Garcia who accompanied my niece and her child from Cadiz."

"So good of you, sir. I am sure." The two shook hands, then Don Pedro sat in a chair between the sofas and Ethan returned to his seat.

Lucia looked around the elegant room. "Don Pedro, your collections are interesting. I would love to hear more about them. I wonder, would it be possible while you and I talk, that Marisol and

Father Garcia could visit your school room? I hear you have the best tutor and classroom in Cartagena. We will one day need to set up a tutor and school room for Marisol's Samuel. We have a small one now for my other niece's child, but look to improve it."

"Of course. You mentioned this in your note and I've already arranged it with my tutor, an English lady I rescued from a sinking ship some years ago. Her name is Señorita Grace." He stood to pull a cord next to the fireplace.

Marisol hoped he didn't see how Father Garcia's head jerked up at the mention of the woman's name. As excited as she, herself, was that they may have found Ethan's sister, discretion was of the utmost importance during this visit.

A servant entered and bowed.

"Please escort the priest and lady to the school room, Marcus." Don Pedro took his seat.

"Yes, sir." The man bowed again, then turned for Ethan and Marisol to follow him up the grand staircase.

They entered a large room with a row of windows on one side which emitted rays of sunshine. The servant bowed, then left, closing the door behind them. An elderly woman and a girl sat in a corner, leaning over an open book. They looked up at the visitors, and the child smiled an eager grin. The woman's frown made it clear she didn't appreciate the interruption.

A sigh sounded from Ethan, but Marisol didn't look at him.

Instead, she spoke to the woman whose face resembled wrinkled beige parchment. "Are you Señorita Grace?" She was much too old to be his sister, but maybe there had been a mistake.

The girl of about ten giggled. "No, this is Grand'mere!"

The woman's frown deepened. "Señorita Grace went to the kitchen to bring this lazy child a cup of milk and a cookie. Otherwise, she may never learn French. What this girl needs is a good caning." She poked her granddaughter with her elbow.

All signs of joy faded from the youth's face and she lowered her head.

Just then, the door opened and a younger woman backed in

carrying a tray. She wore her blond hair pinned back in a neat chignon. Could this be…?

She turned and smiled at the visitors, and her gaze seemed to snag on Ethan. Her face paled. Marisol stepped forward to catch the tray, but she was too late. The dishes crashed to the floor.

"Look what you've done now, you clumsy woman." The older lady glared in their direction.

The young woman pulled a towel from her apron and stooped to soak up the spilled milk. It wasn't hard to see that her hands shook. Ethan strode forward and leaned down to help her. He whispered something to her, and she calmed.

When she stood, her face settled into perfect peace and apology. "I'm so sorry, ma'am. I don't know how I managed to drop the tray." She turned to Ethan. "Thank you for assisting, Father. Perhaps you'd like to go back to the kitchen with me to get more for the child and help bring a tea tray for the rest of us?"

"I would be glad to assist." Ethan's voice sounded normal. He followed her out the door, ignoring the grumbling of the old lady behind them.

Marisol forced her countenance to stay composed, though her heart sang. This had to be his sister, Grace. She even had Ethan's gray eyes.

~

Ethan followed Grace to the hall, then into a small room three doors down. She closed the door without a sound and fell into his arms. "Dear little brother Ethan, how in this world did you find me?"

He cleared his throat and blinked moisture from his eyes. "God gave us a miracle." God, indeed. His chest fairly burst from joy and relief.

She wiped tears from her eyes. "I had almost given up hope." She hugged him again, a joyous laugh bubbling from her. "We don't have time to talk here. Another servant may come down the hall and wonder where I am."

"Then I will come again tonight. Where can we meet to plan your departure?" Ethan stared in the face of his sister, older by seven years, tracing all the familiar lines of high cheek bones, the prim nose, and wide forehead he'd known growing up.

She pulled him farther from the door. "Beyond the two large barns behind the house, you'll see a small older one. No one ever goes there now. It's become my prayer closet. Come tomorrow at midnight when the house will be quiet. But watch for the guards stationed around the estate perimeter."

"Don't worry. I'll get past them." He planted a kiss on her forehead, then followed her out of the room and to the kitchen.

~

On their way back to Blue Mountain Plantation, Aunt Lucia looked from Marisol to Ethan. "Well, was the tutor the daughter of your friend, sir?"

Marisol looked away, hating to be part of another lie to her aunt, but Ethan had convinced her it was the only way to protect her aunt from suspicion and make his sister's escape less risky.

He gave her aunt a warm smile. "Doña Lucia, I want to thank you so much for trying to help. Maybe we'll have better luck another day."

"Well, I'll keep asking discreet questions when I can. But when do you need to return to Spain, sir? Not that you tire us with your company. Not by any means." Lucia patted his robed arm.

Ethan grimaced. "Yes, that's the thing. I must soon head back, but not for another week or two."

Marisol's eyes shot to his. Would he ask her to return to Charles Town with him? How she wished she could discuss everything that had happened with her aunt, including the truth about Ethan. She sighed and gazed out the coach window at the fields of sugar cane waving in the breeze.

~

The next day, the viceroy called again. Doña Lucia had ridden out on the plantation to check some sick slaves, so the servant came for Marisol. She hated the thought of meeting with the man alone, so she told Amy to bring Samuel and come with her.

Don Rafael Castillo rose and bowed as Marisol entered with Amy trailing behind, carrying Samuel. The viceroy, dressed in black again with silver buttons studded with jewels, presented a formidable picture of wealth and power. The shining hilt of the Toledo sword that hung at his side glistened in the afternoon sunlight streaming through the long windows of the sitting room.

Don Rafael grasped Marisol's hand and brought it to his lips. It took everything in her not to cringe before she could retrieve it. She sat in the farthest seat from him that she could. Amy placed Samuel on the thick carpet between the sofas and chairs. The child sat with three fingers in his mouth and turned his full attention on the viceroy.

"He is a fine boy, Marisol."

As if that were an invitation, Samuel crawled toward him. He stopped and sat at the man's feet, then reached for the silver jangles on the black boots.

"No, Samuel. Come back to Amy." Marisol sat forward and motioned for Amy to get the child. But the viceroy surprised them both.

He reached down and brought the boy into his lap. "I told you I like children, Marisol. Mine are grown now, but I always enjoyed them when they were young. Everything is worth exploring at this age. Isn't that so, my boy?" Samuel looked up at him and touched the shining metals on the man's front pocket with his damp fingers. The viceroy smacked his hand away. "But they are not too young to learn a few rules either."

Samuel's face puckered and a pitiful cry slipped out. Anger surged through Marisol as she jumped up and took her son from the viceroy. How dare he touch her child? She held the boy close until his sobs tapered off, resentment building in her chest with every moment.

She had to control herself though. This man held too much power to let her temper fly. At last, Samuel plunked three fingers in his mouth and looked back at the viceroy through long wet lashes.

Marisol turned to the man. "Sir, I am sorry, but I must take my son back upstairs. It's time for his afternoon nursing, and I don't know when I could come back. You're welcome to wait for Aunt Lucia, if you like." Her voice was none too gentle.

Without another word, she left the room and hurried up the stairs with Amy following.

Her dislike for the man had grown to a passionate level. Never, under any condition, would she marry him.

In her room, she sat down with Samuel in the rocker and pondered what she could do if the man persisted in his attentions. How she wished she could talk to Ethan about the situation, but he was busy planning his sister's escape. She must be very careful and wise in dealing with the viceroy. How much power did he possess? Her head ached from the thoughts swirling through her mind.

~

Half past midnight the next evening, Ethan, dressed like a Spanish worker in dark clothing, had no trouble evading the sleepy guards on Don Pedro's estate. He entered the small barn and his heart surged at the woman standing just inside. Grace.

He closed the door behind him just in time to catch his sister as she flew into his arms. The feel of her—here with him, in the flesh—settled a rightness through him, and he sent up a prayer of thanks.

"Ethan, I wasn't sure I'd ever see you again." She clutched him tight for a long moment, then pulled away, laughing and wiping her teary eyes. "Sit." She motioned toward sacks of feed, and he helped her settle herself. He took his place beside her, and she grabbed his hand, as though he might disappear unless she held him captive.

She leveled her familiar gray eyes on him. "I've thought about it, Ethan, and next week will be the best time for me to escape."

Her words tumbled out in rapid succession. "Cartagena will celebrate a special mass. There will be dancing in the streets, parades, and heavy drinking. Don Pedro will be gone most nights until late. We call off the school classes, and I will spread the word I plan to enter into the festivities. Don Pedro gives me a lot of freedom, so no one will notice my absence for at least a day and a night."

Ethan's blood rushed to his head. It was happening. He would rescue Grace, with God's help. "How do you suggest we do this?"

"You're staying at Lucia Chavez's estate, right?"

"Yes."

"Where is your ship?"

"In the bay nearest her plantation."

"Then I will come to Blue Mountain Estate on Thursday evening next week. That's the biggest night of celebration, and no one will pay attention to a Spanish washer woman on the roads or even crossing the fields. I'm familiar with the estate since I once accompanied Don Pedro's daughter there for a child's party."

"Are you sure you can make it there alone?"

"Yes, during the festival I'm sure. Doña Lucia's stable hands will all be part of the celebration in town. You should find me in the stables as night falls. From there, you must have the plan for my escape to your ship."

"Yes, I'll have it. We must both be very careful. Let nothing in our demeanor alert anyone around us."

Grace tweaked his beard. "I can handle it. Can you?" Then her face grew sober. "Ethan, you must know how happy I am to see you. But I need to tell you I'll miss the child I've been tutoring since I've been here. And I hate to leave her at the mercy of Don Pedro's mother." She lowered her lovely gray eyes, so much like his. "And I'll even miss Don Pedro."

"What? You'll miss the man who took you captive?"

"Pedro has treated me well, Ethan. He rescued me from some other hands that would not have been kind, and...he's never accosted me or made me feel like a servant." She paused and turned to face him. "In fact, I believe he would ask me to marry him except for his bitter, proud mother."

Ethan stared in his sister's face, lit by the moonlight from the small window. Had she fallen for her captor? Heaven forbid.

She squeezed his hand. "But that's no matter at this point. We must get back before anyone misses us. Brother, I will see you, the Lord willing, next Thursday at nightfall in the Chavez stables."

That evening in his room, Ethan made his plan for how he would deliver Grace to the *Dryade.* When his sister was safely aboard, he'd come back and ask Marisol to return to Charles Town with them. They would take a normal leave of her aunt after thanking her for her hospitality. Would Marisol come with him? Would Lucia allow her to leave? What reason would satisfy her aunt since she knew him as only a priest? With so much swirling in his mind, sleep was long in coming.

~

Marisol lay in her bed mulling over events. She was thankful Ethan had found his sister. Truly. She prayed they could both escape to the ship and make it back to Charles Town.

But that thought made her heart heavy. What if Ethan didn't ask her to go with them? Did she read too much in his words the night he kissed her? How would she explain to her aunt that she wanted to return to Charles Town?

Then the hard face of the viceroy invaded her mind. Would he try to hinder her leaving Cartagena if Ethan invited her? Then another foreboding thought flooded her mind, sending a chill all the way through her chest.

What if the viceroy discovered Ethan's deception? Would he turn him over to the Inquisition for impersonating a priest? She must do everything in her power to prevent that from ever happening—no matter what Don Rafael Castillo demanded.

~

Two days later, Marisol entered the sitting room to retrieve Samuel and Amy. She'd left them with her aunt an hour earlier while she went riding, and the exercise had renewed her in just the way she'd needed.

A strange, well-dressed woman with her back to Marisol held Samuel in her arms. He gave a happy squeal as he fingered a pearl necklace at the woman's throat.

Aunt Lucia stood nearby, and Marisol sent her a smile. "Thanks for watching Samuel. I see you have a guest."

The woman turned, and Marisol's heart slammed in her chest. Diego Vargas's mother.

Her head went light, and she clutched the back of the nearest chair. She couldn't show her fear. If this woman learned the truth of her son's death, Marisol would see the same fate.

The lady stared at her, and then walked toward her with wide amber green eyes. She stopped two feet from Marisol. "Marisol Valentin, is it really you?" The woman's voice almost squeaked.

Icy fingers seeped into every pore of Marisol's skin. She struggled for words, but her mouth had gone too dry to produce sound.

Lucia smiled. "Yes, this is she. Like I told you, Doña Maria, she delighted me by coming to Cartagena." She turned to her niece. "Marisol, are you well? Did something happen during your ride? Your face looks gray." She turned back to the visitor. "You say you knew Marisol in Spain?"

The woman stiffened and placed Samuel in Amy's lap. "Why yes. She and...my son were once engaged."

"Is that so?" Lucia's brows rose.

Marisol found her voice and politeness. "How are you, Doña Maria? So sorry I'm not feeling well. I hope you will excuse us." With that, she stood and gestured for Amy to follow with Samuel. She forced her wooden legs to carry her out of the room and up the stairs.

Once she reached the safety of their bed chamber, Marisol collapsed on the bed. She could no longer hold her tears in. As hot drops burned down her face, she cried for that awful night. For everything Diego Vargas had stolen from her. For the awful moment when she realized she'd killed him. For all the pain and misery since then. The sobs racked her body, until she had no tears left.

Amy walked back and forth with Samuel, her face a mask of worry.

Finally, Marisol sat up, her face wet and surely swollen. She wiped away the remnants of her emotional collapse, inhaled a steadying breath, then sought for something to say to relieve Amy's concern. "I can't explain it right now, Amy, but I'm not happy to see the woman below. In fact, I hoped I'd never see her again."

Amy took a relieved breath. "Yes, ma'am. We all got one or two of them kind of folks. I can think of a few myself."

Marisol smiled a sad smile that pulled at the tightness of her puffy face. "Why was she holding Samuel?"

"Ma'am, I'm sorry if I shouldn't of let her take him, but I didn't know what to do when she came and seemed so friendly with Doña Lucia. Then she started looking at Samuel and got up and picked him up off the floor and stared into his face. You know your boy. He never meets a stranger. He kinda took to her." The girl's words came out in a torrent, and she resumed pacing with Samuel.

"It's all right, Amy." Marisol arose and moved to the rocker. "You did nothing wrong. Bring him to me."

The girl placed Samuel in Marisol's lap. "She took on about Samuel's eyes. In fact, the lady had eyes similar to his, come to think of it. That amber with a hint of green. Now ain't that odd? Such a rare color."

A sensation of intense sickness and desperation swept through Marisol, and the tears threatened again. Yes, Samuel had his father's eyes. A trait which Diego had inherited from his mother.

~

The next day Marisol received a servant-delivered note on pale yellow stationary with the Vargas coat of arms on the seal. She opened it with shaking hands.

Marisol,
We must meet and talk. I have a plan you need to hear.
I am staying at the Hotel Cartagena on Sayre Street.
Come at three o'clock tomorrow.
- Senora Maria de la Madrid Vargas

Marisol licked her dry lips. She would have to go. The woman held Marisol's life in her hands. And the worst part was that she couldn't even tell Ethan about this meeting. She could only imagine how he would respond if he knew her real past, and the thought tightened the knots in her middle. All her hopes seemed to be dying in the space of a few days.

~

The following day, Marisol walked into the luxurious hotel suite at three o'clock. Doña Maria beckoned her to a small table with preparations for tea laid out. As Marisol sat, the woman poured two cups. Not that Marisol would be able to touch hers with the way her midsection had been roiling all morning.

"I'll not waste words or time, Marisol. Samuel is my grandson. He has Diego's eyes and mine. He's the right age from when you left Cadiz." She sipped her tea and sat the cup back down. "When you left my son murdered with your own small sword in your stables, I guessed what might have happened."

Marisol gritted her teeth and met the woman's gaze, letting her anger give her strength. "Yes, your wayward son raped me and would have done so again had I not found my knife."

Doña Maria's face paled. "I knew my son and all his shortcomings, Marisol. I don't doubt what you're saying. And I can't tell you..." Her voice broke and her eyes filled with tears. "...how happy I am to know about Samuel. That I have a grandson. You might not understand this, but I've been comfortless since Diego died, my only child and heir."

As she watched the woman, Marisol tried to feel pity for her. But the emotion wouldn't come. All she could see was Diego's lecherous green gaze staring back at her.

Doña Maria sniffed and wiped her eyes with a lace handkerchief. "So I have a plan I want to propose to you. Give me the boy to raise. He'll inherit my entire estate, and one day he'll be a wealthy hidalgo, a nobleman of Spain."

Marisol's mouth fell open as shock washed through her. "You think I'd ever give you my son to raise? Look at how Diego turned out."

Doña Maria's face lost its pleasant expression as she took another sip of tea. "You have no choice, my dear. If you don't, I'll expose you as the murderer of my son. Then what will happen to Samuel? As his lawful grandmother, I will take him after your arrest." She sat her cup back on the tray. "Do you want to put the boy through all that?"

Marisol's mind spun as the woman stood and walked to the window. "I'll give you one week to make up your mind."

One week.

Hot tears overflowed Marisol's eyes and she couldn't get her breath. She had to get out of there before she lost her composure completely in front of this woman. This...snake. She stood and strode from the room. And the hotel.

CHAPTER 12

Two days later, when the festival occupied everyone's attention, Marisol, sent by Ethan, found Grace in the stables. She slipped his sister up to her own room while he made ready their trip to the ship.

Grace's easy manner drew Marisol immediately, and in the two short hours they had to talk, their hearts knit together. She even shared her worry about the viceroy, her lesser worry now that Doña Maria had made plain her desire to have Samuel. But she didn't dare share that consuming anxiety with this new friend.

Grace patted her hand. "Come, let us pray about this, and also for mine and Ethan's escape to the ship."

Marisol hadn't knelt to pray with anyone since Mrs. Piper, but as they did so now, the prayer Grace lifted heavenward soothed the raw edges of Marisol's nerves. Surely God would work on their behalf.

~

That night, Ethan led Grace safely aboard his ship with both of them dressed like common laborers flocking to the city for the festival. He took her to his cabin and introduced her to his officers. And, oh, what a joyous dinner they shared that night.

Later, Ethan met with Tim, Ben, and Samson to share what was on his heart. "I plan to go back to see if Marisol, Samuel, and Amy will accompany us to Charles Town."

All three men's eyes widened.

Ben frowned, then his face eased into a smile as he nodded.

Tim punched Samson with his elbow, but Samson's face stiffened.

"You go back? But it verra dangerous, Cap'n." Samson's dark eyes pleaded. They'd developed a mutual respect through the years, and he could see the worry in his friend's eyes.

"Yes, it is perilous, but I'm going. I can't leave Marisol if she wants to come with me." He looked at the three faces who knew him better than anyone, men he could trust, and their concern for him hovered like a cloud around the table.

But he had thought this through. "Here's the contingency plan." He turned to Cullen. "If I'm not back by this time tomorrow, I leave you as captain of the *Dryade,* and I want you to sail away. Take Grace back to Charles Town. Go on to whatever other business you feel led to accomplish. If I'm apprehended, I can only conjecture what the future may hold. I'll try to escape and come to the coast of Panama within three weeks. Meet me there in the cove where we beached the ship to scrape the barnacles the last time we came to this area." He waited for Tim's response.

The man nodded. "I remember the place, sir."

"Wait there one week." Ethan cleared his throat and looked straight into his lieutenant's face. "If I don't appear, the ship is yours, my man."

Tim stiffened, as did the other two listening.

Ethan smiled. "But I think I'll be back here on the *Dryade* in twenty-four hours, so don't fret."

Tim placed his clenched fists on the table, his red brows creasing in a frown. "I appreciate your trust in me, sir. But do you really want to go back with all the risk involved, now that your sister is safe aboard? They'll be looking for Mistress Grace, and Señora Marisol may not even want to return with you." He took a deep breath. "And think of your family waiting for you in Charles Town."

Ethan lowered his head as he gathered his thoughts, then raised it and looked first at Tim, then at the other two. "Sirs, I've counted the cost and I must go back." He smiled. "I have reason to believe Marisol will want to come with me."

Ben rose and laid his hand on Ethan's shoulder. "Then may God go with you, son, and with her."

~

The following morning, Marisol received a summons to the sitting room to receive the viceroy. At least Aunt Lucia would be with her this time. She placed Samuel in Amy's lap and walked with slow steps down the stairway. She would make an appearance, then find an excuse to leave.

When she opened the door and entered, she swept her gaze around the room. Where was her aunt?

The viceroy grinned and stood. Dressed in his usual black and silver adornments, his presence filled the room.

"Sir, it's not proper that we meet alone." She turned to leave, but he came forward and closed the door behind her. He took her hand and pulled her farther into the room.

His grip was solid, squeezing her fingers. She tried to withdraw from his hold, but he cast his strong arms about her and drew her close. Panic surged in her chest, welling up her throat. His hot breath reeked of tobacco and rum, blasting her face so she couldn't breathe. His sword clanged against her side.

She turned her cheek away as he tried to kiss her. "Sir, release me at once."

"I will never release you, dear Marisol. You haunt my dreams and hinder my work. I can't even force myself to leave Cartagena for my Columbian silver estate until you promise to come with me." His hoarse voice sent a shiver of fear through her, and his thick arms pressing her close made breathing almost impossible.

"I'll scream if you don't let me go. How embarrassing will that be for you? The servants will come, and my aunt." She pushed hard, arching her face as far away from his as she could.

"Scream. No one will come. I've seen to it. Now give me one kiss and then we'll plan our wedding day."

The man's strength was an iron band that held her captive no matter how hard she struggled. But then a violent twist freed one of her hands. She slapped him hard, but his inky beard deflected the blow. He laughed and drew her closer until she could hardly breathe. With her last good breath, she screamed.

The door flew open and Ethan stepped in. He cast one glance at them, and his face turned hard and threatening.

The viceroy spared him only a single quick look. "Go back where you came from, Father. This is none of your business. I intend to make this little lady my wife, but I have to convince her."

Ethan cast off his robe and reached for his sword. "You're wrong. This is my business."

Don Rafael Castillo's dark eyes narrowed and his face turned a mottled red. He flung Marisol aside and drew his Toledo sword from its scabbard, then aimed it at Ethan. "So you show your true colors, sir. You are not a priest, eh? The Inquisition judges will delight to get their hands on you, if I don't kill you first."

He stormed toward Ethan and their swords joined. Sharp clicks, clangs, and heavy breathing filled the room as the two lunged across the floor, thrusting and deflecting thrusts. Marisol's pulse thundered as she sat up from the sofa where the viceroy had flung her. Both men appeared well-matched in skill, and chairs and small tables fell over as they crashed around them.

Ethan. Trying to gather her senses, Marisol placed her clenched fist to her mouth to stop the scream rising in her throat. The viceroy would have soldiers and guards who accompanied him anywhere he went. What chance would dear Ethan have, even if he could prove the better swordsman?

She bent to reach for the sword in her boot.

Don Rafael grunted as Ethan's blade nicked his chin, drawing first blood. But it was also to be the last. Four soldiers in their red and silver uniforms stampeded into the room and surrounded Ethan. He struck out at them, slicing with his sword. One of the men howled with pain, but the other three soon disarmed him.

Marisol replaced her own sword and watched, her heart rending in two, as they slapped chains on his wrists, then marched him out of the room.

The viceroy glanced at her as he pushed his blade back into its scabbard and wiped the blood from his chin. "I will go take care of this mongrel puppy, but I will be back tomorrow, Marisol."

"What will you do with him, sir?" Her voice trembled, but she no longer cared.

"Turn the imposter over to the Dominicans and the Inquisition Court, of course. They have swift retribution for anyone who poses as a priest. He may be a spy."

Marisol stood and swallowed the nausea rising in her throat. "But, sir, you are signing his death warrant, and it won't be a quick death with them."

He paused in adjusting his cravat, and stared at her. The cords of his thick neck stood out as his lips thinned. "What's it to you? Who is this man?"

Marisol didn't meet his gaze. He'd know in an instant if she looked at him, and things would go all the worse for Ethan. She curled her hands into fists until the nails bit into her palms, but it still didn't stop the tears.

Don Rafael strode over, took her by the shoulders, and shook her. "Was this man your lover?"

She shook her head. "No. He was just someone who...has shown kindness to me, and I would hate to see him harmed."

He stepped back and considered. "I have great power here, Marisol. His life is in my hands. What's it worth to you to spare him?"

She clenched her eyes shut. "Anything."

He nodded. "Will you marry me of your own free will if I spare his life from the Inquisition? There is one other option I can exercise as viceroy. I can take him as my personal slave to work in my silver mines."

She opened her eyes as a sliver of hope birthed in her heart. "Yes. I'll marry you of my own free will if you spare him. He's strong. He can work in your silver mine." *And I will help him escape.*

"What has happened here?" Lucia strode into the room, eyeing the knocked over chairs and the small table. She looked at the viceroy. "Sir, I am not happy over what has taken place here today."

He smiled at her, a grin like a satisfied lion licking its paws. "Never fear, Señora Chavez. I will replace anything broken. And all is now well. We had a little skirmish with that false priest you were entertaining." His eyes narrowed. "If you do not speak of this, the Dominicans need not know who you were harboring in your house."

"False priest? Father Garcia?" Lucia looked from the viceroy to Marisol.

Marisol nodded and dropped onto the nearest sofa. Her legs had lost so much strength, they wouldn't hold her much longer.

The viceroy looked at Lucia and smiled. "You will be happy to know that your niece, Marisol Valentin Perez, has agreed to marry me."

Lucia gasped.

Marisol couldn't meet her gaze, so she sank lower in the cushions.

"I'll be back tomorrow to discuss wedding plans and our coming journey. We'll want the nuptials to take place at my Columbian estate." The viceroy bowed to Lucia, then to Marisol, and strode out the door, his chin thrust out and his sword jangling at his side.

~

Anger surged through Ethan as he was led down a shadowy dungeon corridor. Or maybe it was fear that washed through his veins. What would happen to Marisol now? What would happen to him?

His wrists were chained behind him, and men on either side gripped his arms.

"I won't struggle." He spoke through clenched teeth, then shrugged against their hold. Thankfully, they released his arms, but their presence around him smothered. In this dank place, the putrid scents of fear, sweat, and human excrement curled his nose. The guards stopped at an empty cell, opened the door, and shoved him in.

He had to scramble to catch himself, and when the heavy door clanged shut, he sat on the straw cot and dropped his head into his hands. Was this where it would all end?

His memories marched through his mind—studying for the priesthood, he and his parents caught up in Martin Luther's movement, their becoming part of the Presbyterian movement, meeting Olivia and answering a call into the ministry, their good years in Charles Town pastoring the small church there, the birth of Joshua. Would he ever see his son again? Pain slammed against his chest, but he did his best to push that particular thought aside. Dwelling on Joshua's chubby smile would wreck him.

He'd do better to think of his ship. Of his men—Tim and Ben and Samson. Would they do as he'd instructed? Then Marisol's sweet face filled his mind to haunt him. What would happen to her? To her child?

This was his greatest regret. He'd saved his sister, but he hadn't been able to help Marisol. He had not even told her he loved her.

But he did love her.

That was a thought to dwell on. He never thought he'd love again, but she had awakened his sad heart, drew him back to real life and hope.

He raised his head and took a deep breath. The first ray of hope since his arrest. Surely the God in heaven he'd known and preached wouldn't allow him to love again, then have it end with an Inquisition trial.

Hours later, voices flowed from the corridor, drawing closer. A lantern appeared down the way, and he watched the light approach. Should he be afraid? Relieved? It hardly seemed to matter, since he had no control over what his visitors would do. In front of his cell, the light beamed through his bars, and he blinked against its brightness.

A Dominican priest held the lantern, and the viceroy stood beside him. The priest spoke. "Why don't you turn this heretic over to us? We'll get his story fast." His voice was harsh, uncaring.

"Sir, I have made up my mind to take him as my personal slave. He's strong. He'll last for some time in my silver mine. The Indians don't last long there, and you know His Majesty is awaiting the next big shipment of silver and gold. Let me have him. After all, I apprehended this imposter."

The white-robed priest frowned, and seemed to ponder for a moment. Then he nodded. "You may take him if you wish."

The viceroy cast mocking eyes at Ethan through the bars. "You hear your fate, good sir? It's to the silver mines for you through the jungle, with a string of other scoundrels I've apprehended. We leave at the end of the week."

~

The next day, the guards pushed two new prisoners into Ethan's cell. He overheard the two men talking about Spain and the ship they'd just arrived on. The captain had them arrested for insubordination when the ship docked. As the hours passed, the two talked much about their homes in Cadiz, Spain. Ethan listened with one ear until he heard the name *Valentin*.

He looked at the smaller man, who reminded him of a weasel with his dark, furtive eyes and short stature. "What did you say about a Valentin family in Cadiz?"

The man stopped chewing a piece of straw, his face turning eager. "I said them authorities there believe the Valentin daughter murdered that Vargas nobleman, because she fled the city the same night with her maid. Came to the New World, some say."

"How long ago did this happen and do you remember the daughter's name?" Ethan searched the man's face. Could he believe anything this scoundrel said?

"I'm thinking it were less than two years ago." He scratched his jaw. "As fur as her name goes, it were something like Maria or Marisol. I heard it from a stable hand who worked there. He found the body stabbed to death in the stables. I say good riddance to any nobleman who treats sailors like peons. I've seen enough in my day. Hope she's never caught." The man spit out his straw and turned over on his cot to sleep.

A pain shot through Ethan's chest like a knife thrust. Marisol wanted for murder in Spain? Was everything she'd told him a lie? She was skillful enough with a sword to kill a man. That he knew well. This fellow's story added up with what little he knew about her.

Bile rose in his throat. A murderess. And he thought he had fallen in love with her? He could wash that idea from his heart. At least it was unlikely he'd ever see her again, locked in the silver mines as he would be.

His miserable, jagged thoughts kept sleep from his eyes. But one relief made him thank God. He had escaped the Inquisition judges. That was something to keep his mind unwavering and hopeful, whatever lay ahead.

Several days later, after a slim breakfast of watery porridge, Ethan marched in a line to the wharf, chained at the waist to forty other prisoners. A sloop flying the Viceroy's flag bobbed in the surf beside a much larger galleon with the same emblem. The guards standing in armed groups around the captives spoke freely, and he was able to overhear that they would be sailing to Portobello. From there, they'd start the arduous journey through the jungle, with the slaves on foot hacking a path for the horseback riders and pack mules to the Columbian silver estate of Don Rafael Castillo.

~

That same morning from her window, Marisol's heart ached as she watched the viceroy's carriage arrive at Lucia's door for their departure. This was it.

Two days before, he had explained to her and Lucia, who had asked to travel with her niece to the viceroy's Columbian estate, that they were to bring only necessities needed during the journey. He assured them they would have no need of anything once they arrived in Columbia. With the fate that lay ahead of her, extravagant possessions hardly seemed to matter.

Marisol, with Samuel in her arms, found her place in the carriage with Lucia and Amy. She tried to feel relief that leaving Cartagena meant she was escaping from Doña Maria Vargas and her threat. It was the only ray of light in the otherwise dismal prospect ahead of her.

She had wept and prayed for two days that Don Raphael had spared Ethan from the Inquisition. But could she trust the man's word? She had shared the truth about Ethan and her own true story with Lucia. Her aunt, rather than being shocked, had patted Marisol's shoulder and assured her prayer could change anything. Aunt Lucia's love was truly a gift from God through these dark days.

The carriage stopped at the wharf, and servants unloaded their few trunks, wheeling them up the ramp to the viceroy's flagship, the *Salvador*. Marisol stepped out of the carriage. The smells, shouts, and curses from the milling workers loading cargo up and down the dock overwhelmed her senses. Some of the crates even included squawking or bleating animals.

Further down the wharf, a line of chained prisoners were being shuffled into small boats, about ten at a time, and rowed out to a sloop anchored next to the galleon. Was Ethan among them? She strained to make out his form.

Don Rafael came up to her and took her elbow. "Come with me, Marisol." He led her toward the line of ragged, chained, dirty prisoners.

Then she saw him.

Ethan looked up at that same moment. His countenance showed no sign of despair or defeat, even though one eye was bruised. Nothing in his strong build or stance beneath the torn, blood-stained clothing offered his enemies anything to gloat over. He held his dark head high.

But when he saw her, his face hardened into a mask. Then he looked at the man standing beside her and his nostrils flared. He turned away without another glance in her direction.

She blinked back a tear. *Ethan, please don't hate me for what I must do. Thank God you've escaped the Dominicans.*

Don Rafael's lips tightened as his eagle eye witnessed the exchange. "These are my prisoner slaves, Marisol, which will follow our ship to Panama. From there we will travel by foot and mule train to my Columbian estate and silver mine. Do you believe me now that I have spared your friend?" He turned to look down at her.

"Yes, and I'm grateful." She looked again at Ethan, but he wouldn't turn his face toward her. Did he hate her that much? Couldn't he understand why she was with the viceroy?

Don Rafael smiled, drew her arm through his, and turned back toward their waiting ship. Lucia, Amy, and Samuel were already on board, as well as their trunks. Marisol walked up the gang plank. On deck Rafael left her to see about the ship making ready to sail.

She stood at the railing for a moment and watched the last prisoners loaded in boats and rowed toward the sloop. Casting her eyes over the people milling below on the dock, one pale, angry face under a black mantilla caught her attention.

Doña Maria de la Madrid Vargas.

The woman looked straight at her, and a chill traveled up Marisol's spine. Would Diego's mother follow her to Columbia? Surely, she wouldn't dare confront the viceroy. Would she?

Marisol left the deck and hurried down the steps to the cabins. She saw Amy entering one, and she followed close behind her and shut the door. Everything in her needed to hold her son. To know with her own hands that he was safe.

She took Samuel into her arms and hugged him close. Tears of relief slipped down her cheeks, but she didn't care. The boy looked up at her with wide amber eyes. He pulled small fingers from his mouth and touched her cheek.

No matter what happened now, her every effort had to be focused on keeping her son safe. He was the only thing she had left.

CHAPTER 13

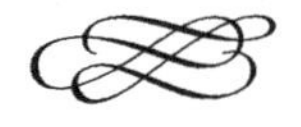

A week later, the viceroy's ships docked at Portobello. Marisol stood on deck with Samuel in her arms, and Aunt Lucia and Amy nearby, watching the preparation for the overland journey they would soon undertake.

"How in the world will we make it through that jungle?" Lucia scanned the thick green growth that stretched out of sight beyond the city.

Marisol stared at the chained prisoners being herded across the dock, hoping for a glimpse of Ethan.

Don Rafael walked up behind them. "You'll go by horseback, my dear, as will we all. Made possible by my slaves hacking out a path for us." The man leaned on the railing close to Marisol.

She flinched, but forced herself not to move away. Thankfully, she had managed to avoid seeing him alone on the packed ship. Samuel reached out toward the shining metals on the viceroy's chest. Marisol grabbed his hand and shifted him out of reach of the objects.

"You have made this trip through the jungle several times, sir?" She forced herself to look into his dark bearded face, handsome to most, if the stares and smiles of the other women and wives aboard were a sign.

"Many times." He glanced at Samuel. "But I haven't made this journey with a child his age. You must keep him close to you at all times. The jungle is full of dangers."

~

They left Portobello early the next morning, with their entourage of horses, wagons, slaves, and soldiers making quite a noise. Don Raphael placed Marisol and her little group toward the back of the line in a covered trap he'd bought to protect them from insects. Soldiers rode beside and behind them, and two cook's wagons moved in front.

Don Rafael rode ahead with his men behind the prisoners. The guards around the men carried muskets as they began the long trek overland to Panama and to another waiting ship. Marisol had listened to the plan at dinner the night before. There they would board a ship on the Pacific Ocean that would take them to the coast of Columbia near Darien and the silver mine estate.

She'd never seen country like they passed through. Once they left the environs of Portobello, scorching, humid jungle growth surrounded them. The prisoners hacked a path through with machetes and brush hooks, while mosquitoes attacked in buzzing clouds. How was Ethan making out with the hard labor, heat, and insects?

The second evening, Marisol left Samuel with Amy and Lucia after they camped next to a river. She needed to stretch her legs, and going to retrieve their dinner was as good an excuse as anything. The cook's open fire lay somewhere up ahead, and the savory smell of roasted meat filled the air as she followed the man-made path.

Sounds from ahead made her stop. That must be the murmuring of men, and the clinking? Surely not chains again after a hard day's work. The prisoners came into sight, herded close to the river bank. As she'd feared, after laboring all day hacking the dense growth, they were back in irons. The soldiers around them gnawed on roasted meat, but the prisoners held no plates of food.

Outrage rushed through her. How dare the men who'd worked so hard be denied their equal share when the soldiers ate? She marched toward the captain. "Why are the prisoners not being fed?"

Dozens of dark eyes turned toward her, from soldiers and the prisoners alike. The captain stopped eating and gave her a slight bow. "By the order of General Luis de Martinez, Señora."

A fresh batch of anger surged in her chest. What kind of animal had the viceroy put in charge of the prisoners? She raised her chin and let the man see the fire in her eyes. "Then he is inhumane. These men have worked harder than anyone in the hot sun. How do you expect them to continue without food? Did you feed your mules and horses?"

"Yes, but I'm sorry, Señora. I must follow orders." He looked toward the cook. The soldiers behind him smiled.

"Bring them food at once. If you don't, I will. Someone must feed them, and if you try to stop me, I will call Don Raphael myself." She moved past him and strode toward the fire.

Soldiers stepped out of her way, but their eyes darted over her. A few appreciative whistles broached the thick jungle air, surely something the men would have never dared if the viceroy were in earshot. The cook stood back as she took over his fork and knife, then cut and piled the roasted pork on tin plates. The heat and fire smoke were almost too much to bear, and several times she had to stop to cough. When she'd scooped enough, she carried the plates to the prisoners.

The men stood to meet her with chains clanking.

"You're a real angel, you are."

"May the Lord bless you, Señora."

Marisol looked around the gathered faces of prisoners. Where was Ethan? Then she saw him standing back, next to a tree. Even though his damp shirt hung in rags, and gashes and welts crossed his arms and chest, he still had the proud stance of a prince.

She swallowed hard, walked to him, and held out the plate of food. His gray eyes seared her, but he took the plate and began to eat.

He wiped his mouth with his hand. "You're a brave woman, Marisol. Aren't you afraid the viceroy will hear of this and cast you aside?" His voice, hard with bitterness, made her wince.

"Ethan, I'm only doing what I can to help you, to save you..."

"Don't bother. Your kind of help is something I don't need or want." He finished the food and handed the plate back to her, then sat down at the base of the tree.

Dismissed. Moisture formed in her eyes, and she turned to walk back to her place in the wagon train.

Don Rafael, on horseback, met her as she left the prisoner camp. "Marisol, what are you doing in the slave camp?" His harsh voice rolled over her.

"I was here feeding the prisoners, sir. Your captain and soldiers filled their stomachs and fed the mules and horses, but ignored the men who have worked so hard hacking our way through the jungle."

A deep frown creased his tanned face, but he reached a hand down for her and she slid up behind him in the saddle. "Marisol, General Martinez knows what he is doing. If they weren't being fed, it was for some infraction of the rules, or to keep the prisoners from breaking and running while we are still close to Portobello."

"You mean to keep them too weak to break and run?" Marisol couldn't withhold the scorn from her voice, and her heart hammered with the injustice.

Don Rafael stiffened in front of her. "Whatever you think, Marisol, you must never intervene again in anything that goes on with the prisoners. If you do, it will go even harder for them." He glanced back at her. "And for one you know well." His hard, authoritative voice matched the expression in his dark eyes and the solid set of his jaw. He spurred the stallion into a canter, almost unseating Marisol as they charged back to her camp.

Forced to wrap her arms around him, she turned her face away from the moon rising over the river as a tear slid down her cheek. When they arrived back at the covered trap and their tent, she slid off the horse and wiped her face. Don Rafael rode away without a backward glance.

Her aunt's soft voice came from her cot. "Marisol, are you all right? Don Rafael's servant delivered our food. Did he bring you back?"

"Yes, and all is well, aunt." She checked the sleeping Samuel and Amy, and made sure the mosquito netting protected them well. "I saw Ethan," she whispered as she dropped onto her cot and adjusted her own insect shield. She had not eaten, but seeing the hungry prisoners being fed was enough for her.

Before her eyes closed, she noted the two guards stationed around their little campsite to keep them safe. Or was it to keep her away from the prisoners?

~

One morning a week later, before Lucia and Amy awakened, Marisol took Samuel and walked to the cooler river's edge near their campsite. Ethan's bitterness when she'd fed the prisoners still bruised her heart.

She sat down on a rock as the morning rays of sun filtered through the jungle growth above them. Samuel slid down from her lap to sit and splash his bare feet in the shallow water lapping over the rock edge. He gave a happy squeal as he bent and splashed the water with both hands.

His laugh soothed her worries every time, but as she lifted her gaze to the water around them, a movement caught her attention. Two red eyes just above the water's surface swam in the river toward them. Her heart stopped, then leaped forward as her body sprang to life.

She screamed and scrambled to grab Samuel. A crocodile slithered toward them, its body emerging from the water. Marisol grabbed up her son, clutching him in her arms, but her legs wouldn't move. As the beast padded toward her, all she could do was look on in terror. Like an awful nightmare, her legs were paralyzed.

The next moment became a blur of movement—a raggedly clothed body swinging a machete, slicing into the crocodile, once, twice. The injured animal swished back into the river.

Marisol backed away and sank onto a large log on the bank, clutching Samuel tight against her. He'd started crying, but as she rocked and worked to soothe them both, his tears ebbed. He pointed at the river and the man with the weapon, still standing on the bank, looking at them.

Ethan. Almost unrecognizable with his long dark hair and beard, and his hard, muscular limbs. He'd been sturdy before as a ship's captain, but every part of him now seemed to be carved of muscle.

And his face. His anger may as well have been carved in stone. "Marisol, for God's sake, never come down to this river again. In fact, stay next to your campsite at all times when not moving in the caravan. This jungle is full of death."

The words were almost difficult to discern between his jagged breathing, but the harsh emotion in his tone was impossible to miss. He swiped sweat from his face with his ragged shirt tail and ran a thick hand across his dark hair. Then without another word, without waiting for a response from her, he turned and left.

Two guards, their eyes wide, emerged from the bank to escort him. One of them laughed, swung his musket to the side, and clapped Ethan on the shoulder. *"¡Vaya! Tienes agallas."*

Marisol understood his Spanish. "Whew, man, you got the nerve."

And he did. *Thank you, Ethan.*

Later, Don Rafael took her aside and gave a warning similar to Ethan's. "Do you want me to post a daily guard on you and

Samuel?" He stepped nearer. "I would hate to lose you, Marisol, before we can even wed."

She stepped back, but he drew her close and lifted her chin. His dark eyes devoured her, making her feel dirty. And sick—from his closeness, from the near terrible accident, and from Ethan's cold stare.

She endured Don Raphael's kiss, then turned and walked away, wiping her mouth. Would this be her fate forever?

~

Two weeks later, Marisol stood on the veranda of Don Rafael's Columbian plantation house. She whispered her thanks to God that the horrible journey was over. First through the jungle to Panama, then the ship on the Pacific side to the Columbian port and on to the estate.

How had Ethan fared? She'd not seen him since he'd saved her and Samuel from the crocodile. The prisoners had labored, hacking through the tangled growth and she'd been told they now recuperated before being transported to Don Rafael's silver mine up the mountain behind the hacienda.

She took a deep breath of the warm, humid air, laced with the gardenias that grew at the edge of the portico. Did she dare go down to the slave quarters to seek Ethan? With Don Rafael off attending to business with neighbors, this might be her only chance to sneak down without him knowing.

Before she thought more about it, her feet took her down the side steps, across the green expanse and garden, to the outer perimeter of the estate. A long row of slave shacks surrounded by a bamboo wall faced the hot evening sun. The door was open in the shack on the corner, and no one seemed to be around, so she moved that way.

As she reached the open door, a guard stepped around the corner to bar her way. He held a musket across his thick chest, and an odor of sweat and uncleanness drifted from him.

She touched her nose with her handkerchief, then wiped perspiration from her brow. She raised her chin to show she was the woman of the place. "Will you please call the man named Ethan?"

The guard smirked at her, and his dark eyes devoured her, scanning from her plaited hair wound around her head down to her trailing yellow skirts. "Ma'am, I'm not to let anyone talk to the slaves, unless it's a servant bringing food or the old doc."

She reached into a pocket in her skirt and brought out a gold piece of eight. "This will be yours if you do."

His eyes bulged, and he turned and went into the enclosure, pulling the door closed behind him. She heard him calling out Ethan's name. She let out a long breath. The man likely didn't see coins of this value very often. Hopefully it would also buy his silence.

He soon returned, pushing a bedraggled man at the point of his rifle. Even through his long knotted hair and beard, she'd know Ethan anywhere.

His eyes widened when he saw her. "Marisol, what are you doing here?" Then his expression changed, his gaze cooling as his hooded eyes assessed her.

"Ethan, I have so much to tell you." She looked at the guard and fished out the piece of eight from her pocket. "I will give you this now if you'll let us talk alone." He grabbed the coin and moved about a dozen paces from them, then slouched down in his chair with his gun on his knee.

Ethan leaned against the bamboo wall. His ragged clothing barely covered him, but he still had the look of a strong, undefeated man. She would talk to Don Rafael about replacing the prisoners' clothing.

"Ethan, do you not understand why I'm here in Columbia?"

"I guess you fell for the viceroy, huh?" He smirked.

"No, I didn't fall for Don Rafael. I...promised to marry him of my own free will if he would save you from the Dominicans and the Inquisition Court. That's why you're here to work the silver mines."

He dropped the straw he'd been chewing on. "Have you married him?"

A fresh ache struck her chest. "No, that's taking place in three weeks when all his family arrive."

His eyes didn't soften. "A Dominican priest visited me in the dungeon, and Don Rafael talked him into letting him have me, so what you say is probably true."

The guard looked toward them and motioned for Ethan to return to the slave quarters.

Ethan's eyes burned toward her. "Do you want to marry him, Marisol?"

"No—but to save you..."

"Then don't marry him. Not even to save me. There's no reason for you to do this."

Tears gathered in her eyes. "Do you think I can stand by and see you delivered into the hands of the Dominicans?"

"There's no reason for you to do this," he said again, his lips tight.

"No reason?"

"I can't say more."

The guard came up with his gun gripped in front of him.

"Promise me, Marisol." His gray eyes bored into her soul. "Vow to me you will not do this, no matter what."

"I promise," she whispered. But how she would keep that promise, she had no idea.

The guard poked Ethan's arm with his musket, and he turned back toward the door.

Marisol stumbled up the garden path toward the hacienda. How could she deny the viceroy? Would he turn Ethan over to the Dominicans? And how could she return to Cartagena after Doña Maria's threat to expose her and take Samuel?

As soon as she could get Aunt Lucia alone for a private word, she confessed her dilemma. As usual, her aunt's kind eyes brought comfort. "I see we're in quite a pickle here in the middle of Columbia, Marisol, but nothing is impossible with God. He can take care of Ethan, as well as Doña Maria and her threat. And He can turn the viceroy's mind to release you. Let us make this unbearable situation a matter of intense prayer."

Wise words, indeed. As Marisol lifted up her petitions to the Father that evening, she couldn't help adding a special thanks for this aunt He'd placed in her life just when Marisol needed her most.

~

Three days later, Marisol learned of Ethan's escape.

Her heart sang, even as she tried to hold in her giddiness so the servant who'd informed her wouldn't be suspicious. That was what Ethan had meant when he told her there was no reason for her to carry out her plan. *Thank you, Lord.*

Even though the slave overseer and his crew commenced a search with vicious-looking dogs, they didn't bring Ethan back that day or the next.

She and Lucia prayed for his safety, seeking God's direction about what they should do. And with growing certainty, she felt His leading. Yet the plan God placed in her heart brought with it enough dread to make her palms grow clammy.

Still, she had to. It was the right thing.

The next morning, Marisol asked an audience with the viceroy.

CHAPTER 14

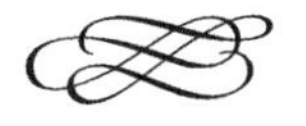

A servant escorted her to Don Raphael's study. He stood in front of the window like a statue of a conquistador. The only thing missing was the steel armor and plumed helmet. Thick arms strained the sleeves of his black doublet.

When he turned to see her, his tanned, bearded face creased in a smile, his dark eyes brightened, and he gave her a short bow. "To what do I owe this pleasure, Señora?" He came forward, took her hand, kissed it, and indicated a red leather chair for her to sit in.

She pulled her hand away. She couldn't sit, so she stood before him. Her heart raced, but she did her best to hold her composure as she spoke. "Sir, I regret to tell you, but I have changed my mind about the marriage."

The viceroy took a step back, and his countenance manifested a complete transformation. Blood rushed to his face and his thick brows drew together in a scowl. His black eyes raked her with a look that was anything but loving. "Changed your mind? Señora, I will not allow it. My whole clan will arrive next week for the ceremony."

She lowered her chin. "I'm sorry I didn't tell you sooner, but I cannot marry you, sir. I wish to return to Cartagena."

He stormed across the room, then turned and marched back to stand in front of her, a picture of the pride and arrogance of Spanish nobility, his face like granite. "So you heard about that mangy false priest escaping and now you want to back out?" He came closer. "I tell you, Señora, we will find him. And when we do, we will hang and quarter him. I promise you will never see him again. If we don't get him, the jungle will. What do you say about that?" His gravelly voice rolled over her.

She shrank from his fury. Would he strike her? "Sir, again, I have no wish to cause you embarrassment with your family, but I must return to Cartagena. I'm sorry I cannot marry at this time."

He moved behind his desk and shouted for a servant. Two pushed through the door and bowed before him. "Take this woman and pack all her things. I want her and her aunt and the two children off my estate before nightfall. Send only two guards with them to our Pacific coast. From there, they're on their own." He sank down in his chair, his face so dark and ominous, a chill swept through her.

Marisol hurried from his presence before he changed his mind.

Within the week, Marisol, Lucia, Amy, and Samuel arrived by ship from the Columbian coast to Panama to await the next overland mule train to the Atlantic coast. It only took three days for a caravan to arrive—the quick timing surely a gift from God.

Only the thought of heading home helped Marisol endure the trek through the jungle from the city of Panama to the Atlantic port of Portobello, and from there to secure a ship to Cartagena. Along with the mosquitoes and perspiration, she swatted away the worry of whether Doña Maria would be waiting in Cartagena. Surely the woman had returned to Spain after seeing Marisol leave the city under the care and protection of the viceroy as his fiancée.

At last, they arrived at Portobello late in the evening. They left the mule train and headed down the main street in search of lodging.

Lucia sniffed and frowned as she looked up and down the

street. "It's too quiet here. Not the usual bustle we saw on our earlier trip through this place."

Marisol followed her toward the entrance of what passed for an inn. At least, the sign said it was an inn. When they came to the desk to register, the clerk seemed surprised and his dark eyes darted over them. "Señora, I am not happy to see travelers come to our city. We are battling an onslaught of fever here. Where are you headed?"

Marisol, holding Samuel, stepped forward. "We will want passage on the first vessel headed to Cartagena."

The man shook his head. "But I am sure they are all booked, Señora."

"We will check to be sure. Give us a room, but, please, not one that has been exposed to fever."

The man's eyes passed from Marisol to Samuel, sucking on his three fingers, and he smiled at the boy. "That I can do, Señora, and may the Blessed Virgin help you find passage soon."

Samuel reached a wet hand toward the man and almost touched his beard as Marisol signed the register.

A servant picked up their baggage and proceeded to the nearby staircase. Amy took Samuel from her, and followed Marisol and Lucia as the man led them up the steps.

Lucia patted Marisol's arm. "Tonight we will pray for quick passage on a ship and that none of us contract the fever." Her aunt added an encouraging smile. "I believe the Lord will provide for us. He hasn't brought us this far to quit helping now."

Lord, let her be right. Don't abandon us in this foreign, disease-ridden place.

~

Ethan hacked his way through the jungle trail that he and the other prisoners helped clear on the way to Panama. The plant growth almost covered it again, but he managed to keep locating the cut notches he had made on certain trees their first time through.

In several days, he made it to the cove where he was to rendezvous with his ship and crew near Nombre de Dios.

He trudged across the sand and looked out over the blue waters. The sight before him raised the exhaustion that weighed his every limb. He let out a whoop. The Atlantic had never looked so good.

He was one day late, if his calculations were correct. Had they waited? He walked along the white sandy beach where they had once careened the *Dryade,* then gazed out to sea again. Nothing but blue sky and cerulean waves met his eyes as far as the horizon.

This was a good private place to beach a ship, scrape the barnacles from its hull, and make any other repairs needed. Would Tim be able to find it again?

That night, he lay down on a bed of rushes he'd gathered, and looked up at the stars until he fell asleep.

~

Ethan awoke to voices.

He crawled into the shadows and listened. Through the bushes, he saw three men disembarking from a longboat. One turned his face toward the rising sun. Ben Thompson. And Tim and Samson just behind him.

Ethan gave a loud whoop as he struggled to his feet.

The three men were crouched beside the boat with their guns pointed at him when Ethan emerged from his hiding spot. "Hello, lads. You looking for pearls or escaped slaves?" All three grinned and rushed to him.

"You're the pearl, my man." Ben Thompson gave him a great hug, then scanned his ragged clothing and wrinkled his nose. "Maybe I should say the smelly crab we've found."

Tim and Samson laughed, a most welcome sound to Ethan's ears.

He turned to his lieutenant and navigator. "Is all well on the *Dryade,* Tim? How's our crew? Bet they're hoping to go after another Spanish treasure ship." He couldn't keep the grin off his face. He'd escaped, and now here were his men and his ship.

"Oh, we kept them busy enough. After we took Grace home to Charles Town and headed back, a French ship in the Caribbean refused to raise the white flag, and we, uh, made them regret it."

"Lose any of our men?"

"Only one, our surgeon, but we found some good plunder."

"Sorry to hear we lost George Johnson, even though he wasn't that good at his doctoring, as we all knew. Right, Ben?" Ben and the surgeon had never gotten along well, due to George staying half-drunk most of the time.

Ben nodded. "One other piece of news, Gabriel Legrand somehow escaped during the battle. We think he hid somewhere on the French ship before we released it."

"Well, that's good riddance as far as Legrand is concerned." Ethan kicked at the scrap of a satchel he'd travelled with from Columbia. "I can't wait to get a good hot meal and a decent bed on board the *Dryade*."

"And how about a bath, shave, and hair trim, my man?" Ben clapped him on the shoulder, grinning.

"Yeah, I can use those, too."

Ethan, Ben, and Tim climbed into the longboat, then Samson pushed it from the beach and jumped in. He made short work rowing to the *Dryade* hidden around the bend.

~

Marisol dropped into her bed at Blue Mountain Plantation the evening they arrived home. She was too tired to think about anything, but not too weary to thank God for the miracle of their obtaining ship passage.

And Ethan. He never strayed far from her thoughts. Had he

made it to safety? Would she ever see him again? Why had he been so cool to her at their last meeting?

At least one worry had receded. Doña Maria's ship was not in the harbor when they sailed into Cartagena, unless it was well hidden somewhere down the coast. Lucia assured Marisol she doubted that the woman would have stayed in Cartagena after seeing Marisol leave with the viceroy.

The concern about Diego's mother and her threat faded even more as one day flowed into another on the plantation. Her aunt kept busy with her overseer and the sugar harvest. Marisol rode horseback almost every day. Samuel, now seven months old, delighted her and Amy daily with new things he could do—or at least attempted to do. He could crawl well, he would turn his head at the sound of his name, and he liked porridge more and more. Another heartwarming thing for Marisol...he had learned to say "Mamá."

One morning in late August, she returned from her ride and skipped up the stairs to the room she still shared with Amy and Samuel. As soon as the cool trade winds blew that afternoon, she'd take her son for a walk in the garden.

Opening the door, she looked around the empty bedroom. Amy must have taken Samuel for a walk already. As she started to leave and search for them, a noise from the chifforobe caught her attention. Had mice found their clothing? Sucking in a breath to keep her squeamishness down, she walked over and opened the wardrobe.

Marisol jumped back as Amy fell out onto the floor, her hands tied behind her back, a gag in her mouth.

The scream Marisol had planned to hold in swept through the air as her heart raced into her throat. She knelt beside the girl and ripped the gag off her mouth. "Amy, what happened?"

The girl began to cry. "Oh, ma'am, they came and took Samuel. I put up the best fight I could, but she had two servants with her." She sobbed into her hands.

"They took Samuel?" Marisol couldn't breathe through the

weight pressing on her chest. Through the fear surging up her throat. She clutched Amy's shaking shoulders. "Who took him?"

"That woman with eyes like his, and...your cousin, Adriana, allowed them upstairs, since you and Señora Lucia were out."

Adriana.

Marisol staggered toward the rocker, gasping for breath. "Not my Samuel." She cried out the words as all the strength slipped from her body. She slipped to the floor beside the chair. He was all she had left. Everything to her.

Feet pounded up the steps and concerned faces of servants peered through the door. She couldn't face them. Couldn't face anything. Samuel had been taken? *Oh, God. No!*

As Amy murmured to the others, Marisol wrapped her arms around herself. There was no way she could hold back the tears. But she had to pull herself together. Had to go after her boy.

She wiped her face. "How long ago, Amy? Maybe we can catch them." She struggled to her feet and pushed through the gaping servants. "Order the carriage for me."

Amy ran to her side. "Ma'am, it were about half hour ago, near as I can tell. And I heard something about a ship standing ready."

She forced the fog to clear from her mind. "To the dock. We must get to the dock." She ran down the stairs and nearly collided with Lucia coming up.

"Marisol, what's wrong?" Her aunt gripped her forearms.

Amy spilled the story in a rush, and Marisol tried to push past her aunt, but Lucia's hold was strong.

When Amy stopped for a breath, Aunt Lucia turned to Marisol. "I can't believe Doña Maria and her servants had the nerve to come into my house and take Samuel, even with Adriana granting them entrance. God will help us find them. I'm coming with you to the dock."

Lucia's strong, confident voice did little to still the storm raging in Marisol's chest, but she nodded. They had to get moving. Every second mattered.

When they reached the front door, Adriana stood there weeping. "Please believe me, Marisol, I had no idea they planned to kidnap your boy. I tried to stop them leaving." The woman reached out a shaking hand.

Marisol only shot her a burning glance. She would deal with the woman later. Just now, she had to find Samuel before he was loaded on a ship.

Pedro rushed a light carriage toward them in the drive, stopping just long enough for them to climb in. He spared no effort to run the horse all the way into Cartagena. The young mare galloped onto the wharf and reared to a stop as harbor workers scattered away from them.

Marisol jumped out and ran to the wharf's edge, scanning the few ships nearby. A Spanish galleon was making its way out of the harbor toward the open sea. A glimpse at the flag made her heart clutch in her chest. The Vargas insignia waved proudly.

"Lord, no!" She fell to her knees as a numbness spread through her. *Samuel, my dear boy.* Her eyes wouldn't even cry tears, her mind simply repeated the words over and over.

Lucia ran to her and took Marisol into her arms. "Dear, I'm so sorry. Let's check with the Cartagena authorities. Maybe they can help."

She was right, but Marisol couldn't summon the strength to stand. She simply watched as her aunt marched up to the window where the harbor officials sat. "Sirs, we need you to set out after that ship." She gestured to the vessel now far out in the harbor. "They've kidnapped a child." She pointed to Marisol. "Her child, a boy of seven months. She is my niece."

The nearest man in a stiff red and gray Spanish uniform leaned out to scan the ocean beyond the dock. He looked behind him at two other officers. "Señora Chavez, are you referring to the *Nuestra Señora de Vargas?"*

"Yes, sir, that is the exact vessel."

The man rubbed his bearded chin. "Señora, the ship's papers were in order. Their destination, Spain."

Lucia stamped her foot. "We're wasting time. We must rescue my niece's child."

"Was this child the grandson of Doña Maria de la Madrid Vargas?" The other two soldiers looked on with faces grown tight. Another sitting in the back now listened.

Lucia's lips tightened. "Yes, but she had no right to kidnap him from my house and his mother."

The other officer arose and came forward, and the other men saluted him and retreated. This new soldier wore a more decorated uniform, and he bowed to Lucia. "Señora Chavez, I am most sorry, but there's nothing we can do. Señora Vargas declared the child her grandson she was taking home to Spain. She holds a paper from the King granting her great privileges in any Spanish port. We dare not send a ship out to hinder her journey, or we'll hear from His Majesty. You understand?"

Marisol's head dropped to her chest. Every breath brought pain to her body. The ship with her precious Samuel aboard was on its way to Spain, and the harbor authorities would do nothing about it.

As she knelt on the dock, great sobs racked her body. She was powerless to stop the ship. How would she ever get her son back?

Amy ran and bent to touch Marisol's shaking shoulders. "Ma'am. You'll make yourself sick."

Marisol lifted her wet face and looked once more out to sea. Another ship approached the harbor. Something familiar about it caught her attention. She struggled to her feet, and would have fallen off the dock except for Amy's firm grasp on her arm.

"What is it, Marisol?" Lucia came to them and looked out at the approaching ship.

Her heart surged. "It's the *Dryade.*" Could it be Ethan coming for her? Marisol broke loose from Lucia and Amy, then waved at the ship. He was here. Hope bloomed in her heart as she waved frantically, running along the dock so Ethan would see her.

CHAPTER 15

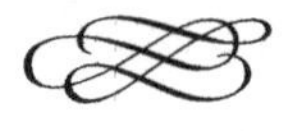

Ethan stepped up beside Tim Cullen, who stood at the ship's rail as they approached the wharf. "Take a look at this, sir."

Ethan took the eyeglass his friend handed him and trained it on the young woman running up and down the dock. His heart leaped. "It's Marisol, Tim. I'm sure it is her. Something must have happened. Pull in to the dock as quickly as you can."

As soon as his ship nudged the wooden planking, Marisol screamed out, "Ethan, she's taken Samuel to Spain. You passed her ship on the way in."

His heart hammered in his chest. Her words didn't make sense, but the panic in her voice meant something was very wrong. "What?" He hollered back. "Who's taken Samuel?"

Instead of answering, Marisol bent her arms around her middle and fell to her knees on the wharf. *Dear, Lord.*

Ethan jumped from his ship to the pier and ran to her. He raised her up and held her by her trembling shoulders. "Calm down and tell me what's happened." He looked from Marisol to Lucia, who only shook her head, her lips thin lines.

Marisol wiped tears from her pale, constricted face. Fear, stark and vivid, glittered in her blue eyes. "Ethan, Diego Vargas' mother has kidnapped Samuel and is taking him to Spain. That was her ship you must have seen as you came in."

Dread clutched his own chest. Little Samuel had been taken? He had to help. "We'll go right after her, Marisol. You can tell me who she is later."

That name. Diego Vargas. Where had he heard it before?

Ethan stood and ran back to his ship, shouting orders as soon as the men could hear him. Within an hour, the water casks were replenished and stored aboard, and the *Dryade* put to sea upon its desperate chase.

~

Marisol, with Amy and Ben Thompson by her side, waved goodbye to Lucia on the quay, then dropped her head onto her arms at the railing. She shook as images of Samuel blasted her mind…crying for her, hungry, and frightened. "Oh, my boy, my precious boy. God take care of him. Help us catch them."

Ben Thompson placed his arm around her trembling shoulders. "Our Lord will take care of Samuel, and if any captain can catch a Spanish ship, Ethan Becket is that man."

Marisol lifted her face to look at him. "But I still nurse Samuel twice a day. He has only started on porridge. How will he survive?"

Amy spoke up, her voice a shade happier. "Ma'am, I just remembered I heard Doña Maria ask one of the men with her if the wet nurse was aboard the ship, and he said she was."

Marisol slumped forward and breathed a prayer of relief. She held tight to the railing, staring at the water sluicing off the side of the ship as it pressed its way through the blue-green Caribbean ocean.

Go faster, dear Dryade. Every bone in her body ached from crying.

Ben patted her arm. "Marisol, why don't you go to a cabin? Lie down and rest. You can't help Captain Becket, he's doing all that can be done. You hear our sails booming and flapping in this brisk wind? We're making good time. I believe we'll catch that ship and soon."

Amy walked close beside her as they descended to the same cabin they'd shared before. Marisol fell onto the cot, her body totally spent. It seemed impossible to sleep, but the rocking of the ship soon had her eyelids drifting shut.

An hour later, she awoke with a start. When the memory of Samuel's kidnapping crushed down on her, she pressed her hand over her mouth to keep a scream from escaping.

Amy came to sit beside her on the cot. "What can I do to help you, ma'am?"

She wrapped her arms around herself. "Oh, Amy, my baby. My baby in the hands of people he doesn't know. How frightened he must be." Tears burned her eyes again. How could she have any left to cry?

"Ma'am, I think I need to remind you that your boy never has met a stranger. And much as I would love to strangle that Doña Maria, I don't think she'd let him come to harm. She seemed real taken with him."

Marisol wiped her tears and gulped down her sorrow. What the girl said was probably true. But what compassion could that woman have to take a child from his mother?

She stood, and Amy followed her back on deck. They walked to the quarterdeck where Captain Becket stood looking through his eyeglass. Tim Cullen stood with him, and they both turned as Marisol and Amy approached.

"What do you see, Captain? Any sign of a Spanish ship?" Marisol held her breath and fought more tears gathering.

Ethan handed the eyeglass back to Tim. "I don't see a sail yet, but I'm sure that ship will stop at Hispaniola to restock. I know the treasure ship route they'll pursue from there, if they sail back to Spain." He offered a sad smile as his gaze met hers. He understood, she could see it in the gray depths of his eyes.

Marisol breathed in his calm confidence like a person dying for air. "I have no doubt they're headed back to Spain." She searched the horizon again, hoping to see a sail.

"After dinner, I want you to tell me how this happened, Marisol, and who this woman is." His eyes traversed her face like a warm, welcome trade wind.

She nodded because she had to, but then she turned away, lowering her chin. How could she tell him the truth? She headed back to the cabin, dragging her feet.

At the captain's table that evening, Marisol couldn't lift a bite to her lips. And her stomach knotted, knowing the conversation she must soon have with Ethan. Would he hate her when he knew the truth? Would he turn from her, and even from rescuing Samuel?

~

When all others had left the cabin, including Amy and Ben Thompson, Ethan lit his pipe and gazed at Marisol. What story would she concoct now? He had lost count of the lies she'd told since he met her. If she wasn't a widow whose husband had died defending her, who was she? Did she murder a man like the cellmate told him? Who and why?

He cut to the heart of the matter. "I heard in prison they want you for murder in Cadiz. Is this true?"

She lifted reddened eyes to his and her lips parted. It wasn't shock in her gaze, but he couldn't quite read her expression.

He waited.

She lowered her head, and he almost didn't catch her muttered, "Yes."

He slammed his fist on the table, his pent up anger and disappointment flooding him. How could he have thought he loved her? *A murderess.* He dropped the pipe into its dish and shook his head.

"Tell me why, Marisol." He stood and paced across the cabin. Then he came back, leaned over the table, and stared at her. "Tell me the truth. All of it." He'd know if she lied now.

Her chin trembled, but then she pressed her lips together, raising her eyes to his. "Diego Vargas attacked me in our estate stables. I didn't mean to kill him." The hurt in her deep blue eyes was impossible to miss, and it speared through Ethan's chest. "I only wanted to make him stop hurting me."

He studied her, searching for signs she might be lying. Could this be the full truth? The pain marking her face couldn't be denied, yet she didn't shy away from his gaze. He'd spent much of his adult life learning to read people, and he only saw truth in her expression.

He dropped into his chair and expelled a long, hard breath. "He attacked you?" He should be angry with the scum of a man who would attack an innocent maiden. And he was. But his relief over Marisol's honesty won over everything else.

"Yes, he's the father of Samuel. It's his mother who has taken my son."

A load as heavy as the ballast bricks balancing the ship's hold lifted from Ethan's shoulders. "Then it was self-defense, not murder, Marisol. Why did you flee?"

She pressed both hands over her eyes. "He was a nobleman of Spain, and his family was—*is*—very powerful. They would never believe my story." She sighed and dropped her head onto her arms on the table.

He touched her dark hair, loose and lying in tangles over her shoulders. She no longer seemed interested in wearing her usual neat braids and coils. Since she'd boarded his ship, it hung about her shoulders and down her back like a thick, curling mane. His heart overflowed in compassion…and relief.

She spoke from her bowed head. "You don't hate me, Ethan? For all the...lies?"

He swallowed and took a ragged breath. It was all he could do not to pull her up into his arms. "I'm not angry, but the truth will take time to digest, Marisol. And we must talk about what we'll do when we catch the ship we pursue." He stepped back away from her.

She lifted her head to stare at him. "What we will do? We have to rescue Samuel."

"Yes, but what if she threatens to expose you? With a warrant out for you in Spain, you could never live free again."

"I don't care what she does. Samuel and I will never go back to Spain. We'll make a new home...somewhere safe."

He swallowed. *Somewhere secure with him in Charles Town.* But the words wouldn't come out.

She stood and nodded at him. "I'll take my leave now." Then she turned and practically fled from the cabin.

Ethan banged a fist on the table. Why didn't he take her in his arms and assure her she and Samuel would always have a place with him, a place of safety?

~

Marisol ran to her cabin and sank onto the edge of the cot, glad that Amy was somewhere else. She had told Ethan the truth, but somehow she didn't feel he'd forgiven her for the lies. She clenched her eyes, trying to forget how handsome he looked pacing the cabin, the gentle touch on her hair. How much she wished he'd pulled her into his strong arms and comforted her.

But he hadn't. And she wouldn't think about it. Rescuing Samuel was all that mattered.

She forced herself up, bathed, and brushed her hair. She would keep her sanity for the day they rescued Samuel.

But the following days passed as if she had to drag each one from a quagmire of grief. The nights took even longer as thoughts about Samuel plagued her. Was he being cared for, kept dry and warm? Did he cry for her?

The third day, Marisol managed to eat and keep down both a morning and noon meal. Later, she laid on her cot, half-praying, half-complaining. Pulling her knees up to her chest, she could almost touch the sore spot around her heart, as if she'd fallen and wounded herself deep inside.

At other times, the pain of losing Samuel would bend her over —the ache clamping down her throat and stomach. The tingling burned behind her eyes where no tears remained.

One of those times when she lay on her cot, shouts and running steps on deck interrupted her dark thoughts.

Amy stood from her chair where she mended a dress. "Ma'am, would you like me to see what's 'appening on deck?"

Marisol rose. "No—yes. I'll go with you." Her heart leaped. Had they spied a sail ahead?

They hurried up to the quarterdeck where Captain Becket, Tim, and the lookout stood staring out to sea. Ethan gazed through the eyeglass. He glanced at Marisol and Amy, then handed the tool to Tim. "It's not a Spanish ship. My guess is she's flying the French flag."

Marisol's heart plunged. Not Spanish. Not Samuel's ship.

Tim turned from scanning through the eyepiece. "Yep, and it's heading our way, Cap'n. Fast. Could it be pirates? They sail against all flags and won't honor our English colors."

"Could be. They won't raise the Jolly Roger until near us. We'll take no chances. We don't want to risk damage to our ship." His eyes flickered to Marisol's. "We're on a chase of our own, so we'll try to out-run whoever it is." He cocked his chin at Marisol and Amy. "Ladies, please go back to your cabin. This could get dangerous."

Sitting in the cabin, Marisol wrapped her arms around herself and tried to pray. What if pirates overcame their ship, or even damaged it? They would lose Samuel forever to Spain, where she could never attempt to rescue him without the threat of arrest. Then it would not matter what happened to her. Nothing would matter. She hung her head as hot tears dropped onto the front of her gown.

A cannon boom jerked her to attention. But the ship didn't jolt, which told her the shot fell short of the *Dryade*. She paced and prayed. Amy fell back on her cot and pulled a pillow over her head.

~

Ethan stood overlooking the main deck. "All hands to quarters!" His roar reverberated over the ship, and men swarmed across the deck and into the rigging. Some climbed high into the shrouds, others locked down deck items.

He followed with, "All hands make sail." Topgallants and royals rolled out over the ship, flapping and snapping in the current of air. The crew stretched every stitch of canvas to catch the wind, and the *Dryade* gave her best effort to outrun their pursuer. Water sheeted off her sides as she plowed through the troughs of the Atlantic.

But the ship behind them still gained.

Tim came up on the quarterdeck. "We'll show them our stern, sir, then turn and spit in their eye. Is that the plan?"

Ethan trained his eyeglass again on the fast-nearing ship to estimate its distance away. The pursuer's lighter brigantine could move faster than his galleon, but it only boasted half the guns of the *Dryade*. His brows knitted and his lips thinned into a tight line beneath his mustache.

He hated the thought of a battle with women aboard. But he had no choice. "Yes, it looks like that's what we need to do, Tim." He leaned over the railing and shouted the orders to slow and turn the ship to face their pursuer. But this meant a full side of the ship would be open to cannon shot as they turned. Ethan prayed they were turning before the *Dryade* was in cannon range of the vessel chasing them.

Two minutes later, a shot splintered their bowsprit.

Ethan shouted, "Man the guns."

The sound of the crew pushing cannons toward the gun ports rumbled across the decks like thunder, interspersed with the commands of the gun crew leader. "Swab out them barrels, lads. Put in the powder. Careful, now, you lackeys, with that wadding. Ram it home. Run it out!"

~

Below, Marisol understood those movements and sounds. "Dear God, we're going into battle. We didn't outrun whoever is pursuing us." She stared at her companion.

Amy sat up from her cot, her face pale and eyes rounded. "But this ship has many guns. Surely it will be a short battle, milady. I trust Captain Ethan to win it fast."

Cannon blasts drowned out further conversation. The cabin shook and creaked as if it would split apart. Amy ran and dropped on the cot beside Marisol, then clutched her hand. The odor of burnt gunpowder filled the room. Smoke poured through their porthole as if an entrance to Hades yawned before them. Marisol coughed, then covered her mouth and nose with a handkerchief.

Would she ever see her son again?

CHAPTER 16

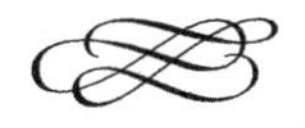

A dreadful explosion on the sea rocked the *Dryade.* Then a strange silence followed. Marisol drew her hand away from Amy's. "What could that have been?

They waited. The faint scuffle of men moving around above sounded like nothing more than the normal efforts of sailing. No strangers boarding the boat, stomping across the deck.

Five minutes passed. Then ten. Marisol paced. What could be happening? Did she dare sneak up the stairs to see?

It must have been thirty minutes from the original blast when the familiar noise of a single pair of boots marching down the stairs sounded. Then a fist banged at their cabin door.

Amy was already at the door, so she opened it a crack, then wider as she stepped back.

Danny stood there, smiling with his chest thrown out. He stuck his head in and addressed Marisol. "It's all over but the plundering, milady, since that good shot we got in." His bright brown eyes moved from Marisol to Amy, who had her hands braced on her hips.

"Plunder? What kind of plunder you talkin' about, boy?" Amy

arched her back and lifted her chin. She was a head taller, but his same age.

"I don't know 'zackly," he admitted. "But Captain Becket, he looked real happy when the boarding crew came up out of that ship with three chests. It were a pirate ship."

That night at the dinner table filled with Ethan's gloating officers, Marisol learned that a cannon shot from the *Dryade* ignited gunpowder stored in the forecastle of the attacking ship. No one knew why it was stashed there and not in the hold. But the explosion crippled the vessel and they surrendered.

The other ship's captain was Gabriel Legrand, who'd died in the attack. They released the rest of the crew to repair their ship the best they could, and sailed away.

Legrand. She shouldn't speak ill of the dead, but he'd caused trouble once again by hindering their chase of the *Nuestra Señora de Vargas*. How much farther away was her beloved Samuel now?

Their stuffy cabin still reeked of gunpowder which made it impossible to sleep. For her anyway, Amy didn't seem to have the same problem. Marisol pulled on a light cape and walked up to the deck for a breath of air.

She stood near the stern, hidden in the shadows, and watched the white foam forming by the *Dryade's* hull as it cut through the dark waves. Under a half moon and blinking stars, a welcome wind snapped the sails and cooled her troubled brow. Would they ever catch Doña Maria's ship? Was her Samuel sleeping in peace, fed and dry? Was he missing her?

Marisol wrapped her arms around herself to ease the pain of grief that rose like a tidal wave in her heart.

"You cold?" Ethan's deep voice rolled over her. He came to stand near, but didn't touch her. The sword at his side jangled as he leaned against the railing.

She looked at his handsome bearded face in the moonlight, a marble statue with its chiseled cheekbones and strong chin. But something like gentleness gleamed in his gray eyes, clear even in the shadows.

She turned her face away and swallowed as her breath came faster. "I wonder how much farther away Doña Maria's ship is after this battle today. Have we lost it forever?" She trembled and fought the tightening across her chest.

He touched her shoulder. "We won't lose it. I happen to know where Spanish ships stop to re-water and take on supplies in the Caribbean before starting the long trip across the Atlantic."

She turned to face him. "Where is that?"

"You never mind. Let me handle this rescue. The open sea is our best chance, but I even have an alternate plan. If we don't catch them at one port, we'll catch them at the next one." His confident voice raised a flag of hope in her heart.

She gazed at his profile, willing his words to be true. "Do you think it's really possible? If those are Spanish ports, how would you board a Spanish ship in their own port?"

He smiled. "I have a plan, Marisol. Pray we have a chance to initiate it. It worked well one time when I was part of His Majesty's Royal Navy." Now he looked into her eyes. "Don't fret. It'll only make you sick, and then what will your boy do if we rescue him and you're too ill to take care of him? Make that *when* we rescue him."

She clenched her eyes shut to stop tears of relief gathering. He was so strong and she needed his strength, his confidence. His warm hands moved to her shoulders and pulled her to him. She leaned into his chest and a wayward sob escaped her lips.

"Shh...it's going to be all right, Marisol." He touched her hair, then bent and kissed her forehead. "We *will* rescue Samuel."

His touch was so warm, so reassuring. Yet the longer he held her, the more her awareness shifted to the gentleness of his caress. The nearness of this man she'd come to love against all odds.

He lifted her chin and her eyelids closed. He brushed them with his lips, then trailed kisses down to her mouth. His touch was ecstasy, feather soft, yet warm enough to send a tingle all the way through her.

His lips brushed her mouth in a tender kiss, then deepened,

setting her senses on fire. It took all her will power to break away from his kiss, but he still held her tight in his strong arms.

He rocked her back and forth a moment, his heartbeat thudding against her cheek. "We'll find Samuel. I'll never give this up. Do you understand?" His hoarse voice rumbled up from his throat.

She absorbed his strength, but then he released her, and her knees almost folded. He chuckled and caught her. If he could see her face in the shadows, he'd probably see bright red as heat flamed to her cheeks. She needed to get control of herself.

In her tired state, she couldn't process what had passed between them, but hope fluttered in her heart. Ethan said he would never give up. He would find Samuel.

After making her way back down to her cabin, she dropped onto her cot without changing clothes. The kiss tingled on her lips as she fell asleep.

~

One day passed into another without any sign of a ship on the horizon ahead of the *Dryade*. Marisol worked hard to keep hopeful when she lay on her cot each night.

One morning, she awoke with a headache and feeling too warm. She threw the coverlet back.

"Ma'am, your cheeks sure are red this morning." Amy stood over her.

Marisol looked at the girl and wondered why her face seemed foggy. "I think I'll just rest here for now. I must not have slept well."

"I'll get something to soothe you." Within minutes, Amy placed a cool compress on her forehead. Every so often, the girl replaced it, but nothing brought Marisol relief from the fever and chills.

In and out of consciousness, she fought through cobwebs of nightmare-filled sleep, drenching heat, and shivering that made her teeth rattle.

Amy's anxious voice brought her back. "Ma'am, I'm doing all I can, but you're still hot and then you start shivering. I've put all the blankets we have on you. What else should I do?" Fear, stark and vivid, glittered in the girl's eyes.

Marisol licked her dry lips. She wanted to calm the girl, but couldn't get her words together. Only bits and pieces came out.

Amy froze when the garbled words spewed forth. "Oh, ma'am." She dropped the compress and ran out the door.

~

"Cap'n Becket!" Amy burst into Ethan's cabin.

He looked up from the chart in front of him. "What is it? You look petrified. Don't know that I've ever seen your eyes so wide."

The girl wrung her hands. "Sir, Marisol has the fever. I know about that sickness. My ma and pa died of it." Her words tumbled over each other. "When we got to Portobello, they was having a plague of it. And, sir..." Her voice rose an octave. "I'm afeered to nurse anybody with the fever." She jerked a handkerchief from her pocket and covered her face as a sob hiccupped from her.

Ben Thompson, who had entered the cabin behind Amy, waited near the door. His eyes flew to Ethan's. "And us without a surgeon."

"Ben, help calm Amy and keep her away from the others."

He stood and turned to the trembling girl. "I'll check on Marisol. Ben will find you a new cabin. Don't return to yours, and you must repeat none of this to my crew. Do you understand, Amy?"

The girl sniffed and nodded, then Ben motioned for her to follow him.

Ethan grabbed the surgeon's bag he'd stowed under his bed, then hurried to Marisol's bedside. She lay curled on her cot, tiny wet ringlets of her dark hair plastered against the side of her pale face.

He pressed a hand to her forehead and his heart lurched. She was burning up, with sweat beading along her brow and temple.

"Marisol?" He stroked her skin, so soft, even with this horrible illness.

She didn't move. Only the slight rustle of breath escaped through her chapped lips.

He moved his hand to her shoulder and gave a gentle shake. "Marisol. Wake up."

Still no answer. The pressure in his chest made it hard to breath.

Then her shoulders began to tremble. A chill. He pulled the covers up higher around her, but her fragile body shivered so badly she made the little cot shake.

He did everything he knew to do, but nothing seemed to help her. Energy balled up inside him, and he stood and paced the floor, pressing the recess of his mind for something that might help. A spontaneous prayer flew from his lips. It had been a while since he'd uttered a fervent prayer, but this felt right.

Ben Thompson stuck his head through the door. He glanced at the quaking figure on the cot. "Is it yellow fever?"

That's what he should determine. Ethan removed his coat and rolled up his sleeves. "Get me the medical book from the surgeon's cabin. I'll try to find out."

"Aye, sir."

Now that he had something to do, he slipped back into his captain role as easily as a worn coat. "I'm quarantining this cabin. Keep Amy and everyone else away. We mustn't let the crew know. You understand?"

Ben nodded.

"Only tell Tim what's happened, and for him to take over until I know what we're dealing with here."

"I understand, Ethan. We don't want fear running rampant over the ship. I'll be praying. But what about you, sir? What if you catch —?" Ben's lips tightened.

"I'll take that chance. Now bring me the medical book."

Ben ducked his head and closed the door.

He returned in about fifteen minutes with the medical journal, handing it to Ethan without entering.

Ethan dipped the cloth in water from the bedside bowl and wrung it out to place on Marisol's forehead. Her hair hung in damp ringlets around her lovely face, now bright with heat. Long dark lashes lay on her cheeks. He placed the cloth on her smooth brow. Her flawless skin transformed from the heated pink to translucent as the fever changed to a chill. He removed the compress and pulled the blanket up to her chin, but she still shook. Two mumbled words escaped her heart-shaped lips. "Samuel. Samuel."

His heart ached as he dropped into the only chair and picked up the book. He turned to the chapter entitled, "Fevers."

Sometime later Ben looked in again. "Find anything to help, Ethan?"

Ethan let out a sigh as he looked up from his intense study. "Found some hope. Yellow fever and swamp fever have the same symptoms in the beginning."

"How do you know which it is?"

"If it's swamp type, it will break in seventy-two hours and it's not contagious. If it's yellow fever..." Ethan looked at Ben without finishing the sentence. Ben raised his brows, then stepped back and closed the door.

During the night at her bedside, Ethan tried to keep the blankets on Marisol when the chills came. He sponged her face and the edge of her thick hair.

Her occasional moans gave him hope. At least she was still alive and had a chance. He dropped off to sleep in the chair once about midnight, but her chills shaking the cot awakened him. He stood and replaced the blanket on her.

Once when he was adjusting the cover, her long tapered fingers touched his. He clasped her hand for a moment, his heart surging even as emotion clogged his throat. He couldn't let her die. Maybe he should be guarding his heart from her, protecting himself from another loss, but he'd already given too much of himself to her. His heart was no longer his to guard.

The next morning, he had Ben bring a bowl of broth, and he got a few swallows past her lips while he held her head up. As he laid her back on the pillow, the blanket slipped, exposing her creamy neck and thin gown. He forced his eyes away from the feminine loveliness and pulled the blanket back to her chin.

He lost track of time, and only knew it was becoming night again when daylight faded through the porthole.

The second evening, when he leaned over to look at Marisol, his throat went dry at how much paler she'd grown. Her cheeks, lips, small nose, and eyelids looked like someone had fashioned them out of porcelain. The tapered fingers lay lifeless at her side.

His heart stilled as he struggled to discern if she breathed. Was she dying or already dead? He pressed a finger over her lips, and barely felt the brush of breath.

Something in him shattered. He fell to his knees in front of his chair. "Oh God, have mercy. Spare her." His hoarse voice echoed across the room and out the porthole.

But the covered figure on the cot didn't stir.

A cold settled around his shoulders and a mocking voice spoke in his mind. *He didn't spare your wife, did He? Why do you think your prayer might work now that you're a backslider?*

Ethan clenched his fists, then took a deep, shaky breath. He knew that evil voice, but he also knew how to fight it.

Repentance.

Scriptures he'd once preached to others flowed into his mind.

"Be zealous therefore and repent."

"...ask for the old paths. Ask where the good way is...and find peace for your souls."

"...His compassions fail not, they are new every morning."

The words rumbled from his heart, softened by humility. "I'm sorry, Father God. Please forgive me for blaming You for Olivia's death and the babe's, and going my own way like a horse with the bit between its teeth. Forgive me for turning my back on your calling. Help me find the old paths, the good way, and peace again."

In one long acknowledgement of failure, he laid himself bare before God. He held nothing back of all the bitter months he'd lived almost like a heathen.

As he ended his prayer, peace drifted through him, settling over his heart to replace the weight that had pressed so hard.

He stood, wiped his wet face, and glanced at the still figure on the cot. He leaned close and watched her upper body rise and fall with shallow breaths. His heart lifted. "Lord, please heal Marisol, and help us find and rescue her son."

~

The next morning, after he sponged Marisol's face and arms, he again managed to get liquid through her dry lips. Ethan handed Ben the empty bowl at the door. "Today we'll know. If it's swamp fever, the heat should break. Is everything well with the ship?"

"Oh yes, not to worry there, sir. You know what a good man Tim is. And he started the rumor among the crew that you were busy concocting a plan to stop Doña Maria's ship."

Ethan nodded, trying to summon the remnants of a smile for his friend. "Yes, that's what's at the edge of my mind."

He closed the door behind Ben and dropped into the chair. Weariness made his bones ache. If he leaned back in the seat, he would fall asleep in an instant, but he needed to stay awake for when Marisol needed him.

Running his hand over the three-day stubble on his chin, Ethan turned his mind to stopping Doña Maria's ship. Maybe a drogue device would work. A well-crafted drogue applied underwater, out of sight, could cripple the *Nuestra Señora de Vargas* at sea, away from any Spanish port.

In his former British Navy stint, the tool had worked well to stop a slaver, and he'd been in on the plan and creation of it. The device need be no more than a large sea anchor and a bolt of number one canvas sewn into a funnel, then reinforced to stand the strain with Doña Maria's ship going at twelve knots. They would attach the contraption to one of the lower pintles of the rudder underwater.

Attaching the drogue without being discovered by the ship's crew was the tricky part. But once it was in place, the weapon would tear the rudder clean away when the ship started sailing full speed at sea. It would render the vessel helpless. Dead in the water.

A deep sigh came from the cot, followed by two whispered words. "Amy. Samuel."

Ethan stood and moved to Marisol. She no longer shivered or tossed. Her face had regained most of its color, and her chest moved with regular breaths. He rested his palm against her forehead. Finally cool and dry. *Thank you, Lord.*

As much as he wanted to be here when she awoke, there was much he needed to do. He slipped out the door and headed toward his own cabin.

Ben greeted him at his cabin entrance. "Ethan, my man. How's Marisol?"

"The fever's broken. Send Amy to her."

"Thank God. This is an answer to prayer."

Ethan turned to look into his face. "Yes, I've no doubt it is, my friend. God is good."

Ben's brows rose, and he clapped Ethan on the back just before the captain kicked off his boots and fell into his corner bed.

~

Marisol sat on the cot after her bath and let Amy brush her hair. "Thank you so much for taking care of me during my sickness, Amy."

"Oh, but, ma'am, I didn't nurse you." She dropped her head. "I was afeared of catching the fever like my ma and pa had."

"You didn't?" Marisol turned to look at the girl. "Who took care of me?"

"Why Captain Becket did. He was the only one. And he never left your side."

"How long was I sick, Amy?"

The girl shook her head. "Three days, ma'am. That's how the

captain said he knew it was swamp and not yellow fever. It broke in three days."

Marisol's eyes widened. Ethan spent three days alone with her in her cabin while she was abed with sickness? Her hand fluttered to the top edge of her gown and spread over the expanse of exposed neckline.

~

The next evening, Marisol took her first stroll on deck since her sickness. The cool breeze lifted her hair, refreshing her like only the sea air could do. She walked up the quarterdeck steps, and Ethan turned and smiled at her.

"It's good to see you up and about, Marisol. You gave us a scare." His intense gray eyes perused her face, causing a tingling in the pit of her stomach.

She gripped the railing and looked out at the white-capping waves. Warmth rose in her cheeks at the thought of his taking care of her. "I didn't know you were a doctor, sir."

"Oh, I'm not a doctor. I just read the medical book we have on board and prayed what afflicted you was swamp fever and not the other."

Prayed? She looked into his eyes. There was a difference there. A peace? A new confidence? "Well, I owe you thanks for helping see me through when others would fear catching what I had. And for your losing sleep all that time."

Ethan grinned. "Sleep is one thing sailors learn to do without when necessary. Many things can happen aboard a ship, and you have to stay awake to stay alive."

"Have we had any sight of Doña Maria's ship?"

"Not yet, but they should stop soon to re-water."

Marisol turned to follow his gaze out to sea. She could only pray God would make a way for them to recapture her son when they finally found the vessel.

~

Two days later in the early evening, Ethan's man on watch high in the eagle's nest sighted the first green sliver of Hispaniola on the horizon. As they sailed in closer, flying a French flag, Ethan kept his eyeglass trained on the ships in the harbor.

He shouted the command to strike colors and topsails as a sign of courtesy and nonaggression to the Spanish authorities. Half a dozen three- and four-masted galleons were riding at anchor when the *Dryade* closed with the land. Giving the Spanish ships a wide berth, Ethan yelled the command to drop anchor.

A ship anchored below them at the far end of the dock caught his attention. Just as he had hoped, the *Nuestra Señora de Vargas's* captain had stopped to re-water and take on supplies. If Ethan's plan was to work, he would have to ensure Marisol didn't see the vessel.

He had no doubt she would do everything in her power to board it and demand her son. But this was a Spanish port. Doña Maria de la Madrid Vargas held all the cards in her rich, noble hands. The harbor authorities would back her and arrest Marisol if a dispute ensued.

Their only real chance to get Samuel back would be on the open sea. And with the falling darkness, they had a good chance to carry out his secret plan.

He called Tim Cullen to his side. "Marisol must not guess we are this close to Doña Maria's ship or she might try to go aboard and end up arrested. She and Amy are having dinner in their cabin. Don't let anyone tell her what port we're in. For another safety measure, I want you to post Samson at her door and tell her it's because we're in the pirate-infested port of Kingston to re-water, and we're taking precautions for having women on board. Tell them they must not leave their cabin until we're at sea again in the morning. We're only stopping to take on water."

Ethan wiped the sweat from his forehead and paced across the quarterdeck. "Hurry back and I'll share with you a daring plan we'll initiate tonight."

He had lain awake many nights as they sailed in their pursuit, thinking of the possibilities for the drogue device. And he'd finalized the idea when sitting at Marisol's bedside.

Now as the opportunity seemed imminent to put it to work on Doña Maria's ship, the old symptoms of adventure, as recognizable as ever, assailed him—the quickened heartbeat, the heat under his skin, and a great restlessness. Would the plan succeed? Or would they lose Doña Maria's ship and Samuel forever? He couldn't let that happen.

Later in his cabin, when the *Dryade* had taken on her needed water and all grew quiet, he laid out the plan to Tim and three handpicked trusted, sailors. "When darkness falls, you three men will lower a boat and row it around the *Dryade,* as if to stop crew members jumping into the bay and deserting during the night. That's what we've told the port authorities. But just past midnight, you will also have another little mission."

Tim and the three men nodded, their eyes glued to his face as he described the drogue they would construct and secretly attach underwater to the rudder of the *Nuestra Señora de Vargas.* "We'll need a large sea anchor and a bolt of number one canvas sewn into a funnel, one end larger than the other, and a chain sewed around the mouth to strengthen it. I've seen this thing work well when I was part of His Majesty's Navy." Ethan took a deep breath. "Questions?"

One crewman crossed his arms and grinned. "This thing will slow down the ship, maybe even stop it at sea when she sets full sail and the strain comes?"

"That's right. We must get the ship out from this Spanish port's protection before we have any hope of capturing or boarding her." Ethan looked at the excited faces. "And, yes, before you ask, when we capture and board her we will not only rescue Marisol's son, we'll also take as our prize any valuable cargo. But we won't destroy the ship. In fact, it's my hope we'll not have to fire a single shot once the drogue does its work."

One man slapped his thigh and whooped, then settled down as if remembering he was in the august presence of his captain.

Soon other men entered the cabin and set to work making the device that Ethan sketched out. The sail maker, the carpenter, and the boatswain did their part by lantern light as darkness enveloped the *Dryade* and the other ships swaying at anchor in the bay.

Ethan set to work on the other details. He summoned powerful swimmers who could work underwater, an armorer's mate who could attach the final shackle in the chain in the darkness, and strong rowers to move the longboat fast on its errand.

On the quarterdeck, just past midnight, Ethan watched the boat push off in the darkness, carrying the drogue and the men who would attach it to the rudder of Doña Maria's galleon anchored further down the dock. The word was that the Spanish ship would sail with the morning tide.

So would the *Dryade.* At a respectable distance.

Three hours before dawn, the boat returned and reported success in their mission. Ethan expelled a relieved breath and instructed Tim to prepare for sailing at daylight just after Doña Maria's galleon headed out to sea. He lay down in his cabin berth without removing his clothing.

At the first glimmer of daylight, Ethan strode back onto the quarterdeck. The sounds of the *Nuestra Señora de Vargas* making ready for sea echoed over the surface of the water. The *Dryade* also made ready, but with secrecy and stealth.

As streaks of pink, green, and yellow fanned over the eastern sky, the *Nuestra Señora de Vargas* pulled anchor, cast off, and moved out into the channel.

Ethan waited a short interval, then commanded the *Dryade* to do the same. The Spanish galleon cleared the channel and held a course northward.

The *Dryade* stayed at a distance, following the *Nuestra Señora de Vargas,* which soon sailed far ahead. Then came a breath of different air. Ethan felt the gust on his warm face long before the wind made it to the white sails. It was not the heated air of the land breeze, but the fresher breeze of the trade wind, clean after its passage over three thousand miles of ocean.

The sails flapped and shivered as the full gusts filled them. Now that they had caught the trade wind, they could thrust their way northward and gain on the heavier Spanish galleon. Ethan reveled in the warm sunshine glistening on the Atlantic rollers and how the *Dryade* plowed its way over them at a quick speed.

Marisol walked across the quarterdeck, her thick blue skirt rustling with every step, and tiny curls about her face lifting in the breeze. "Where are we heading now, Ethan?"

He lowered his eyeglass from the ship ahead of them, which was becoming more and more visible on the horizon. He looked at her pale, thin face, her lovely blue eyes dulled from anxiety. She had lost weight. Dare he tell her what he hoped would soon happen? That Doña Maria's ship would flounder, and they should be able to board without firing a shot? Yet what would happen if he raised her hopes and the drogue failed to work? Could she stand such a let-down?

Perhaps it was best to share only a part of the good news. He handed her the eyeglass. "Take a look at that ship."

She looked through the glass for a moment as the *Dryade* drew ever closer in its pursuit. Suddenly she screamed, and the tool flew from her grasp. "Ethan, it's Doña Maria's ship. Is it? Am I seeing right?"

Ethan grabbed the eyeglass before it flew overboard. He smiled and stored it in his belt. Slipping an arm around her trembling shoulders, he confirmed her words. "You're seeing right. It's the *Nuestra Señora de Vargas.* Of that I'm sure."

"Oh, Ethan." Tears overflowed Marisol's eyes. "This close. This close to my dear boy."

Ethan turned her toward him. "Marisol, I must ask you to do something difficult."

She eyed him and wiped her cheeks with both hands. "What

could be harder than what I've already gone through?" She gave him a shaky smile, her beautiful blue eyes glimmering.

"The next couple of hours will be critical in this rescue. I need you to go to your cabin and let us do what we need to. It could become dangerous."

"Oh, Ethan, you...won't fire on the galleon, will you? You know my Samuel is on board." Her voice tightened with a strain he could almost feel.

"I hope we don't have to fire a single shot, Marisol. That's the plan, but until I know for sure, will you please go back to your cabin and stay there until I send for you?"

At first she shook her head, then a new light came into her eyes. She took a deep ragged breath. "Yes. All right. I know I have to trust you." She turned toward the quarterdeck stairway. Before starting down, she looked back and gazed at the ship on the horizon one last time.

The yearning in her heart was visible in every line of her form, and his own heart swelled with urgency. *Lord, please don't let me make the wrong move here. Guide me.*

CHAPTER 17

Ethan watched Marisol go below deck, then ran out the eyeglass again. Blood pounded in his veins and his breath came in spurts as he viewed the *Nuestra Señora de Vargas,* now slowing ahead of them. The drogue must be working.

Tim Cullen strode onto the quarterdeck, staring across the capping water toward the Spanish ship. "She's setting her topsail, sir." His voice overflowed with excitement.

"Yes, that's a good sign." Ethan kept the eyeglass trained on the ship. "We'll soon know. When the drogue comes into full action, she'll have to come to a standstill."

"Cap'n!" The lookout yelled. "She's flown up into the wind. She's all aback. There goes her topmast, sir."

"And so goes her rudder," Ethan muttered, his lips in a tight line. A terrible situation for any ship to find itself in. But good for him.

Tim danced on the deck, his face beaming. "It worked. The drogue worked." A cheer rose up from the ship's crew below them.

"With her rudder damaged, she'll never be able to hold a course," Ethan said.

The *Dryade* seemed to catch the excitement and sailed ever

faster toward the floundering galleon. Ethan took a deep, satisfied breath. They were approaching the ship at a clipping speed, and she was a pitiful sight with her fore topmast broken off clean.

"Fire a shot across her bow," he shouted from the quarterdeck.

A boom, followed by a trail of smoke, echoed across the waves. The good shot landed just over the bow of the Spanish ship. The red and gold flag of Spain came down in surrender.

A surge of elation washed through Ethan and he turned to Tim. "Go bring Marisol on deck."

When she came and looked out over the water at the surrendered ship, a cry escaped her lips, followed by a sob. "Oh, Ethan, thank you." She stood at the railing as the *Dryade* pulled alongside and threw boarding hooks onto the captured ship's deck.

The Spanish officers remained at attention on the foredeck, their faces hardened into bronze masks.

After his crew boarded and herded up the captives, Ethan helped Marisol swing over to the deck. Now that his men had taken over command, it should be safe enough for her on the Spanish ship. And one look at her face proved she wouldn't be held back.

The proud Spanish captain, with his silver helmet under his arm, came forward and offered his sword. Ethan received it and looked into the hard eyes darkened by defeat. "You have a woman and child aboard, sir?"

The man clicked his heels and threw out his chest. "Yes. Señora Maria de la Madrid Vargas and her grandson."

Marisol stretched to her full height, and her blue eyes blazed at him. "He is *my* son and Doña Maria kidnapped him. Bring him to me at once."

But Ethan's crew had already gone below, and now they brought Doña Maria on deck. She stood there, her face a wash of fear and shock. She clutched Samuel in her arms and glared at Ethan and Marisol, her aristocratic, coiffed head erect.

When Samuel caught sight of Marisol, he reached out his little arms. "Mamá."

With a squeal, Marisol darted to him, tears streaming down her face. She pried him from Doña Maria's arms, and even across the distance, Ethan could see the fierce glare Marisol sent the woman. "How could you take a child from his mother? You—"

Samuel laid his dark, tousled head on Marisol's shoulder and plopped two fingers into his mouth. She stopped mid-word, and turned all her focus to her son, showering him with kisses. "My boy, my dear boy."

Ethan swallowed the lump in his throat. Ben Thompson and several of the *Dryade's* crew coughed as they looked on.

The guarded Spanish captives also stared as they jostled against each other. The bumping of their silver helmets held under their arms sounded across the deck.

Doña Maria drew a lace handkerchief from her cuff and wiped at her eyes. "I took good care of him, Marisol. Surely you knew I would." Another woman stood quietly beside them. "Here is the wet nurse I hired for him."

Marisol ignored both women and hugged Samuel tight. She sniffed as she flicked at the stream of tears coursing down her cheeks.

Doña Maria's face crumpled into deep crevices as tears leaked from her eyes. "I love your boy, Marisol. I'm his grandmother. He is the only one left in my family line. Can you forgive me for the love that drove me?"

Marisol's jaw flexed, and her eyes shot daggers at the woman. "I'll never forgive you."

Ethan turned to Marisol, hoping she'd see his imploring gaze, but she didn't appear to soften at all. He crossed his arms and looked back at Doña Maria, now a broken old lady, not appearing noble or powerful at all.

The woman wiped her eyes again. "Marisol, I want Samuel to inherit my estate, and it includes your father's estate that Diego won from your uncle the night you..." She swallowed and continued. "I have my lawyer on board. He can draw up the papers. I only ask that you allow me to see him on occasion. Would you consider this?"

Ethan's eyebrows rose. The woman's offer sounded almost too good to be true. It would secure Samuel's future for the rest of his life. And even more than that, Marisol could be free…

Even though Ethan's crew was busy loading goods—or rather, plunder—from the Spanish ship's hold onto the *Dryade,* he stayed nearby to hear Marisol's response.

Her voice, when it came, was as brittle as splintered glass, each word like a shard to cut both coming and going. "I want nothing to do with you or your estate, Doña Maria."

She was too emotional in this moment. Maybe she didn't see all the possibilities here. Ethan touched her arm and pulled her aside.

She turned red-rimmed, pain-filled eyes up to him, which pressed so hard on his chest he could barely draw breath. "She kidnapped my child. I hope I never see her again."

Samuel reached out his arms, and Ethan took the boy, pulling him close for a tight hug. Lands, he'd missed this boy. He'd not known how much until now. The lad patted Ethan's beard, and he took the small hand in his and kissed it.

Then he turned his focus to Marisol, letting her see his hope in his gaze. "Marisol, what if you can add whatever you want to this document? Such as a sentence saying she'll never prosecute you for any reason. You could be free."

~

Marisol stared at him, speechless. Her breath caught in her throat. She understood what he was saying, but it took a moment for her reluctant mind to wrap around the idea. Could she ever be free of the murder of Diego Vargas? Then she shook her head and reached to take Samuel back in her arms. Nothing was worth the safety of her son.

"Don't decide this too fast, Marisol." Ethan's serious gray eyes held hers captive. He touched her shoulder.

Her heart hammered against her ribs as his magnetism and strength played their usual part in attracting her. A plethora of emotions—confusion, doubt, fear—gripped her. But behind it all, a glimmer of hope rose like a small beacon on a storm-tossed sea.

Doña Maria came up beside them. "I heard what you said, Captain Becket." She wiped her eyes again and her face lightened. "Of course, I would agree to never bring charges against my grandson's mother. How would that benefit him or me? That can be written in the legal document." Her wobbly voice held none of its usual superiority.

Marisol glanced at the pale, tight face, the hair not so neat, the rich clothing limp on her angled form. But this woman had kidnapped her precious Samuel. She stiffened and swallowed a wave of nausea rising in her throat. How could Ethan think they could ever trust such a person? She turned away, wearied by indecision.

Ethan addressed Doña Maria. "Your ship has floundered, Señora, but we will not leave you here alone and unaided. I'll be glad to take you, your lawyer, and one of the ship's officers close to the nearest Spanish port, where you can bring back help for your ship or belongings."

"Thank you, Captain. That is very generous of you. I'll speak to my captain to see who he'll send ahead." Doña Maria swished toward the captured crew and its leader. Her silk skirts rustled behind her.

Marisol, holding Samuel close in her arms and kissing the top of his head every few moments, watched Ethan direct the removal of the ship's store of gunpowder and the sabotage of the cannons so they couldn't fire on the *Dryade* after they departed. He also confiscated all the guns of the crew.

Within the hour, Ethan, his crew, Marisol, Samuel, Doña Maria, her lawyer, the First Lieutenant of the Spanish vessel, and another strong rower boarded the *Dryade*.

~

The next day, a happy wind—to Marisol's thinking now with her son back—moved the ship with ease over a glassy sea. She stood on deck at the railing, breathing in the fresh, salty air after feeding Samuel and putting him down for a morning nap with Amy watching over him. One of Ethan's men guarded the cabin door. How could she ever feel Samuel was safe until they dropped Doña Maria and her party off at the next Spanish port? Then they could sail toward their eventual, long-awaited goal—Charles Town.

Ethan had informed the Spanish noblewoman and her three compatriots at dinner the night before that he would endeavor to sail near a secluded coast of Cuba. There, he planned to put them ashore in one of his small dinghies within a day's rowing distance of the port of Santíago.

They accepted the offer.

Now, Ben Thompson came to stand beside Marisol at the railing. "How's your boy, Marisol?"

"He's fine, sir. Sleeping, with Amy watching him and Samson at the door. Thank you for asking." She turned to look into the older man's eyes. "And thank you for praying. Only God could have made his rescue a success."

She looked up and saw Ethan on the quarterdeck with his eyeglass trained in the distance. Had he glimpsed the coast of Cuba? She started to ask that question of Ben, but a movement behind her and a voice she hated interrupted her thought.

"My dear, I have the document I mentioned to you yesterday."

Marisol whirled around to face Doña Maria and her short, wiry lawyer in his blue silk waistcoat, stockings, and white wig. The woman's tired, drawn face hinted at lack of sleep.

Ben nodded to her and the lawyer. "Good morning, Señora and Señor."

The mother of Diego Vargas continued to stand in place, but Marisol couldn't look at her. Not yet. She turned toward the railing —away from that woman.

She could feel the weight of Ben's gaze, could hear the crinkle of paper as he took the proffered document. "Give us a little while to examine this, if you don't mind, Señora. I read Spanish, but slower than English."

"That will be fine, sir." The swish of skirts and quiet tread of boots died away as the two walked toward the deck steps to the cabins.

Ben moved beside Marisol and looked out at the white-capping waves. "You know Ethan and I both think it might be a good idea for you to consider this offer." He gestured to the paper.

She sighed. It would be too good to be true if she could hope to escape her terrible deed. To be free of it and all her past life.

And that was just the point. Doña Maria wanted to stay in her life, in Samuel's life, forever. *Or until the woman dies.* Marisol tightened her jaw to push away the grim thought. Losing Samuel had hardened her more than she'd imagined. She turned to Ben. "All right. Let's go to the captain's cabin and look at it."

An hour later, Marisol slumped in her chair at the big table, drained after hearing Ben read and point out the wise conditions written in Doña Maria's document. He recounted the main points to her for the third time.

"She's agreed never to prosecute you for what happened to her son. She even admits he was a disappointment to her with his carousing and gambling." He looked up at Marisol. "That took courage to write."

Marisol shrugged and rubbed her stiff neck.

He continued, "She only wants to see Samuel every two years at a place and time you can choose. And she wants to send him gifts at Christmas and on his birthday."

"I will never let him wear any clothing she sends." Marisol couldn't keep the loathing from her voice.

Ben's brows rose. "And she has a whole page here, her Last Will and Testament, if you please, describing her estate and all her possessions she is bequeathing him at her death. She gives you permission and requests you give him the Vargas last name to simplify matters."

Ben laid his hand over Marisol's, which rested limp on the table. "My dear, I know you're battling a lot of conflicting emotions, but what can you lose? You have all the cards, actually the whole deck in your hands, so to speak. And one day, Samuel could be a rich young man. Would you deny him that?"

Marisol looked into his face. "Do you believe I should sign this? Will Ethan agree?"

"Agree about what?" Ethan strode into the cabin, his sword clinking at his side. His wind-blown curly hair stood on end. He ran a hand over the unruly strands as he sent her a gentle smile. "Agree on what?"

Then his eyes fell to the obvious legal manuscript on the table. He walked over, picked it up, sat, and read through both pages in short order, his Spanish being much better than Ben's.

He nodded as he reread sections. "I think she and her lawyer have written this pretty well, and you have a lot of say so. In fact, just about all of it. The lawyer will be the go-between. You won't have to deal directly with her about the visits, or choice of place or time, or anything I can discern. Of course, you'd never leave Samuel alone with her. It specifies an hour visit once every two years near his birthday. And you could be present the entire time." He stopped and glanced at Marisol.

She took a shaky breath, stood, and wrapped her arms around herself. "What hope has a mere woman against the two of you?" She lowered her head and sighed. "How do we do this?"

Ben stood. "I'll fetch Doña Maria and her lawyer. Ethan and I can witness both your signatures."

Within the next thirty minutes, all was finished.

Marisol trudged back to her cabin carrying her signed copy of Doña Maria's pledge and will. She placed it in her trunk and walked over to pick up Samuel, who had sat up on the bed, his rosy face rested and happy. Was he a rich heir now because of the document? She shook her head, groaned, and hugged him tight.

She could only pray she wouldn't forever regret her decision.

~

Early the next morning, a knock sounded on Marisol's door. She had just finished dressing herself and Samuel while Amy still slept. "Who is it?" she called out.

"It's me, Marisol." Ethan's strong voice sent the usual flutter through her chest.

She opened the door with Samuel in her arms. She had just nursed him, and his green eyes glowed with a dash of topaz. The boy reached to touch Ethan's beard. "No, Samuel." She moved back a step and looked into the captain's face.

A smile spread across his chiseled cheeks. "We're lowering a boat for Doña Maria and her men to row into the Santíago harbor. She asked that you come and bring Samuel so she can say goodbye to him." He reached out and placed both hands on her shoulders, then gazed into her face. "It's almost over, Marisol. When they pull away in that boat, you can be at peace."

Marisol inhaled a deep breath, and the tight bands around her chest began to break away. "I'll come."

Amy, now awakened, sat up on her cot. "I will, too, ma'am, if you don't mind."

The Caribbean dawn showered pink, blue, and purple strands across the sky. Doña Maria stood huddled in her gray silk cloak with her hair piled high under her silver mantilla, as her group prepared to disembark in the row boat.

Marisol approached her with Samuel.

Tears overflowed from the woman's dark eyes, and Samuel reached over and patted her cheek. Before he could reach for her jeweled mantilla comb, Doña Maria took his hand and kissed his fingers.

With her other thin hand, she reached into her pocket and pulled out a small gold and silver toy soldier and held it up to him. The child squealed and grasped it in his pudgy grip. She reached into her clothing again and brought out a heavy gold ring on a chain. She leaned close and proffered it to Marisol.

"What is this?" Marisol couldn't keep the coolness from her voice.

The woman pressed the chain and black onyx ring into Marisol's hand. "This ring with the Vargas insignia will guarantee you safety in any Spanish port, Marisol. Or whoever bears it. Our name still carries authority..."

Before Marisol could hand it back to her, the older woman sat in the chair that would swing her over the railing to the small boat. As they lowered her down the side of the ship to the dinghy below, her eyes never left the boy, so long as she could see him.

Marisol slipped the ring and chain into her pocket and breathed a deep sigh of relief. It was over. She glanced at Ethan and Ben as they watched the small boat pull away. Hugging Samuel tight, she walked back to the cabin.

Amy followed and leaned forward to look at Samuel's gift. "That toy soldier looks like it might be worth something. Looks like gold and silver to me, ma'am."

"Keep your voice low, Amy. I want none of this crew coming to our cabin to look for it. It's a chess playing piece."

"What is chess?" Amy's brow wrinkled as they entered the cabin.

"It's a game with a board and pieces to move about. Wealthy people play it in Europe." Marisol stored the chain and its ring in her personal box and sat down in the rocker with Samuel on her lap. The child, absorbed with his new toy, uttered a happy sigh.

Marisol slept well that night and awakened so refreshed, she realized just how exhausted she'd been the past stressful weeks since Samuel's kidnapping.

She could at last breathe without pain crossing her chest. Looking at her boy sleeping in the smaller cot Ethan had made for him beside her bed, Marisol smiled. She arose and busied herself bathing with the tepid water in the bowl, then donned her best gown—the yellow silk. Today was a day to celebrate. All was again well with her world.

Thank You, Father God. Thank You for bringing my son back to me. You're my Lord and Good Shepherd. I choose You and Your ways forever. A weight lifted from her heart.

Amy sat up and yawned. "When will we get back to Charles Town, ma'am? Are we getting close?" Her voice was low, not to disturb the sleeping child.

"We're definitely on our way. I'm going up on deck for some air. Please watch Samuel and come get me when he awakens."

"Yes, ma'am." The girl dropped back on her pillow.

Marisol walked up the quarterdeck steps with a sense of floating on air.

Ethan turned toward her as she swished across the deck to him, and a wide grin creased his face. "I thank God you're looking more like yourself, Marisol. Beautiful, if I might say so." His deep-timbered voice and his gaze washed over her, affecting her breathing even more than usual.

Heat climbed up her neck and spread to her cheeks. She met his dancing gray eyes, and a delicious magnetism sparked between them. How had she ignored him the past month? With his white shirt billowing in the trade wind that filled the sails of the *Dryade*, his handsomeness swept through her with a visceral ache.

Ethan placed an arm around her waist and pulled her close, out of sight of the crew below. His eyes traveled over her face, searching. His tender gaze and nearness made her senses spin.

"Marisol, I love you and Samuel. I want to take care of you the rest of our lives."

Her breath caught in her throat and her heart hammered in her ears. But the old wound, the lies she'd heard from Diego, flashed back through her mind. Could she ever trust another man? She tried to push away from him, but he wouldn't let her go.

Instead, he leaned closer. She breathed in his manly scent of sea and spice, an aroma that smelled so right. "Whatever happened in the past, let it go, Marisol." He whispered the words in her ear, his breath caressing her skin.

A dizzying current raced through her. "I don't know if that's possible, Ethan." She tried again to push back, but he held tight.

"Can't you see that God brought us together? I didn't understand how bitter I had become after my wife and child died, but I've repented and opened my heart to Him and to you. Love chased the bitterness away. Let His love and mine do the same for you." His voice turned husky as he leaned back and searched her face.

The smoldering flame in his gray eyes leaped into her heart. When he drew her close, she felt his pulse beat against her cheek. She was powerless to resist any longer.

Something broke loose deep inside her. All her fear, distrust, and misgivings lifted like a dead weight from her shoulders.

"I'm asking you to marry me, Marisol." His voice rumbled in her ear. "To become my wife and build a new life together in Charles Town." He lifted her chin with his thumb. "And I'm thinking of returning to my church, leaving the sea. What do you say?"

She was having difficulty breathing, much less speaking. But when she opened her mouth, the words tumbled out. "Yes. I say yes, Captain Becket."

His mouth claimed hers in a kiss as powerful as the trade winds driving the *Dryade* north by northwest over a glassy sea.

EPILOGUE

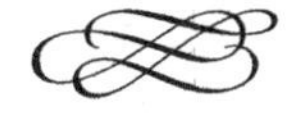

Charles Town

Marisol laid Samuel down for his morning nap and looked again at the lovely dress hanging on her chifforobe door. A fresh flutter lit inside her chest. She would wear it in a few hours when she and Ethan pledged their vows in the little Presbyterian Church down the lane. The current pastor, longing to be with his grandchildren in England, didn't hesitate to express his joy when he heard the news that Ethan would return as pastor after his marriage.

She strolled over and fingered the pale yellow silk skirt with its rows of lace ruffles, offset with pink rose buds every few inches. The silk bodice, with its modest neckline, boasted a matching ruffle, as did the flowing sleeves. She had never seen so fine a dress when the dressmaker from Bay Street brought it to show her and Mrs. Piper.

Ethan had surprised them by walking into the kitchen while they were admiring the gown. His gray eyes glowed as he looked from Marisol to the dress. "It's perfect, as though she made it for you, my dear wife-to-be."

Pink had come into the dressmaker's cheeks as she glanced at Mrs. Piper, who ducked her head to hide a smile. But Marisol could only glory in his love. Her husband-to-be.

More than a handful of well-wishers had met the *Dryade's* arrival in Charles Town two weeks earlier. Ethan's sister Grace and Ben Thompson spread the story of their Spanish Main adventures, and the entire community buzzed with it.

It was wonderful to see Grace adjusting well with her parents in the Charles Town house. She'd settled into Cousin Emma's former room, since their cousin had met and married a soldier in His Majesty's service who'd been posted to Charles Town for two months. She and her son had returned with him to England.

As Marisol descended the stairs, the delicious scents of Mrs. Piper's and Grace's baking tantalized her nose and made her stomach growl with hunger.

She walked into the warm kitchen and glanced at the sweet rolls and breads lining up on the buffet, ready for the coming wedding guests. "Dear ladies. You're working so hard, can't I help do something?" A smile that came fast these days spread across her lips as she looked at the two women, now her dearest friends.

Mrs. Piper looked up from slicing a loaf for the tea sandwiches. "Not on your wedding day, young lady. But help yourself to a breakfast roll. Got to keep up your strength. Ethan ate three before he headed over to help get the church ready." She turned back to her work.

Grace leaned over a pot, stirring something savory bubbling on the fire. "Please rest and enjoy this special day, Marisol." She wiped strands of damp hair from her forehead and laughed. The sound was like a happy tinkling bell. "Tomorrow and thereafter, you may stand right where I am."

Marisol walked over to Joshua, who played with his toys in the corner. "Young man, how would you like to take a walk in the backyard garden while we wait for Samuel to wake?" The boy stood and toddled to her, then reached for her hand. His sweet trust never ceased to warm her all the way through.

They exited by the back door and walked on the path toward the garden, with its grassy play area and sand box under a tree. Marisol sat on the bench and watched Joshua playing until it was almost time for the mid-day meal. Just as she was ready to return inside, the sounds of Samuel waking drifted from the open upstairs window.

"Come, Joshua, let's go get Samuel and find something to eat." Ethan's son, two years older than Samuel, was always ready to eat. He was a head taller than the younger boy, but that might not be the case for long. Samuel ate hardily, too.

Ethan's parents and Grace took charge of Joshua and Samuel after lunch and planned to bring them to the church for the ceremony.

At three o'clock, with help from Mrs. Piper and Amy, Marisol donned the lovely wedding dress. A knot of emotion gathered in her throat as she stared at her reflection in the mirror. If only her parents could be here for this special day. She added one last touch to the shoulder of the dress—the Valentin ruby brooch. As she attached it, her mother and father seemed nearer than before.

The housekeeper peered at it. "Oh my dear, what a lovely pin. From your family?"

"Yes." Marisol adjusted her mantilla and its lace veil. Had Ethan finished getting ready? He was dressing in his own room downstairs.

From her window a few minutes later, she saw him leave the cottage and head down the path to the church. Her heart flipped at how handsome he looked in his dark blue waistcoat and snowy cravat.

Soon, the carriage came for her and the other women, driven by Ben Thompson, who had asked to give Marisol away. They alighted at the front of the little church, and Mrs. Piper hurried inside.

Marisol, with her hand on Ben's arm, waited at the back of the sanctuary until the strains of music heightened. She only had time for one glance at the gathered guests. Several of Ethan's crew had come—Tim Cullen, Samson, the carpenter, and some others whose names she didn't know. All their faces beamed at her as she started down the aisle on Ben's arm.

Then Ethan walked from behind the pulpit area, stealing her gaze as she took in every part of him. She came to stand beside him at the altar, and still couldn't take her focus from her strong, handsome, husband-to-be. *Thank you, Father.*

With a twinkle in his gray eyes, he took her hand, pulled it through his strong arm, and moved her closer to his side.

Marisol felt as if she were floating on a frothy wave, but managed to respond at the right times to the minister during the ceremony. Ethan, whose smile never left his face, helped by pressing her hand when she needed to speak.

When the minister pronounced them man and wife, Ethan drew her into his arms and pressed her lips with his—a chaste kiss, but with a strength that promised more later. His crew erupted in shouts and whistles.

Samuel gave one of his happy squeals, slid out of Grace's lap, and crawled up the aisle to grab hold of Marisol's skirt. Ethan bent and lifted him to his shoulder, and they walked back down the aisle. As they passed Joshua in his seat, the boy slipped out and took Marisol's hand, falling into step beside her. Together, they exited the church, a family at last.

Later, when all guests had left and Mrs. Piper had both boys asleep in her room, Ethan and Marisol strolled hand in hand through the garden and sat on the warm bench. Moonlight lit their faces and the strumming of crickets filled the night.

He leaned close, turning her face to his just before he lowered his mouth in a kiss. Tender and oh so loving, but not nearly long enough. He lifted his head to whisper, "I love you, Marisol. I think I loved you from that day I first saw you standing on the indentured servant's platform."

She smiled into his handsome face. "And I tried to hide it, but I was attracted to you even while I stood out among that terrible crowd of men."

"Were you really?"

She leaned her head on his shoulder. "I knew something about you was different."

He winced. "I'm afraid I was backslidden from the faith at that time, my dear."

She looked up into his face. "But you still had some goodness about you. You may have left the Lord, but I don't think He had left you. I didn't even know Him at that time."

He snuggled her closer against him. "Thank God you do now, Marisol. I'm sure after all that happened to you, it would be hard to trust God, if you felt He allowed all the hurt."

She sat up straight. "I know now we have an enemy who plans the bad things that happen to us. But our mighty God can take whatever happens and work it for our good if we trust Him. He worked all the bad things that happened to me for good. He gave me Samuel and helped me find you." She touched his firm cheek and traced her finger down to his fine lips.

He sucked in his breath. "I'll never tire of your touch, dear wife."

She smiled, but then removed her hand and looked out across the garden. "I still don't know how I feel about Doña Maria and her attachment to Samuel." She turned to look into his face. "Do you have any idea how that legal paper we signed will work out in the future? I mean, do you think she'll really want to visit him and leave her entire estate to him? I would never want to think of Samuel going to live in Spain. Do you think he ever would when he grows up?"

~

Ethan took a deep breath, not wanting to even think about Doña Maria or anything else—not with Marisol so close and soft and wonderful in his arms. "That's what she attested to in that legal document and with witnesses. And as far as our Samuel, I don't know what that young man might want to do one day. He's already shown he has an adventuresome spirit. Being kidnapped didn't seem to daunt him, and he never seems to meet a stranger. So I guess we'll have to wait and see how all this will turn out, my wonderful, darling wife." Those last words grew husky.

"But enough of this talk." He stood and pulled her up to her feet. "Besides, I have a surprise for you. Go pack a bag. We're going to spend our wedding night on the *Dryade*."

"On your ship?" Marisol looked up into his face, her lovely skin almost glowing in the moonlight.

"Yes, but first, this." He tipped her chin up and trailed kisses across her brow, her cheeks, then captured her mouth with his. The kiss, like the soldering heat that joins metals, sent a burn all the way through him.

And it must have done the same for Marisol, because she gasped. He planted a tantalizing kiss in the hollow of her neck and started to let her go, but her knees gave way. He chuckled and swooped her up in his arms, then walked toward the house.

~

On the *Dryade* the next morning, Marisol sat with Ethan as they finished the morning meal the ship's cook had served before disappearing.

Ethan leaned forward and studied her. "I've decided to keep the ship, dear wife."

"But you said you were leaving the sea." Marisol's brows drew together. Yet even his words couldn't dispel her love for the man across the table from her. Nor memories of the passionate night before that still brought warmth to her cheeks.

"I am, except for an occasional visit here." He smiled at her. "Like last night, for example."

Her color heightened more, and she ducked her head, but couldn't stop a smile.

"And who knows whether Joshua or Samuel may one day find a love for the sea flowing through their veins? The *Dryade* needs to stay in the family. I'll partner with Tim Cullen to sail her and run a merchant business while I pastor."

He reached for her hand and pulled her up from her chair into his strong arms. He kissed her soundly then pulled back and groaned. "For now, we need to get back on shore to check on our two little future sailors."

She had no way to respond as he leaned close again and caressed her face with kisses, then held her for a few more wonderful moments. In his arms, she sighed in perfect contentment. The picture of their new beginning began to form in her mind's eye. "I can see it, Ethan."

He pulled back to look into her eyes. "See what?"

"The fresh beginning I've dreamed of since I left Spain—a happy new life I thought was impossible for me. I can scarcely believe He's begun it."

He hugged her closer. "Yes, He has, my dearest wife, and we give Him our great thanks and praise."

VOCABULARY APPENDIX

1) Andalusian Horse

This breed, also known as the Pure Spanish Horse, is from the Iberian (Spanish) Peninsula, where its ancestors have lived for thousands of years. During the 15th and 16th centuries these majestic horses with their long manes and high stepping gaits became a status symbol of the royal courts throughout Europe. As the importation of horses from Spain became more difficult, the Vienna Court decided to develop their own breeding farm. In 1580 they brought nine stallions and 24 mares from Spain to Lipica. These horses became the foundation for the famous Lipizzan breed and the Spanish Riding School in Vienna. That's why it is called "Spanish" school, even though it is located in Vienna. One interesting historical note: During WWII the Germans confiscated the Lipizzaners and moved them, but our American General Patton rescued them and returned them to Austria. Today there are over 200,000 registered Andalusians worldwide.

2) Pirate vs. Privateer

What usually set privateers apart from pirates was a piece of paper known as a Letter of Marque. Governments bestowed these commissions on privately owned ships during times of war as an inexpensive way to weaken the enemy. Privateers—a term that refers to a ship, a captain, or a crew—preyed on the merchant ships of a specific country's enemies. In exchange for providing the privateer with a safe haven and license to attack, the issuer shared in the profits.

Sometimes privateers turned to piracy, especially during times of peace.

2) Tricorn

A man's hat with its brim turned up on three sides, making three points, worn by men in the 18th century.

3) Draught of a ship

The draft or draught of a ship's hull is the vertical distance between the waterline and the bottom of the hull, with the thickness of the hull included. Draft determines the minimum depth of water a ship or boat can safely navigate.

6) 'Swounds

An interjection. An exclamation contracted from God's wounds, used as an oath.

7) Ballast Bricks

During the crossing of the seas in the sailing years, captains used the bricks as a weight and balance method in the hold of the ship. After arriving at their destination, the ballast bricks were unloaded and replaced with fine goods for the return.

8) Drogue

A device to slow a boat down and even cause it to stop after it reaches a certain speed. It is generally constructed of heavy flexible material in the shape of a cone.

(Research credit given to *Admiral Hornblower in the West Indies* by C.S. Forester.)

9) Burgoo

A shipboard fare for lower echelon crew members. It was a mix of oat gruel and beef grease cooked all night, usually for breakfast.

10) Hardtack

Dry, unleavened bread served aboard ship to the lower crew members and sometimes served with salt beef pickled in barrels of brine along with salted peas. The hardtack was a survival biscuit made with three simple ingredients: flour, water, and salt. It was a solid survival bread that held up well to rough transport and kept nearly indefinitely.

12) Brigand

A member of a gang that ambushes and robs people in forests and mountains.

13) The Spanish Inquisition (1478 – 1834)

The Holy Inquisition was a very successful institution created by the Holy Roman Catholic Church in 1478 for the purpose of suppressing supposed heresy—a belief or opinion contrary to orthodox Catholic teaching. The priests responsible for hunting out and convicting heretics were called Holy Inquisitors and the Dominicans were given the primary charter to do this worldwide as Spain planted colonies. Their methods of uncovering supposed heresy were brutal and chilling. Several types of torture were used to get "confessions" of heresy. It included purging of prophets and dreamers (the charge that led to the burning at the stake of Joan of Arc). Tortures included starvation, burning coals applied, the rack, or being buried alive. Family members were pushed and tortured to testify against each other. The wealth of the dead victims was then transferred to the Church. Besides Catholics being examined for heresy, Jews, Muslims, Protestants, the Knights Templar, the Waldensians, were hunted down and became victims of the Inquisition. Estimates today of the death toll during the Inquisition worldwide during the 250 years of its existence range from 600,000 to as high as 9,000,000. The Inquisition was formally abolished July 15, 1834.

Did you enjoy this book? We hope so!

Would you take a quick minute to leave a review where you purchased the book?

It doesn't have to be long. Just a sentence or two telling what you liked about the story!

~

Don't miss *The Sultan's Captive*, book 2 in the Charleston Brides series!

Prologue

1755
CHARLES TOWN

"Will you kiss me if I win the race?"

Twelve-year-old Georgia Ann Cooper stopped dead in her trek across the plantation's wide, verdant lawn. She cast a look at the grinning fifteen-year-old Samuel Valentin Vargas striding beside her.

The children following them halted, and a collective gasp washed through them. Some of the girls pressed their hands across their mouths and squealed at Samuel, while several boys forced out their breath in shrill whistles.

Georgia Ann studied Samuel from under her long blond lashes. With his windswept black hair, tanned face, and scent of sea and leather, he looked every bit the sailor he had become sailing on his stepfather's former ship, the *Dryade.*

Samuel twirled his green tricorn in his hand, awaiting her

response. His tiger green eyes, bright and mysterious, met hers as he swiped a thick lock of dark hair from his forehead.

Who did he think he was? Besides being a late arrival, as usual. Whatever he was after with his scandalous words didn't matter. She would win the foot race, hands down, just like she'd won over every other guest at her birthday party.

Joshua Becket, the oldest of her guests, frowned and stomped up in front of Samuel, his step-brother. His dark eyes flashed and his lip curled in his pale face. Two years older, but an inch shorter, he stretched to his full height. "Samuel Vargas, that is no request to make of a young lady, *sir*." He emphasized the last word with a heavy dose of scorn.

Samuel cocked his chin in response but didn't take his eyes from Georgia. A slow grin spread across his mouth. "Let her decide."

His voice, warm and deep, sent a ripple of awareness through her.

Joshua uttered a hissing sound.

Georgia tossed her curls and looked over at her guests, then back to Samuel. "Maybe I would, maybe I wouldn't, but what does that signify, Mister Vargas? You will not win." She straightened herself with as much dignity as she could muster.

A hush fell on the group.

Joshua glowered at Samuel. "I refuse to have a part in this kind of race."

Georgia's twin cousins stepped forward. "We'll take care of it," John offered. "I'll drop the starter stick and Jeremiah can be at the finish to declare the winner."

Georgia moved to the starting point and lifted her skirts in preparation. When John swung the stick to the ground, she sprinted forward, as fast as a doe. Her yellow satin birthday dress ballooned behind her like a daffodil waving in the wind. Matching silk shoes skimmed the tops of the grass.

But Samuel won the race.

All the children ran across the lawn to join Georgia as she stood catching her breath a few yards apart from Samuel. She glanced at Joshua, hanging back, his brow black as a thundercloud.

Georgia's best friend, Abigail, flew to her side and whispered, "Are you going to let him kiss you?" She glared at Samuel, and said in a louder voice, "If he's a gentleman, he won't dare require this."

Samuel strode to stand in front of Georgia. "Why don't you let her make up her own mind? And I doubt I am a gentleman." His husky voice sounded deeper than usual.

She looked up into his face. Before she knew what was happening, he bent and brushed her lips with his own. Her eyelids closed of their own accord and stars exploded beneath them. A shock traveled the length of her frame.

The birthday guests burst into whoops and clapping.

All except Joshua Becket. He kicked a rock several yards into the grass.

"Georgia Ann Cooper, what are you doing, young lady?" Her governess's sharp voice brought Georgia Ann back from the starry place she visited. The woman marched across the lawn toward them, her face an angry mask.

Georgia blinked. Then she lifted her hand and slapped Samuel Vargas right across his hard, tanned jaw.

~

Chapter One

1760
Charles Town

Georgia Ann Cooper stood on the Charles Town dock in the early morning light, blinking back tears. She clutched the ruffled brim of her white hat to keep it from blowing away, and drank in the handsome figure of Samuel Vargas as he spoke to his step-brother Joshua. Samuel's newly outfitted brigantine, the *Eagle*, bobbed in the Atlantic behind them with its fresh paint and rigging.

She and her father had come with Samuel's family to bid him Godspeed on his coming voyage to the Spice Islands in the East Indies.

A venture she had tried her best to discourage.

Joshua clapped Samuel on the shoulder and laughed. "Brother, if you get arrested for piracy, I'll do my lawyer best to keep you from hanging."

Georgia frowned. Not a possibility she wanted to consider.

Samuel shrugged and moved on to his mother and Reverend Ethan Becket, his stepfather.

Marisol Becket took one of his large hands in hers and pressed it to her cheek. She looked up into his animated face. "Son, you will be careful? Not take unnecessary risks?"

He bent down and hugged her. "You know I will, Mother. And I'll bring back spices for you and Mrs. Piper like you've never seen." He kissed her cheek, and then looked back at Joshua with a smile. "And I won't be needing any lawyers to get me out of trouble, either."

Ethan cleared his throat. "Samuel, I never dreamed letting you spend so much time on the *Dryade* with Tim Cullen these past years would go this far, definitely not to the far reaches of the of the globe." He grinned and gave Samuel a hug, and then shook his hand. "Our prayers will go up daily for your safety and success. Write when you can."

Traffic had increased on the dock with so many ships planning to sail with the morning tide. Animal odors and sounds floated across the water as slaves pushed carts of squawking chickens, squealing pigs, and other goods toward multiple gangplanks. Well-frocked ship owners strode by their group, nodded, and proceeded to their own vessels, their voices giving final orders to their captains filled the air.

But Georgia Ann pushed the background noise away and focused on Samuel.

Dressed in his privateer outfit of a crisp white shirt, blue breeches, and plumed tricorn, Captain Vargas made quite a picture of manly strength. His rough, virile attractiveness always made her heart quicken and her palms sweat. And today, her breath caught, her head swam, and her stomach clenched at the thought of him sailing to the other side of the world. Would he miss her during the two years his journey might take? His three-masted *Eagle* bobbed in the dark water, ready to sail. The *Talon,* his partner ship, rose and fell with the tide farther down the row of vessels. Georgia's father had mentioned that sailing preparation for it, too, had been completed the day before sailing. Samuel had always been a careful planner.

As if he felt her gaze, Samuel turned and strode toward her. "You look like an English rose waving in this fine Atlantic breeze, Georgia." He took her hand, kissed it, and turned her chin up with a thumb. His keen, sea green eyes searched her face, making her heart race. He flicked away a tear escaping down her cheek and grinned the familiar grin he'd used on her since they were children. "I'll be back before you know it. Two years is not that long."

He took off his tricorn and ran his fingers through the top of his dark hair. "And you'll be busy with all the usual balls and soirees of your coming out." He looked deep into her eyes. "You'll probably forget me before the summer is over. Will you?"

She turned her head to swipe the wetness from her face. "Samuel, I could never forget you. Why won't you listen to reason and forget those Spice Islands?"

His lips tightened as he looked toward his ship crew standing ready, and then back to her. "We've gone over that, sweet one, several times." He put his hands on her shoulders and smiled.

She breathed in his scent of sea, new rigging, and leather.

"Do you think I might get a smile to remember? I promise to bring you and Mammy June spices and silk like you've never seen."

Her father, Alistair Cooper, walked down the gangplank of the *Eagle* toward them.

Samuel dropped his hands and turned toward him.

"Son, I did a quick inspection, as you requested, and your ship passes muster. But you be careful, especially around the Canary Islands. I've had more than one of my ships come under attack there by the Spanish, but you have to restock on one of the islands."

"Yes, sir. That's our plan, and I've got a good crew I can depend on whatever turns up, as well as a great partner ship."

The man glanced at his daughter and then proffered his hand. "Our prayers go with you."

Samuel shook his hand. "That's what we need, sir. Goodbye to you both." He slid his gaze to Georgia.

She managed to give him a smile, maybe not the one he wanted, but the best she could do with misery so acute a physical pain pressed her chest.

As Samuel turned and strode up the gangplank to his ship, the piercing notes of pipes announcing the captain boarding sang across the Charles Town Harbor.

The lonely sound only accented the sadness cloaking her. She swallowed to steady her voice and turned to her father. "Why are they piping him aboard? His ship is a merchantman not a British vessel."

"To honor him, I'm sure. Shows they think a lot of him." Her father took a deep breath and scratched his bearded chin. "If I was about twenty years younger, I swear, I'd love to go with him."

Georgia tapped her slippered foot and muttered, "You men."

Papa patted her arm. "Daughter, he'll be fine, if I know Samuel Vargas. I'll see you this evening." He turned and headed back to his merchant's office above the dock.

Georgia grasped the side of her trailing gown and marched back to their family carriage.

Joshua hurried to her side and helped her climb in. He leaned toward her. "Will you give me a little time, Georgia, now that my sea-roaming step-brother is back to his sailing?"

She ignored his question and watched the *Eagle's* sails unfurl, then snap and swell as the strong morning breeze filled them. Sailors ran up and down the rigging.

Samuel stood on the quarterdeck and threw up his hand in a wave as the ship moved out of the harbor.

An acute sense of loss flooded her, and she bit her lip until it throbbed like her pulse.

When it became a distant speck on the horizon, Georgia swallowed the despair in her throat and glared at Joshua, still standing beside the carriage. "Why did you have to mention pirating? Samuel is a privateer." She could not bridle the annoyance in her voice.

He grinned. "Sweet Georgia, you know, under the law, there's hardly a hair's breadth of difference."

She shook her head and called to her driver. "Home, Solomon."

Joshua moved aside and crossed his arms.

The servant clapped the reins across the backs of the matched bays and the horses headed back toward Windemere Plantation at a rapid pace, but not fast enough for Georgia Ann. Once they passed through the harbor area and the cobbled streets to the open road, she let her pent-up tears fall unheeded. Would she ever see Samuel Vargas again?

~

ONE YEAR LATER
THE SPICE ISLANDS

Standing on the quarterdeck of the sun-drenched *Eagle*, Samuel breathed in the tantalizing fragrance of cloves permeating the sea breeze. Finally, they'd arrived in the southern Indonesian archipelago, home of the fabled Spice Islands. He swung his arms out as if to embrace the wonderful scent and whispered a prayer. *Thank you, Father God, for bringing us here through all the dangers.*

The elder man who stood beside him grinned. "Didn't I tell ye we would smell the spices ten miles out from them islands?"

"You did, sir, but I didn't believe you. Finally arriving here is a dream come true." He turned to look into the gray-bearded, leathery face of Luis da Gama, a Portuguese sailor he had run across at the Charles Town dock many months earlier. The seasoned sailor had taken some ribbing from the *Eagle's* crew after he joined at Samuel's invitation. Some of them persisted in calling him Vasco da Gama, after the Portuguese explorer who, over two centuries earlier, found a new route to India and the spice trade by sailing around Africa's Cape of Good Hope.

Finding Luis had been an answer to Samuel's prayers for this risky trip to seek the Spice Islands. The man's knowledge had proved invaluable from day one.

"Captain, sir." Luis da Gama leaned closer. "You do remember the dangers I shared of landing on these islands?"

"Yes, I do, my man." Samuel leaned over the deck railing and shouted, "All hands on deck."

Shawn Edwards, his First Lieutenant, and Samson, boatswain, repeated his order over the ship. In two minutes, all the stalwart Charles Town mariners who had survived the long dangerous crossing gathered in front of the quarter deck.

"Men, we are about to arrive at our destination, the fabled Spice Islands. I'm real sorry for those we lost on our way due to storms and sickness. And the *Talon* being blown off course. Hopefully, they made it back to port. But finally we are here."

Cheers erupted from the men, as well as a "Thank God, we'uns made it."

"Captain, what is that blessed scent we be smelling?" A tough, old sailor from the back yelled, and other voices rose in assent.

"It's cloves, my man, and we hope to fill our hold with them. If we do and make it back to Charles Town, all of you will have some gold to jingle in your pockets."

Cheers and stamping boots filled the hot midday air.

Samuel projected his voice so every man could hear. "Men we

are now heading toward a landing on one of the Maluku Islands. We're told by Luis, here"—he gestured to the Portuguese beside him—"that all these islands are really volcanic atolls, and most of their harbors are ringed by sunken reefs. I don't need to tell you many a vessel has been dashed to pieces on the razor-sharp coral, so we must be careful as we try to sail in closer."

Samuel didn't mention another aspect of the danger Luis has shared with him—that some of the isles were inhabited by headhunters and cannibals, who were feared and distrusted throughout the East Indies.

The cook, Hobbit, who boasted a wooden leg, shouted, "Well, who's gonna help git us through without wrecking?"

"Luis has sailed here before. He will direct the *Eagle* where to drop anchor, then we'll go ashore in the longboats. Not every one can go. But after the officers, we'll draw lots for who will set out with us. Those who go or stay aboard will share equally in the cargo we carry home. Does everyone understand? We have covered this before and all of you signed articles."

"Aye, aye, Captain," filtered through the gathering.

~

The next day, with the *Eagle* safely through the dangerous waters by taking constant soundings of the depth, they anchored some distance from the shore. Samuel lowered and entered a longboat, with a crew selected by lot, and rowed toward the verdant island and its strip of tan beach. Rice, cloth, and tools for trading floated behind them in the second longboat with its two oarsmen.

"Captain," one of the oarsmen called, "Do we all disembark or wait at the shore for you to return?"

Samuel clicked his tongue. The man had already forgotten the instructions. "You stay with the boats, as will all the crew, until Luis and I decide what we should do."

As soon as their boats touched the rocky beach, two tall dark-skinned natives, clothed only in loincloths, arose from the bushes and strode forward, holding large spears. But they made no aggressive movements, and kept the weapons pointed downward instead of toward their visitors.

Samuel spoke before his crew could draw their pistols. "I'm sure they've watched us since we left the ship. Stay calm—we outnumber them if it comes to a confrontation." He disembarked and bowed to the young men now standing a few yards away. Luis did the same. Each pulled up a bolt of red cloth from the longboat and held it out for the natives to see.

The two men stepped forward, touched the bright material, and conversed with each other in excited words Samuel didn't understand.

"Please, take us to your chief." Luis spoke slowly and pointed behind the natives.

The strangers tipped their heads as if not sure they understood, so Luis repeated the words. The two nodded and turned back the way they had come. Samuel and Luis followed, swiping sweat from their foreheads at the fast pace. He could only pray they weren't being led into a trap.

They soon arrived at the edge of a village of small thatched-roofed dwellings. The two men shouted something to the women and children who gathered in their doorways as the group proceeded down the shell-strewn street. Finally, the guides stopped at a larger hut.

A lighter-skinned man with a mane of gray hair and a long beard sat on large rock beside the door, smoking a long-stemmed pipe. He wore faded, ragged breeches, but no shirt or shoes. From the way the two men spoke to him, he must be the chieftain of this village.

Samuel laid the bolts of cloth at his feet and bowed to the man. Two women peeking from inside the dwelling spoke in excited, unknown words, and pointed to the red fabric.

The man pulled the pipe from between his teeth. "Saw your ship enter the bay. Who are you and where are you from?"

Samuel did his best to contain his surprise as he moved forward. Not only did the man speak English, but he had blue eyes. "I am Captain Samuel Vargas. We sailed from Charles Town and have come to trade for cloves."

"Charles Town?" The man looked at him blankly. "Not England?"

"It's a colony of England in the New World. Are you English?"

"Aye, arrived here as a boy after the Portuguese ship that took our British vessel captive wrecked on the reef more years ago than I remember. I alone survived." He placed the pipe back between his lips and puffed.

Samuel sent Louis a glance to see if he was feeling the same wonder flooding Samuel's chest. Only God could bring them to an island with an English-speaking chief. *Thank You, Father.*

~

After a week or so, the villagers seemed to lose their awe for their island visitors. One hot afternoon, Samuel found himself surrounded by a group of them who kept pointing at him and jabbering to each other in their language he couldn't understand.

The chieftain approached. "They have never seen anyone with green eyes like yours, Captain."

Samuel laughed and backed away, shaking his head.

During the following two weeks, Samuel worked hard to keep the crew out of too much trouble, especially with the friendly island girls. He had his own work to do to keep several of the women from following him around the island.

The natives traded many hemp-woven bags of dried cloves for the rice, cloth, and tools Samuel brought from the *Eagle*. They restocked the ship with fruit, dried meat, salt, and water for the long trip home.

The leader shared interesting facts about cloves with Samuel. He told how the village families planted a clove tree in honor of each child born. He explained the growth stages of cloves on the adult trees, which start out as yellow flower buds. They turn brown for harvesting and drying to be used whole or ground into a powder.

The day came when all trading was finished and Samuel gave the order for the *Eagle* to set sail with its fragrant cargo, minus the goods it had brought with which to barter. Every man, woman, boy, and girl from the village stood on the beach with their chieftain waving goodbye. Samuel had expected the white chieftan to return to Charles Town with them, but the man elected to stay on the island.

~

Samuel breathed easy as all passed fairly well on the return voyage and the water and supplies restocking stops they made at Java, Sumatra, and Nicobar, in the Indian Ocean. But at Socotra, because of the strange umbrella-shaped Dragon Blood trees, some of his superstitious crew refused to disembark. On their earlier stop when headed to the Spice Islands, the natives had told them they believed the blood red sap of the tree was dragon's blood.

Two days after they sailed from Madagascar toward Africa's Cape of Good Hope, a terrible storm arose and tossed the ship a night and day between mountainous waves.

Samuel hated to give the order but to save the ship, after they had thrown every other possible thing overboard to lighten it, he had no choice. "Throw half the sacks of cloves into the ocean," he shouted through the dark, pelting rain.

He stood behind the helmsman helping him steer the strained vessel through the waves as high as their topsail one moment, then shooting them down into an endless gulley the next.

"Aye, aye, Sir." came the unhappy reply. Shawn Edwards slid down into the hold and threw up the sacks to Samson with a rope around his thick torso tied to the mast to keep him from being washed overboard as he tossed the fragrant sacks into the sea. They had to throw some more before the storm abated.

Two weeks later, sailing toward Charles Town after a Canary Islands stop to restock, Samuel stood on the quarter deck watching the blue-white water sheet off their hull. Georgia Ann flowed strong into his mind—her azure blue eyes and golden curls, her soft lips, her tears at their parting. Had she forgotten him during the year and half he'd already been gone?

A cry came from the lookout high in the shrouds. "A sail, a sail to starboard."

Samuel whipped out his eyeglass. As the vessel bobbed up and down on the waves, he recognized the flag flying from her mast and noted her size. A Spanish mercenary, most likely. He scoured the horizon for other ships that might accompany her, but she seemed to be alone, perhaps lost from the squadron that might have travelled with her. She was heading back toward Spain and maybe loaded with West Indies treasure to make her nobles wealthy and fund their war against humanity with their presumed blessing from God.

As always, his gut clenched as he thought of the Spanish Inquisition destroying lives daily in the name of heresy—maybe even the life of his own grandmother years before. His mother, Marisol Valentin Beckett, had told him she believed her English mother had become the victim of the Inquisition judges when she disappeared from their Cadiz estate when his mother was twelve. To Samuel's thinking, any Spanish ship attacked and plundered was one less enemy ship against England, and less money and manpower for the Inquisition horrors against mankind.

Shawn Edwards ran up to the quarter deck from below, and Samuel handed the eyepiece to him.

"Sir, it's a Spanish ship for sure. It's flying the Cadiz flag of arms. Wonder if they are on their way back to Spain from the West Indies?"

Samuel snapped the spyglass closed and pocketed it. His thin lips spread in a slow grin. "My thinking exactly. Wherever they're headed, they're fair game." He leaned over the quarterdeck railing and shouted, "Make clear and ready for engagement."

Amid whoops and jostling, crew members scrambled to their assigned tasks. They stowed hammocks and sea chests at the bulwarks to help stop shot and splinters. Men quartered at the guns knocked gun ports loose from the caulking that kept out seawater, and they rigged the train tackles. The gunner checked the charges in each cannon to make sure they were dry, and laid out loading materials and ammunition. His musketeers brought up small chests of muskets, pistols, and cutlasses.

Aloft, the boatswain had his crew adjust the sails to fighting sail so the vessel could be managed with only a few men.

A loud cannon blast from the approaching ship shattered across the water, and a shot splashed less than a hundred yards from the *Eagle's* bow—a warning to show colors.

"Post colors," Samuel trumpeted across the deck.

"Which flag, Cap'n?" a sailor yelled.

"The Spanish, of course."

Blood surged through Samuel's veins. They would let the coming ship think they were friendly until the *Eagle* drew close enough to make every shot of their cannons count.

WATCH FOR *THE SULTAN'S CAPTIVE* AT YOUR FAVORITE RETAILER.

Charleston Brides ~ 2
The Sultan's Captive
ELVA COBB MARTIN

GET ALL THE BOOKS IN THE CHARLESTON BRIDES SERIES

Book 1: The Pirate's Purchase

Book 2: The Sultan's Captive

Book 3: The Petticoat Spy

Book 4: The Sugar Baron's Governess

ABOUT THE AUTHOR

Elva Cobb Martin is a wife, mother, and grandmother who lives in South Carolina with her husband and a mini-dachshund. A life-long student of history, her favorite city, Charleston, inspires her stories of romance and adventure. Her love of writing grew out of a desire to share exciting stories of courageous characters and communicate truths of the Christian faith to bring hope and encouragement.

Connect with her on her web site at http://elvamartin.com.

Other Books by Elva Cobb Martin:

In a Pirate's Debt
Summer of Deception

Want more?

If you love historical romance, check out our other Wild Heart books!

Waltz in the Wilderness by Kathleen Denly

She's desperate to find her missing father. His conscience demands he risk all to help.

Eliza Brooks is haunted by her role in her mother's death, so she'll do anything to find her missing pa—even if it means sneaking aboard a southbound ship. When those meant to protect her abandon and betray her instead, a family friend's unexpected assistance is a blessing she can't refuse.

Daniel Clarke came to California to make his fortune, and a stable job as a San Francisco carpenter has earned him more than most have scraped from the local goldfields. But it's been four years since he left Massachusetts and his fiancé is impatient for his return. Bound for home at last, Daniel Clarke finds his heart and plans challenged by a tenacious young woman with haunted eyes. Though every word he utters seems to offend her, he is determined to see her safely returned to her father. Even if that means risking his fragile engagement.

When disaster befalls them in the remote wilderness of the Southern California mountains, true feelings are revealed, and both must face heart-rending decisions. But how to decide when every choice before them leads to someone getting hurt?

~

Lone Star Ranger by Renae Brumbaugh Green

Elizabeth Covington will get her man.

And she has just a week to prove her brother isn't the murderer Texas Ranger Rett Smith accuses him of being. She'll show the good-looking lawman he's wrong, even if it means setting out on a risky race across Texas to catch the real killer.

Rett doesn't want to convict an innocent man. But he can't let the Boston beauty sway his senses to set a guilty man free. When Elizabeth follows him on a dangerous trek, the Ranger vows to keep her safe. But who will protect him from the woman whose conviction and courage leave him doubting everything—even his heart?

~

Rocky Mountain Redemption by Lisa J. Flickinger

A Rocky Mountain logging camp may be just the place to find herself.

To escape the devastation caused by the breaking of her wedding engagement, Isabelle Franklin joins her aunt in the Rocky Mountains to feed a camp of lumberjacks cutting on the slopes of Cougar Ridge. If only she could out run the lingering nightmares.

Charles Bailey, camp foreman and Stony Creek's itinerant pastor, develops a reputation to match his new nickname — Preach. However, an inner battle ensues when the details of his rough history threaten to overcome the beliefs of his young faith.

Amid the hazards of camp life, the unlikely friendship growing between the two surprises Isabelle. She's drawn to Preach's brute strength and gentle nature as he leads the ragtag crew toiling for Pollitt's Lumber. But when the ghosts from her past return to haunt her, the choices she will make change the course of her life forever —and that of the man she's come to love.

Made in the USA
Middletown, DE
04 August 2022